The PLAYER

BOOK ONE

K. BROMBERG

The Player
Copyright 2017 K. Bromberg

ISBN: 978-1-942832-07-2

Editor: Madison Seidler Editing Service and Help Me Edit
Cover Designer: Helen Williams
Interior Design and Formatting: Champagne Formats

Published by JKB Publishing, LLC

PRAISE FOR THE NOVELS OF K. BROMBERG

"An irresistibly hot romance that stays with you long after you finish the book."
> —# 1 *New York Times* bestselling author Jennifer L. Armentrout

"Captivating, emotional, and sizzling hot!"
> —#1 *New York Times* bestselling author S. C. Stephens

"Bromberg is a master at turning up the heat!"
> —*New York Times* bestselling author Katy Evans

"K. Bromberg is the master of making hearts race and pulses pound."
> —*New York Times* bestselling author Jay Crownover

"Sexy, heartwarming, and so much more."
> —*New York Times* bestselling author Corinne Michaels

"Super charged heat and full of heart. Bromberg aces it from the first page to the last."
> —*New York Times* bestselling author Kylie Scott

OTHER BOOKS BY K. BROMBERG

DEDICATION

This book is dedicated to those women who love sports. The ones who didn't think twice about getting grass stains on their tights as little girls, and now that they're older, have no shame in sitting down to watch a game with the guys.

I've always been a sports girl.

The book is dedicated to nerd girls. The ones who like to sit at home on a Friday night and get lost in the pages of a good book. The ones who always want to learn new things. Never be ashamed of being smart.

I've always been a nerd girl.

This book is dedicated to strong girls. To the ones who would rather help their fellow women succeed rather than try to bring them down.

I've always been a strong girl.

This book is dedicated to the insecure girls. Yes, *you*. I *see* you. I've *been* you. I *am* you. It's okay to spread your wings every once in a while and see how far you can fly. Nothing ventured, nothing gained.

Look at me, I did.

PROLOGUE

Easton

The rush hits me.

The adrenaline through my body.

The roar of the crowd in my ears.

The mixture of scents—dirt, popcorn, leather, pine-tar—in my nose.

They're my lifeline.

My constants.

The only religion I was ever taught to believe in.

The only thing I was ever allowed to be.

For those few moments before the pain hits—the blinding, excruciating, unending pain—when the dust is dancing around me and I can feel its grit sliding beneath my body, I remember why I love the game.

Everything about it.

And then I look up.

Our eyes meet. It's a split-second connection. But I'm reminded of something. Of someone.

And then it's gone.
Because now there's only pain.
It takes over.
Steals my breath.
Kills my streak.
And hopefully doesn't ruin my future.

CHAPTER ONE

Scout

Four months later

"**H**ow do you want me?"

Hazel eyes.

An arrogant smirk.

Those are the first two things about Easton Wylder that grab my attention when he peeks his head around the training room door.

I open my mouth to speak but fall silent when he walks over the threshold and comes into full view. And it's not just because he's shirtless—that's par for the course in my job—but rather it's *everything* about him that knocks the words from my lips. The bare, tanned, and very toned chest. The low-slung gym shorts showcasing a perfect V of muscles. The happy trail ever so slightly visible, which draws my eyes to where I shouldn't be looking.

But I *do* look.

And that's a problem. Because even if it's only for a moment, it's still long enough for him to notice. I snap my eyes back up and over his dark scruff to once again be greeted with that cocksure smirk that

I swear taunts me and asks if I like what I see.

Another day. Another client. *Another player.*

I shouldn't have expected any less.

He's hot. I'll give him that. Like the mouthwatering, stop-traffic, draw-all-eyes-when-he-walks-into-a-room type of hot. And not only that, but he's a freaking god on the field. One of the best catchers I've ever seen. Batting average, on-base percentage, caught-stealing percentage, pick-offs, pass balls—all his stats say if he stays on this track, he'll be one of the greats someday.

The total package.

But if first impressions are any indication—the arrogant lift of his eyebrows and cocky set of his shoulders—I already know he's going to be like every other *total package* I've worked with before. Great to look at but a bore to work with. Conceited and one-dimensional. If it's not about him, he doesn't want to talk about it.

I hope I'm wrong, or else this is going to be a *long* three months. Not only that, but I've admired his career over the last few years and would prefer to keep admiring the man I perceived him to be, too.

"On my back?" he rephrases his question before I can recover from my thoughts, and takes a step closer. "On my stomach?" He stops and scrubs a towel over his face so that his dark brown hair sticks up every which way, yet somehow it only adds to his appeal.

Give him a chance, Scout. He's baseball royalty. Besides, he might not be that bad. Does it really matter if he's a conceited jerk? There's still a contract, a set timeframe, and he's still your client. So, chop-chop. Get to it and *do your job.*

"Uh," I say as I glance down again, trying not to let that body—the hard, damaged, perfection of it—scatter my thoughts and undermine my professionalism.

"*Uh?*" he repeats, as those multicolored eyes of his laugh at a joke only he seems to understand.

"Sorry, you distracted me." Once the words are out I realize how they sound, giving the implication that his body is the culprit.

"Distracted?" A lift of his brows. A ghost of a smile.

I start over. "I'm the new PT the club contracted to help get you back on the field."

"The *club* hired *you*? I thought they were hiring Doc . . . and you're definitely not Doc."

"Doc's the one who assigned me to your case." My tone is defensive, my soul sagging under the weight of why I'm here and he's not.

"Doc Dalton, Doc?" Disbelief tinges his tone.

"Yeah, Doc Dalton, Doc. I'm his partner."

"*Partner*? Doc's notorious for working solo." He narrows his eyes and studies me unabashedly for a moment. The silent scrutiny has me shifting on my feet, and just as I'm about to speak, he chuckles under his breath at something I'm obviously not privy to. "Which one of the guys hired you?"

"Your general manager. Cory Tillman."

"Cory?"

"Yes. Cory." *Why is this so hard for him to understand?*

"And she even has the name right," he mutters, more to himself than to me, only furthering my confusion. "Nice try, though. My bet's on Drew or Tino. They covered all of their bases with you, didn't they?"

What in the hell is he talking about?

"Not that you care, but I don't need my bases covered. I'd really like to get started."

"No."

"No?" *Is he being serious?*

"You think I'd let *just anybody* touch my arm?"

"Excuse me?" The insult hits me harder than it should. It's one I've learned to expect—the assumption that I can't be as good as Doc—and yet my temper still lights. "I assure you my touch is every bit as magical as Doc's is." *Asshole.*

"I'm sure it is," he murmurs, drawing the words out, while his eyes roam down the length of my body. The look in them—one of pure male appreciation—sets my nerves, already tinged with temper, abuzz. And I don't want them to be abuzz. I don't want them to feel anything when it comes to him and how much of a prick he is proving himself to be right now.

"Try it on someone else, Hot Shot. Your charm isn't going to work on me."

"My charm?" I love the little startle to his head. The one that says he's not used to being called on the carpet.

"Yeah. The 'I'm a cocky bastard' charm. Do you really get women when you act like that?"

"I wasn't aware I was trying to get a woman." His eyes lock onto mine. There's humor in their hazel depths, but all I feel is stupidly hurt as if he'd just rejected me, when I didn't want to be wanted by him in the first place. "And for the record, it works all the time."

What I'd give to knock that smug smirk off his face right now.

"So, what? You just walk up and throw some stats at her? 'Hey, baby, I'm having a killer season, batting three seventy-five with a twenty-game hitting streak. Wanna go out?'"

"Nah." He fights back a laugh, and I hate that even though I know I'm being mocked, that sheepish smile of his draws me in to take a step closer. "I just tell her I have a big stick and I know just how to use it."

"Seriously?"

He shrugs. "No, but you're going to think what you want to anyway, right?"

"Sure am."

"And you have a thing against big sticks, I take it?"

He's taunting me. Seeing how far he can push me. Little does he know, I push right back.

"Nothing against big sticks, but they're worthless unless you know how to use them. And guys who drop cheesy lines like the one you just did definitely don't take the time to learn how to use them properly."

"Are you speaking from experience? Do a lot of men try lines like that on you?" Our eyes war across the small space.

"Not men I'd give the time of day."

"That's a pity. Maybe you haven't met the right one, then." He just stares at me with an unrelenting gaze that asks questions and makes assumptions I'd rather he not make. This conversation has veered way off course from where it needs to be.

Back to him.

Focused on him.

And the irony isn't lost on me that this is the exact opposite of what I wanted moments ago.

"Look, I'm here to do a job. It's probably best if we stick to that," I say in an attempt to reset this conversation for the second time.

"You sure you want to? Your hostility screams how much you're enjoying my company."

"Liking you is not a necessity. I'm good at ignoring people who rub me the wrong way." I follow the dig with a sickeningly sweet smile. "Let's get to it." I motion to the padded table behind him.

He looks at the table and then back to me. "What if I tell you thanks, but no thanks."

"And what if I tell you, you don't get a say? I'm getting paid to do a job, and I intend to get that job done." I take a few steps closer to him and make sure my voice is as authoritative as possible. "On your back."

"Gotta love a woman who knows what she wants." There's no mistaking the suggestion in his words, and it's only reinforced by the intensity of the way he stares at me, as if with each passing second, another layer of my clothing is falling off. "But you'll learn soon enough, I rarely do what I'm told."

"*Pretty please.*" Sarcasm rings through my voice as we wage a visual war of wills, but I'm unsure over what. I'm here to give him exactly what he wants—to be back on the field—and so his defiance is both frustrating and confusing.

5

Because while I may have been questioned by players in the past—underestimated because I'm a woman, tested because I'm not as experienced as Doc—it's so very different this time around.

This time I have Doc Dalton's benchmark career riding on rehabbing Easton Wylder. I have my father's last wishes to fulfill. I have my reputation to solidify.

"Feisty, gorgeous, intelligent, *and* polite," he muses, crossing his arms over his chest so his biceps flex with the movement. Eyebrows lifted, he gives me a full-blown smile to boot. "Because of that, I'll obey . . . but just this once."

Quit staring at me. "Let's get to it." *Quit smiling at me like that.* "On the table." *Quit flexing your biceps.* "Shirt off." *Quit unnerving me.*

"My shirt's already off."

"Oh. Yes. Sorry." Crap. *Nothing like showing you're capable and in control by completely missing the obvious.* "Do you want to tell me where it hurts the most, so I can start there?"

"I've got a lot of hurts." He laughs, and it irritates me that I find the sound of it sexy. "But I'm curious, how do you plan on fixing me if touching the clientele is off-limits?"

"I touch, Wylder. There are no limitations. I throw my hands and my body into it until I've made the pain go away. Then we move on to your next ache and start the process all over again." Ignoring the disbelief on his face, I point to the table behind him. "I thought you were going to obey this once?"

"On one condition."

Condition? *Is he serious?* I have no choice but to play along. "What's that?"

"Stop pretending like you know what you're doing when it comes to my arm." He arches an eyebrow in challenge.

The surest way to piss a woman off is to question her abilities and yet he just did again. "Don't be an ass. You're irritating me. And wasting my time." I raise my eyebrows. "I don't like my time wasted."

"Isn't the customer always supposed to be right?"

"Sit. Down."

"What the lady wants, the lady gets." Resigned, but with a lop-sided smirk that says somehow he's getting what he wants anyway, he scoots his ass onto the padded table behind him, eyes still locked on mine. "One more condition?"

"No more conditions." The man is positively frustrating.

"What's your name?"

"Scout," I answer, already exhausted from this game I'm a player in but don't quite understand.

"*Scout*?"

"Yes. Scout." I opt to leave out my last name. There's no need for him to question my abilities any further.

"That's not exactly the type of originality I was expecting. What happened to Star or Trixie or *Kitty*? Were those all taken?"

What in the hell is he talking about?

"Sorry to disappoint you, but it's just Scout."

"Damn. My bet was on Kitty."

"Nope."

"Scout. Hmm." He nods his head, eyes narrowing as if he's trying to figure something out. "I was wrong. It wasn't Tino. It was Drew. He's the one who hired you, coached you on what to say, and told you what to do, right?" He swings his legs up onto the table, and I swear he says something about there being *no Velcro* but when he props himself up on his elbow and meets my puzzled gaze, all he does is give me a perfectly innocent, choir-boy smile.

"I'm sorry, am I missing something?" *I'm so confused.*

"Don't you worry that *pretty little head of yours*," he says with a smirk. "You're not missing a thing."

I hear him—the mockery in his tone, the alarm bells telling me something's going on that I don't quite understand—but I'm momentarily distracted by our proximity. By the scent of the shampoo in his hair. By the sight of faded scars on his body, more visible now that

I'm closer to him. By the unique color of his eyes, which are a mixture of brown and gray with a ring of blue around the iris.

But it's his wince that pulls me from la-la land. It's a simple motion, the lift of his arm behind his head, but I catch the grimace on his face. My eyes home in on his shoulder. On the vibration of his muscles as he shifts and adjusts to get comfortable and the mask now in place trying to pretend it didn't hurt.

My training kicks in. Takes over. Throws that unwelcome pang of insta-lust I was momentarily mesmerized by out the window. I itch to put my hands on him so I can knead and stretch and try to give him relief from his nagging pain.

But right as I'm about to touch his shoulder, he shifts to look at me and asks, "Don't you need music or something?"

My hands freeze as his words break through my concentration. They hit my ears, and my synapses fire for what feels like the first time since he stepped in here. Everything clicks into place. The hints that have been niggling in the back of my mind suddenly link together and make sense.

The throwback baller.

The All-American do-gooder.

And the notorious prankster.

How could I not have connected the dots earlier? That the man who is known in locker rooms around the country for pranking his teammates—like the ones he named moments ago, Tino and Drew—thinks they are pranking him. Getting him back for the legendary stunts he's done to them.

And he thinks I'm in on it.

Velcro. Music. The ridiculous stage names.

Yep. He thinks I'm a stripper.

Or a hooker.

Lovely.

And while I should be insulted that he thinks I'm here because his buddies hired me to dance for him, at least our conversation makes some sense now.

Why does the thought relieve me? Because it redeems him? Not in the least. But maybe he's not the asshole I pegged him to be. Maybe, just maybe, he was reacting to the situation he assumed and not to me.

But then again, he's still lying down, still letting this play out, still letting me—the woman he thinks is here to strip for him—touch him.

And while I may have worked in enough clubhouses to know this prank is tame in the scheme of things, I also know there is no better way to get a prankster to take you seriously than to prank him right back. So, I make the split-second decision to ride this ruse out. I'll play the part, and then when the time is right, I'll tell him the truth. Perhaps his disappointment that I'm not a stripper will knock some of the cockiness from his smile.

When I meet his eyes again, I hold them just a touch too long, smile a little more seductively. "Do I want music? It's your preference. Do you prefer that I . . . *do it* to music? Or would you rather we do a dry run first—see what feels good to you, what doesn't, and then we can take it from there?" I don't believe my voice has ever purred before, but right now I feel like I deserve the stage name Kitty.

Those thick lashes of his shock open at my sudden change in demeanor. He glances at me and then out of the training room's windows to the empty locker room beyond. He must be wondering where Drew and Tino are, because no doubt they'd be standing by to watch their prank play out.

No dice, Hot Shot. The joke's on you.

"There's no one else here, Easton. Just you. And me." I put my finger on his forehead and push so his head rests back. "And the little workout I'm about to give you."

"A workout? Is that what you call it these days?" His chuckle says it all. So does the quick inhale of breath and the tensing of his muscles beneath my fingertips as I press on the skin atop his rotator cuff to feel for the presence of scar tissue. The first step to try and assess why it's taking his arm so long to heal when it should be far past the wincing stage.

His skin is smooth. Hot. And there's a zap of electricity—a hum of something—when our bodies connect in this most innocent of ways. It's so unexpected and unlike anything I've ever felt before that I have to stop myself from pulling my hand away in reaction.

"I appreciate you pretending to know what you're doing and all, but—"

"Oh, I know what I'm doing, no worries there," I croon to stop his protest. "Let's try this now. Does that hurt?" He resists when I try to lift his arm over his head. At least he has enough sense to question letting a stripper work on his million-dollar arm.

"No. It's just . . . I don't think you should—"

"I assure you I'm more than qualified." There's panic in his eyes, fear over how far this stripper is going to carry on the I'm-a-physical-therapist-routine. So I carry on. "A torn labrum isn't anything to mess around with. Only a professional will know how to make it feel better. And rest assured, I'm a professional."

"Handling me is one thing, Scout," he says with a bit of bewilderment, "but my arm is a whole other matter."

"You don't trust me to fix it?" I walk my fingers up his biceps, and his Adam's apple bobs in reaction as he debates what to do next.

"I highly doubt that's what you're here for."

"No?" I feign innocence. "Then why don't we get down to exactly what I'm here for?"

In a move I use daily to stretch my players, and before I lose the element of surprise, I hop onto the table so that my knees cage the sides of his hips.

"Wait. *Whoa.*" Easton's face is the picture of surprise—eyes wide, mouth opening and closing, eyebrows arching.

"I'm ready if you are." The purr is back as I lean forward so I'm on all fours with our torsos parallel and my eyes locked with his.

"Yes. No." He blinks rapidly as if it will help him grasp the fact that what was all fun and games a minute ago is now very real. A part of me likes that he's hesitant and not all grabby-hands and raring to go with some random woman. The other part of me wonders if I really were a stripper here on a prank, just how far would he let this ride out. "My rehabber—Doc. He'll be here any minute." He stutters out the protest.

"No, he won't."

"*He won't?*" His voice rises in pitch.

"Nope." I shake my head and lift my eyebrows.

"I knew it. I knew Drew and Tino were behind this." He breathes out a laugh that's part disbelief, part relief, but when he starts to sit up, I remain right where I am.

"Nope. Not a prank." That stops him cold.

"What do you mean? You're a . . ."

"A physical therapist," I finish for him.

"That's a good one. Cute. But I call bullshit."

"Actually, it's not." I reach out with one hand, and just as I'm about to touch his shoulder, he yanks it out of my grasp. His hiss from the pain, the kneejerk reaction, is audible. "*And you need me.*"

His eyes bore into mine—gauging, judging, questioning—before that cocksure grin of his returns. "I'm sure a lot of other guys need you . . . Scout, *is it*? But I'm not one of them. I don't need to pay to see some skin."

"First, you're not paying me, the club is. And second, I'm fully clothed."

"Drop the act, sweetheart. The club's not paying you shit. They're paying Doc, and right now, he's somewhere waiting for me, and I need to find him. So, time's up. It was cute, you had me going for a bit, but it's time for you to head out."

I nod in mock resignation as I slowly climb off the table, but my eyes never leave his as I lean down close to his ear. "You get a pass today, just so you can wrap that *pretty little head of yours* around the fact that I'm your new physical therapist. Be here tomorrow. Same time. Same place. Don't let my appearance fool you, because I'll work you out all right, but only so I can get you back on the field." I step back, take in his wide-eyed expression as it morphs slowly from arrogance to the realization that I just might be telling the truth. I smile. "Oh, and leave your assumptions at home. I may not be Doc, but I sure as hell am a *Dalton*. It's been a pleasure."

And with that, I turn my back and head for the door. My hands are trembling, and my body is riding high on something akin to adrenaline, but I'm satisfied that he'll take me seriously from here on out.

"Hey, *Kitty*."

Despite every urge in my body to keep walking and not acknowledge the stripper alias, my feet stop. And I hate that they do, but at least I don't give him the satisfaction of turning around to face him.

"The name's Scout. And, for the record, I'm not sure whether to be flattered or pissed off that you'd think I'd accept money to dance for you *or* sleep with you."

"So, you'd do it for free then?" The chuckle that follows is smooth as silk, full of suggestion, and twists my insides with a potent combination of disgust and lust.

"Not hardly," I lie.

"Good thing I didn't take the bait then. I was ready to kiss you senseless just to call your bluff and prove you were a stripper."

"Good thing I didn't knee you in the nuts because you had."

His laugh is warmer this time around. "Lucky for me, I practiced restraint."

"Remember that term—practice restraint," I say, feeling like I've made some headway. "I won't be easy on you, you know."

"I'll count on it. And Scout? I knew you weren't a stripper."

"Way to try and save face, Hot Shot." *Men and their egos.* "But if that's the case, then why'd you let me keep the act going?"

"Only a stupid man would stop a beautiful woman when she's

straddling his thighs."

"And here I thought you'd redeemed yourself," I mutter through the smile he can't see.

"Redemption's boring. I prefer excitement," he goads.

"Great."

"Tomorrow, Scout."

"Yeah. Yeah."

I walk out of the locker room, the echo of my footsteps down the concrete corridor nowhere as loud as his voice on repeat in my mind. *I was ready to kiss you senseless just to call your bluff.*

If that would be my punishment for being wrong, why the hell would I want to be right?

CHAPTER TWO

Easton

"**I**t's just pain. I've played through it before. I can play through it again."

"And risk ending your career?"

"Look. I know my body better than anyone. I'm not going to risk my career by pushing myself too early, which is why—"

"Which is why the club hired Doc."

"Don't remind me." My laugh is loaded with sarcasm but my thoughts are already back on the athletic brunette with challenging gray eyes and a smartass mouth. The one I've probably thought about more times in the last few hours, while waiting for my agent to call back, than I care to count. "And for clarification, it's not Doc doing my rehab. It's Scout. Whoever the fuck Scout is, because I've made some calls, been asking around, and I can't find shit on her other than she's his daughter. *His daughter,* Finn? Not some topnotch professional who is scheduled out for months in advance because she's everyone's go-to. Look, I'm not one to knock taking up the old man's profession because . . . well, *because pot meet kettle.* But taking over and actually being as good as him are two entirely different things. The club promised they'd get me the best physical therapist after the bullshit I had to put up with from the other one. Second best isn't the best, Finn. This is my arm we're talking about here. My career, so—"

"The same arm you want to chance by thumbing your nose at the club's protocol and declaring yourself ready to go without the therapist's consent, right?"

Fuck. Finn's got me there. I roll my shoulders in reflex and hate that there's that slight stab of pain when I do—my constant reminder that I'm not ready to play, and yet that's all I want to do to get my life back to its norm.

"Easton." He sighs. "You agreed to the terms and have to abide by the parameters now."

His disapproving tone grates on my nerves. "We've gone over this." *What feels like a million times.*

"Well, you're the one who signed the papers—"

"You're goddamn right I did. They carted me off the field and the pain was so brutal I would've signed anything for them to get the oxy quicker to dull it some; so don't chastise me like I did something stupid. You would've done the same exact thing."

His silence is more irritating than his disapproving tone. "I would have at least read the papers first."

"Yeah. Yeah. I know. But I didn't, and now I'm forced into their rehab guidelines. Can they really put a deadline on when I have to return? It's not like everyone heals the same."

"Should they? No. Can they? Well, you signed the paper that said you'd be back by August first, so yes, now, they technically can."

I roll my shoulders, pissed at myself for signing it, at him for his constant nagging over it, and at all the shit that can't be changed. "And if I'm not ready by then?"

"I told you, they can trade you."

"And you also told me during the last negotiation that I had an iron-clad contract, Finn. Eight years with an extension option."

"It is iron-clad. . . but then you went and signed the first papers they put in front of you without reading them, and—"

"It wasn't like . . . you don't understand." Frustrated, I pinch the bridge of my nose and close my eyes to shut out the stadium laid out before me, taunting me. "It doesn't matter. I don't quite understand this new general manager yet, but I guess it's his new protocol."

"What is?" he asks. "Making a player sign something when his arm was just ripped apart? Sounds pretty callous if you ask me. What's the purpose? Is dotting all your I's and crossing all your T's really that important in that moment?"

"You're preaching to the choir, dude."

"Everyone says he's the best there is when it comes to this kind of thing, and there's no way they can all be crazy, so hang in there."

"Easier said than done," I gripe.

"Yeah well, the bright side is that it typically takes him three years to successfully restructure an organization before he moves on to the next one."

"Three years?" *Fuck.*

"Let's just hope all these new policies and strategies are worth it. I expect to see a pennant won before he leaves."

"Always looking for the diamond in a pile full of cow patties aren't you, Finn?

"One of us has to."

"Strategies are one thing, but treating your players with respect is another. Giving me a finite amount of time to rehab and return to the starting line-up is definitely not a way to show me respect." Everything about the situation pisses me off and rubs me the wrong way.

"I know. The timeframe is most likely Cory's way to add a bit of pressure so you get back on the field as soon as possible. After all, you're their star player."

"He does know this is my job, right? Star player or not, I'm a big boy who's well aware of what my fucking obligations are."

"He does. I promise you I gave him an earful over this. But look at the positive, he listened to you and brought in Doc—hired him exclusively for your rehabilitation. That shows just how much the club wants—no, *needs*—you back to help them win that pennant he's promised the city."

"Perhaps. But if they wanted me back so desperately, it would be Doc here, not his daughter."

"She wouldn't be here if she wasn't qualified. You sound like a prima donna. You wanted a different physical therapist and you got one. Suck it up, Wylder. You've got less than three months to get your spikes back between the chalk lines, so use the resources they got for you and quit—"

"My bitching," I finish for him as I scrub a hand through my hair and look out at the empty stadium. "You're right. Sorry."

"Don't be."

"This is getting fucking old. I'm stuck on the DL, being pressured to return on a timeline by the club I've played for my whole career, and all because I decided to go for home and try to score the extra run? Santiago didn't even have the goddamn ball when he blocked the plate. So what? He fucks over me and my arm both in one goddamn dirty play, and all the fucker gets is a hundred-grand fine and a four-game suspension? You want to know why I'm in a crappy mood? It's because I'm getting the shit end of the stick here, with no damn clue why he did it."

I know he's heard it all before. My bitching and moaning over the injury. Over being taken from my game, my life, and forced to sit here on a daily basis and watch it play on without me.

"I can't tell you why Santiago has a beef with you . . . but he does. That's pretty damn evident."

"No shit. Sorry," I say for what feels like the tenth time. "I'm just having a pity party."

"I get it, East. You want back out there."

"Like fucking yesterday."

"I know dude, but I can't make your arm heal any faster. You've had the best surgeons, the best resources, and now you'll have the best physical therapist there is in baseball."

"But—"

"You think Doc's going to risk his career by ruining yours? If he sent his daughter to rehab you, then no doubt she's qualified to get you back. Just ride it out. Put your earphones on if you need to, listen to one of those damn audiobooks that I can't for the life of me understand how you listen to, and tune her out . . . but put in the hours. Get better. And you'll be back before you know it."

Easier said than done.

"Yeah. Sure."

I end the phone call, lean back into the hard plastic of the stadium seat, and prop my feet on the empty row in front of me.

And I dare to look at what I'm missing out on. The nets of the backstop fade away as I stare at the place where I've lived my life—between the chalk lines and behind home plate.

It's fucking beautiful. A blessing and a curse. My pleasure and my pain.

The only thing I've ever known.

The only thing I've ever wanted to do.

I lose myself to my thoughts. Time passes, minutes ticking down to the next Aces' game tonight that I won't be playing in. And like every night my team plays without me, I fight the rage of helplessness that corners my mind.

I know he's there. I can sense him before I hear the creak of the seat a few down from mine, followed by the clearing of his throat. I don't glance his way—unsure if I want to deal with his bullshit just yet—so I nod instead of speaking.

"By the length of time you've been sitting out here, and the fact that you're not in the team meeting right now, am I right to assume you haven't gotten cleared to play yet?"

"Hi, Dad. How're you doing today?"

"I take that as a no?"

"What do you think?"

"Don't be a smartass." There is no humor in his tone. No smile warming his voice.

"I'm not. I'm here. They're there. And it's been two days since the last time you asked the same exact question you asked me three days before that, so do you really think that I've miraculously recovered since then?"

Definitely not in the mood to put up with his shit.

"The team—"

"Dad, there are more things in life than baseball." I look his way for the first time. I give no smile, no nod, just a lift of my eyebrows behind my sunglasses in a half-hearted attempt to mask my need for him to just be my dad and not the baseball great, Cal Wylder.

"Like what, son? Do you have a family you go home to every night? *No.* This club is your family. Your teammates are your brothers. And you're currently letting them down by not showing up to the table with dinner every night."

Ah. Tough love, Wylder-style. Gotta love that. But then again, I shouldn't expect any less. It was always one more fly ball, one more throw down to second, one more *let's do it until you get it right, son,* before we could eat lunch, eat dinner, or go home.

In an effort to avoid the recurring fight between us, I look away and rest my head on the seat back. It's much easier to focus on the blue sky above and feeling sorry for myself than deal with him. "Sorry, Pops. While I inherited your skill with a ball, I sure as hell didn't inherit your godlike ability to heal."

"Maybe you're not putting in enough time at the gym, then. It takes dedication to come back from an injury. You know, if you get the muscles strong around the tear, they will help take the pressure off the cuff."

"Got it." I clench my jaw.

"Every day you're off the field gives another player an opportunity to steal your starting position. You have to be vigilant against that."

"Sure thing."

"I'm serious, Easton. This is important, so you better start treating it that way." Funny how no matter how many times he's used this phrase over the years, it still jolts me back to being eight years old and on the mound in Little League, the tears of frustration in my eyes because I couldn't make the ball hit the strike zone, and him telling me I wasn't trying hard enough. And how, well over an hour after the last inning ended, he sat on the bucket behind home plate and demanded ten strikes in a row before we could go home.

I hated him that day.

I respected him later for it, but I hated him that day.

Kind of like now. Not much has changed.

"I get you're serious. No doubt there, Dad. Good thing the front office is, too, since they just brought in Doc to help my rehab."

"Hmm," he murmurs, and it takes everything in me to keep my eyes closed and wait for whatever I've got coming next. That sound from him is never followed with a benign statement. "Doc, huh? Let's hope you don't blow off three sessions with him like you did the trainer you had before. That'd be grounds for the club to cut you."

"They're not going to cut me, Dad." But he's planted the seed, and I know it will haunt me tonight when I can't sleep. "Besides, I skipped out because I didn't have a choice. I had to take care of Mom."

I wait to hear the disapproval that always falls from his mouth, but it doesn't come. In fact, nothing does, and I'm not sure if the silence makes me grateful or worried.

"It's a shame your mother's . . . *problem* . . . is affecting your career."

I grit my teeth and hold back the sigh I'm certain every child of divorce knows by heart when one parent disses the other. "Yeah, well . . . her *problem* was a result of things beyond my control. She was alone and fell. Someone had to take care of her. And, for your information, I didn't skip out on my appointments. I called in, got my training, and did it on my own time."

He clears his throat, his universal sound for "not buying it," but I don't really fucking care right now. I love him more than anything, but most days I loathe him, and his demanding expectations, too.

"It's not the same. You have to be present, be seen. The club isn't happy, Easton . . ." He lets his phrase fade off, but it will still fertilize the goddamn seed he planted. "Your bat was on fire. You had the streak going, you were picking off runners left and right, and your pitch calls were perfection. Every day you're gone is another day those facts are forgotten, and in a game of statistics, that's worrisome."

"And here I thought you were going to pay me a compliment and just leave it at that. I should have known better."

"Easton." My name is a warning. A demand for respect. One I've heard more times than I can count. And yet there is something underlying it that I can't quite pinpoint.

"Such a shame my rotator cuff was ripped apart. Must have been my fault that prick yanked it backward on the tag. Should I have called time-out on the way down and asked him to hurt something else instead? Break a bone because that heals easier than tendons? Is that what I was supposed to do, Dad? Would that have met your expectations?" My voice escalates with each word, my frustrated anger loud and clear. And fuck, yes, I'm being disrespectful, but so is he, and I'm sick of hearing it.

Silence descends around us in this house I grew up in, under the shadow of the iron giant sitting beside me, who ruled this stadium his entire career. I look out to where his number, twenty-two, adorns the center field wall in retirement, and wonder if I'll ever live up to the expectations he set out for me that day on the mound when I was eight.

I'm not quite sure.

"Look, you're right." He sighs instead of apologizing. "I just want the best for you, Easton. I always have. I hate that you're injured. I hate that your shoulder's not coming along as quickly as it should.

And I hate that I'm here and there's nothing I can do to help you."

I look over to him, see his dark hair with silver at the temples and his eyes that match mine, and know he means well. The hard-ass with a son who can carry on the legacy he left when he retired.

"You can just be my dad. That will help me."

And yet I know there's no separating Cal, the three-thousand-hit player, from Cal, Easton's father.

They're one and the same.

Always have been.

Always will be.

CHAPTER THREE

Scout

Each thump of his stride on the treadmill irritates me more than the last.

Every grunt of exertion adds to it.

And then there's the beep. The one that tells me his thirty minutes of high intensity running is complete, and now it's my turn to get hands on and complete the session.

Lucky me.

I'm irritable. Pissed off. And I'm not sure if my current mood stems from exhaustion after spending too many hours last night Googling Easton Wylder, or the fact that it seems he was doing the same about me.

"So are you actually going to touch my arm today, or is the expertise you bragged about yesterday limited to telling me *treadmill, thirty minutes, level ten*? If you wanted to avoid me, then maybe you should call in sick for the next few months." Sarcasm drips from his voice. His obvious disdain for me makes that even keel I thought we might have found yesterday seem nonexistent.

I need to turn around, to face him, but I stall. The images from

Google are seared in my mind. The charity calendar where the month of April is a picture of him wearing nothing but a strategically placed baseball glove. The ESPN body issue where he's batting—naked—the twist of his legs hiding his package. The ESPYs with him looking dashing in a three-piece suit. All of them are there, floating around, reminding me how all those hard lines and toned edges look in person.

And it would take a dead woman to not be affected by him.

So, I steel myself for the visceral impact of looking at him—hot, sweaty, relaxed—but it doesn't help when I turn around. I'm not sure anything could. Because even in his sweat-dampened T-shirt, he's still breathtakingly handsome with his mixture of all-American and rugged outdoorsman. He still exudes that tinge of arrogance. And the odd thing is how today when I look at him, after I've stared at pictures of him for hours yesterday, somehow the arrogance adds to his appeal.

And then he smirks, and I shake my head and question my own sanity.

"So you actually want me to look at your arm? You mean you'll trust me with it? And here I was under the impression you thought I was just a *trophy* trainer."

"Come again?" He chuckles.

Time to clear the air between us. Being handsome doesn't override being an asshole. "You know, *trophy trainer*—someone good for you to look at, but incapable of much else."

He shrugs. "If the shoe fits."

I take a step closer to him, his sarcastic comeback igniting the embers of my temper he lit yesterday. "Don't be a jerk. If you want to find out if I'm qualified for the job—capable of getting you back in top form—then you *ask me* for my credentials. You want a resume? You want references? I'd be glad to hand you a list of them, so don't go snooping around, making phone calls, and questioning everything about me without talking to me first. *Got it*?"

Our eyes hold as he worries his bottom lip between his teeth to combat the smile he's fighting. "You want me to take my rehab seriously, right? Then don't chastise me for making sure the person charged to do it is up to par and has the right experience. I don't trust my body with just anyone, let alone a rookie trainer still learning the ropes. *Got it*?"

"Touché," I murmur as we wage a visual war of defiance and misunderstanding. "We're wasting time. Let's get started."

Maybe if we begin, I'll forget about the phone calls I received last night. The ones from previous clients and personal friends I'd rehabbed informing me I was being vetted. I was thankful for the heads-up, and at the same time, I was pissed that he was questioning my qualifications.

But he did just make a damn good point.

I grab the ultrasound cart and wheel it toward the table, but he's still standing there like yesterday, still questioning me. Obviously, he doesn't believe I'm experienced enough to do the job, but I shrug it off, knowing after my rebuke of him, he was bound to either respect me or test me, and by the current standoff, I'm guessing it will be the latter.

"Yes?" I finally ask when he doesn't budge.

"You wanna tell me where Doc is?"

"He's got a packed schedule on the East Coast right now. As you know, injury happens without warning." I hold his gaze and hope he doesn't see through the lie.

"Uh-huh." He just nods, but I can tell he's not convinced. He's the one who made the calls last night, so I'm certain he has pieced together that it's been a while since Doc's been around. But there must be something in my eyes he sees—the something I'm trying desperately to keep together—that prevents him from digging deeper. "He's the best there is," Easton says.

"Agreed."

"Should I be worried then?"

"About?" I prompt.

"If he's the best, then doesn't that mean you're second best?"

His remark hits closer to home than I'd like, but it's his body, his career, and his right to ask.

"Second best to Doc Dalton isn't a bad place to be. I learned everything I know from the man. I assure you, he's the last person I want to let down, and you're the beneficiary of that fear, so . . ." I quirk my brows. "Lucky you."

"Lucky me," he murmurs but still doesn't move. "The problem is I still don't know shit about you, and yet you're standing there ready to work on my arm."

"What do you want to know?" I'm getting impatient. Another day, another round of bullshit, and once again, time is wasting. But at least he listened and is asking me instead of snooping around for answers.

"What were your stats in the major leagues?"

"*What*?"

"I asked your stats. Errors. On-base percentage. Batting average. Fielding percentage. You know, statistics."

"I know what statistics are," I respond dryly.

"But if you've never played in the majors, how do you know how my arm's supposed to feel so that you can get it back to one hundred percent?"

He's neglecting the fact that no other trainer has played in the major leagues either . . . but I have a better way to shut him up. "Have you ever been a woman?"

"*What*?" It's his turn to be surprised by an unexpected question. "Of course not. I've got plenty of proof that I'm all man."

I roll my eyes, half expecting him to grab his crotch and equally relieved that he doesn't. "Well, if you've never been a woman, how is it you know how to please one in bed? How do you know if you're hitting the right spot? Getting her off?"

He fights back a bark of a laugh, but eventually lets it escape as he just shakes his head. "Touché," he repeats my word back to me.

"If you're going to bust my chops, Wylder, you should know that I can give as good as I get."

"Point taken. But since you're the one singlehandedly charged with busting my balls in rehab over the next three months, you've gotta admit, it was a valid question."

"It was," I concede, "but it's your job to talk to me, tell me how it feels, where it hurts, and when it feels good, so I can make it better." An unexpectedly shy smile slides onto his lips when he gets the correlation between my question about how to please a woman and my answer.

"Just like sex."

"Perhaps." I smile; it's all I can do as heat flushes my cheeks and the room around us becomes too small for him and this innuendo-laced conversation. "Some men have all the tools in the world, but if they don't know how to use them, they're useless. It's the same with my job. You've gotta know how to use your skills, and I assure you, I do. So, if the I-don't-trust-you-because-you-have-a-vagina-card has been exhausted, can we get started, please?" I lift my chin toward the table behind him while I adjust the settings on the machine.

"You drive a hard bargain, *Kitty*." He chuckles as he sits down and pulls off his shirt.

"You ain't seen nothing yet."

Nothing more is said between us as I apply the ultrasound gel and then the wand to his shoulder, despite being all too aware that he's still staring at me.

I welcome the silence, using it to concentrate on the task at hand as I move the wand over the joint of his shoulder, across the angry red seam there and back, several times over. Players enter the locker room beyond where we are. I can hear their chatter—the low whistles, the suggestive laughs, the one-off comments—but know better than to give them attention. It may be a different clubhouse, but it's basically the same reaction I typically get.

I knew I'd have a tough crowd to win over when I followed in my father's footsteps. I knew being a woman in this male-dominated world wouldn't be a walk in the proverbial ballpark. And so I ignore the comments like I always have and choose to consider them compliments, while letting the more suggestive ones go. In a practiced move, I keep my eyes focused on the player I'm working on and my back to the lockers to avoid any pecker peep-shows, which I learned long ago are inevitable.

It saves me embarrassment and preserves the respect I have to command to be taken seriously.

"Relax," I murmur as I run the ultrasonic waves back and forth to reduce inflammation. For some reason, he keeps tensing up, and it's counteracting the therapy I'm providing.

There's another comment behind my back. Something good-humored about another wand in his jock I could put to better use.

If the guy's going to be a chauvinist, at least he's witty about it.

I stifle a laugh. It's all I can do. But it's Easton who visibly tenses in reaction.

Apparently, he can dish it out, but doesn't want anyone else to.

Interesting.

And sweet.

He seems to be upset on my behalf, and yet yesterday he was the one who thought I was a stripper here to entertain him.

Good thing I didn't take the bait, then. I was ready to kiss you senseless just to call your bluff and prove you were a stripper.

His words come back to me—the ones that repeated through my mind at random times yesterday, which then led to my Google search on him. My hands touch him now, but my mind recalls the charity calendar I found—him in all his gorgeous, naked glory.

Another comment somewhere in the locker room.

Another bristle by him.

And the irony isn't lost on me. He's getting pissed on my behalf, and I'm thinking of what he looks like naked. Well, almost naked. My imagination fills in exactly what is beneath the baseball glove.

And, of course, now *I* blush.

"Where did you leave off with your previous trainer?" I ask to try and break the tension that's becoming more and more evident in the tightening of his muscles.

"We were throwing the ball."

"All out?"

"At about fifty, sixty percent."

"Hitting any?"

"A bit, at about seventy percent."

"Okay." I draw the word out, pleased he speaks my lingo. "Tell me how it felt when you did those things."

"Frustrating."

"If you're going to make love to me Wylder, you're gonna need to do a helluva lot more than that to get me off." His head whips up, shocked hazel eyes meeting my gray ones, and I know I've got his attention now. I continue. "Explain. Why was it frustrating? Did it hurt? Was there a pinch, or was it just tight from not being used? Or was it mental? It's bound to feel different, so is it the fear of reinjuring yourself that's holding you back?"

He struggles with what to say, his eyes narrowing as he looks away. I lower the wand and wipe the excess gel from his shoulder. "How about all of the above?" he finally says.

"That's a fair answer. I tell you what—how about we stretch it today, go through some new exercises that you might not have done yet, and then tomorrow we take it to the field and get a ball in that hand of yours?"

"Really?" He sounds like a little boy finding out he gets to play after sitting on the bench for the last six innings. It breaks my heart and fills it simultaneously.

"Really." I walk around to the back of him and begin to move his arm to feel for any clicking or popping with the movement in his rotator cuff. "Let's get started then."

"So, I think it's on the right track," I say with a conclusive nod, needing to step away from him and the connection that our bodies have had for the better part of ninety minutes.

I've worked his arm every which way and now have a better grasp on what I need to do to strengthen it. How to make a plan of attack.

"It might be a bit sore later and tomorrow. Your hissing tells me I pushed you a little further than your previous trainer did, but I'm pleased with how solid the repair feels. We just need to get you back into the routine slowly, and then the motions will begin to feel natural again."

"Does that mean I get to throw a ball tomorrow?"

"It does, indeed." His smile is lightning-quick in response, and completely disarming.

I've seen Easton-the-skeptic's smile. I've even seen the Easton-thinks-he's-being-played smile. But Easton's I-get-to do-what-I-love-tomorrow smile is bright enough to light up the room.

"Easton. My man. You doing good?" Luckily we're interrupted so I stop staring at him. J.P. Gaston, another player, walks into our training room. He grabs hands with Easton in some kind of handshake and pulls him in for a manly hug before slapping him on the back in greeting.

"Hanging in there. Way to kick ass last night. Your bat's on fire, man."

"Don't jinx me, dude. Bad juju is everywhere these days."

"Look who you're talking to," Easton says with a shake of his head. "I feel like I've been swimming in it for months. My luck has to return soon."

"Fucking bad juju," J.P. says with a laugh before leaning closer to Easton and murmuring so I can barely hear it, "But dude, the DL has never looked as appealing as it does right now."

"Watch Guzman's slider tonight," Easton says, talking right over the comment as if he didn't hear it. "I was studying him against the Yankees the other night, and it's starting to float some."

"Ah, the beloved hanging curveball," J.P. says as he takes a few steps backward toward the door. He slides his eyes my way and offers up a smile before looking back to Easton. "Good thing I know how to swing my stick."

Easton picks up his shirt sitting beside him, balls it up, and throws it at him, just as he darts out of the doorway and past the windows, into the depths of the now-full clubhouse. I avoid the natural inclination to watch him, because the pregame ritual has started out there, and that means men in varying stages of undress, shooting the shit as they mentally prepare for their night of work.

"Hot damn. She's as hot up close? Shit," someone says loud enough for me to hear. Seems that J.P. was the one elected to come on in and get a closer look at the new female trainer.

There's one in every clubhouse.

"Hurt me, baby," someone else cries out.

"Oh, Easton. Let me stretch you and bend you and do naughty things to you," another teammate mimics in a high-pitched voice.

Without glancing up, I lift my middle finger to the men, who I'm more than sure are watching and waiting to see my reaction from their schoolyard ribbing. Laughter rumbles through the locker room at my response, but I hear a muttered, "Goddammit," beneath Easton's breath.

"Let me guess? Tino and Drew?" I ask, completely unfazed.

"Yep," he sighs with a roll of his eyes.

"Good to see they've matured since high school," I say lightheartedly as I continue to put the ultrasound machine away. But when I turn back around, I'm stopped in my tracks by the look on his face. His expression is guarded, and yet there's something about it—a hint of surprise maybe—that holds my feet still and my attention hostage.

"What is it?"

"Just trying to figure you out, is all," he says with a shake of his head.

"There's not much to figure."

"I disagree."

"Well, you're wrong," I say as I spray disinfectant on the table and start to wipe it down, anything to avoid the softening of his eyes and the questions I don't want to answer. "I'm boring. A what-you-see-is-what-you-get kind of girl."

"Except you wear your heart on your sleeve." My hand falters mid-motion then I continue to clean with a renewed vigor, but he doesn't turn to leave like I had hoped. "You come off tough as nails, like you don't let shit get to you, and yet that heart you're wearing says there's a helluva lot more than the tough exterior does."

"And your point?"

"Nothing. Just making an observation."

Those words scrape nerves already raw after the last few months. Comebacks and rebukes all swirl in my head, but every single one of them is on the defensive. And while the defensive implies he's right—*and he is right*—I sure as hell don't want to let him know that.

This is work—the reputation I'm trying to establish. And he's a client who holds the ticket to achieve two of my goals.

"Scout and Easton sitting in a tree, k-i-s-s-i-n-g," someone sings above the fray outside the door.

"Let it rest, guys," Easton shouts over his shoulder.

"It's fine," I say.

"Of course it is. Anything to save you from having this discussion, right?"

"There's nothing wrong with wearing your heart on your sleeve." I may say the words to play it off, but my tone doesn't sound as forgiving.

"Sorry." He sighs. "For what I said . . . and for the assholes."

"Don't be. I'm here for you. Not them." I risk a glance their way and smile. "Hopefully none of them get hurt, because I'd be a lot less gentle if I have to rehab them." I get the chuckle from him I was working for and hope the discussion is now buried.

"Good to know, but I'm sorry, anyway. We can train somewhere else if you want. Or if it bugs you, I'll have a talk with them."

"No need to . . . but thank you for the thought. Besides, it seems like their ribbing is minor compared to the legendary pranks you've pulled on them."

"True." His lips break into a smug smile. "But it's not fair to you."

"Don't worry about me. I'm a big girl. I can handle myself. I've got a sword tucked in my purse in case I need to slay any dragons."

"Your purse?"

"Yeah, it's big and roomy." I smile, more than glad to change the subject, as I grab said purse from the cupboard I stashed it in.

"Keep anything else in there besides a sword?"

"High heels," I joke, earning a raise of his brows. "This girl likes her heels when she's kicking ass."

"Gotta love a woman who's multidimensional. You heading out, too?" he asks, but neither of us makes a move to leave as his eyes continue to ask more questions than I want to answer or even acknowledge.

Suddenly flustered by the intensity of his stare, I begin to ramble. "So, alternate ice and heat every twenty minutes or so for the next few hours. That will help with the swelling and inflammation I caused today. Okay?"

I take a few steps, as if the conversation is over, but Easton doesn't move out of my way. He just stands there, eyes still searching, continuing to pull at parts of me that need to stay put.

I lick my lips. I shift my feet.

"I know the drill," he finally says.

But we still don't move.

"Same time tomorrow."

"Okay."

Quit looking at me like that.

"And depending on how the week goes, we might bump up our sessions to twice a day."

"Okay."

You've run out of things to say, Scout. Time to go now.

"Well, I'll see you then. Tomorrow, I mean." I roll my eyes at myself.

"Obviously. Tomorrow, I mean." A half-cocked smile turns up one corner of his mouth.

Move. Go. Walk.

"You're nothing like I expected." I cringe once I realize I've just blurted my thoughts out and hate myself the minute I do. My cheeks flush with heat, but my embarrassment gives me the motivation I need to take the first step away from him.

"I'm never what anyone expects. It's a blessing and a curse."

His comment begs me to ask more, but I don't. Can't. This space is too small for us—it feels like there's not enough air when he looks at me that way.

"Good night."

"'Night, Scout," he says as I reach the doorway. "Hey . . ."

"Yeah?" I turn around, one hand on the doorjamb, my eyes falling back on him.

"For the record, how is it you know that I know how to please a woman in bed?"

Crap. I walked right into that one.

The cocky grin he flashes me is the lasting image burned into my mind as I walk away without a word.

Because I know.

CHAPTER FOUR

Scout

"Hi. How are you doing?"

"What's the assessment?"

I fight back the tears that burn at hearing his voice again and knowing, even now, he's still putting the business between us. I take a deep breath to control the emotions spiraling out of control, because I know he'll get upset if he hears a waver in my voice when I answer.

"Scouty?"

"Yeah, Dad. I'm here." He may only be a two-hour drive away, but right now it feels like a million.

"And?" he presses.

How are you?

I miss you?

Are you in pain?

Are you getting worse?

I'd rather be there with you than here.

"Clear mind. Hard heart."

I clench my jaw when he repeats the mantra he expects me to

live by, and I sense the rebuke is because he knows I'm about to fall apart. Of course he knows. He knows me better than anyone.

I clear my throat, compose myself, and then try my best to be what he needs me to be right now. "Easton Wylder. Four months post-op from a torn labrum. The onset of injury was due to a questionable play by the opposing team when the patient was sliding into home plate. He was tagged unnecessarily, arm hooked by the opponent and yanked backward with force. The injury presented immediately and surgery commenced within twenty-four hours. Easton completed his initial three-plus months of post-op rehab, but was not cleared for play by the previous physical therapist. Upon initial observation, he seems to have good mobility. I'd say he's at eighty-five percent. The joint seems stiff, as is to be expected after restricted use, but during stretching would allow me to push its limits, which indicates that full mobility is within reach. The patient has indicated that in previous attempts to bat and throw he has felt pain. I plan on getting a ball back into his hand as quickly as possible to work on the mental aspect, because I feel he is holding back for fear of re-injury. Prognosis is good, but I need more time with him to know if my assessment is accurate or not." Confident I've covered the bases, I wait for my dad's feedback.

His rattle of breath reaches through the line and draws out my need for approval.

"You mean *the player*, right?" It's all he says, and I die a little inside.

"What?"

"You said Easton."

"I did?"

"Yes. Twice."

"Yes. Once for the patient introduction and the other was a simple mistake."

"Scout. How many times do I have to tell you that you're to remain impartial?"

"I am. I was. His name's in my notes. I was looking at them and accidentally repeated what I saw."

"Don't let it happen again."

"Yes. I won't."

"And questionable play. Why add that in? It's not your job to decide what's questionable or dirty or accidental. It's your job to get your player back to optimum performance, not to pass judgment."

"I know, but the play was dirty, Dad. You can't argue that."

"Do you like him, Scout?"

The question catches me off guard, and I'm uncertain what exactly he means by it. "I've only just met him." It's a safe answer.

"But do you like him? Is he going to work hard? Does he want to return? Or is he a prima donna riding his dad's coattails with no respect for the sport?"

"You're kidding me, right?" I stutter. "The man plays with more heart than anyone I've seen in a long time. He's a throwback. A real gamer. The guy you want at bat when you're bottom of the ninth, full count, with the World Series on the line."

"You're too close, Scout." It's all he says, but it's enough to make me realize how ardently I just defended a man who, seconds before, I said I barely knew. Did I just prove my dad's point that maybe I'm already too close, because Easton's just another player and it's my job to get him ready.

But he isn't just another player.

He's the player who can give me what I need to fulfill my dad's wishes.

And he's the man who has invaded my thoughts and taken residence there.

"That's the player you're talking about. What about the man?"

It's the oddest of questions for my dad to ask, and yet I feel like there is more to this conversation that I'm not quite getting the gist of. I take my time to respond. "Like I said, I've only assessed him twice, so I don't know him that well. First impression is that he's a good guy. I mean, he stood up for me when the guys were doing their usual bullshit about me being in the clubhouse."

"*Really*?" It's a leading question, but I don't buy into it. If he wants to ask me something, then he needs to ask it.

"Dad, what are you—"

"What's your plan of action with him moving forward?" he asks, as if I never even spoke. And while I hate being disregarded, this razor-sharp focus of his on a player has been gone more days than not, and so I acquiesce.

I sort through my thoughts, explain them point by point, and then outline what I plan to do with *the player*. My dad makes suggestions, and I take notes, heeding his advice on possible drills.

But I catch myself holding the phone to my ear with two hands and just listening. Memorizing the sound of his voice. The timbre of it. The little inflections only he has. I lose myself in the presence of the only person who has ever been a constant in my life.

"Sounds like a good plan, Scouty. You'll need to adjust as he does, though. Nothing good ever comes from setting your plans in stone."

"I know," I whisper, thinking of all the plans we'd made over the years for when he retired. And now that he unofficially has, we'll never get to fulfill them.

"Scout." It's a warning. A reprimand. A plea for me to toughen up.

I clear my throat. "He seems eager to return," I say to save face, in the hope that he'll see I'm unaffected by Easton. But before I can finish my thought, he erupts into a fit of coughing.

It sounds worse than last week. That's all I can think as that rattle makes chills race across my skin and dread sink in my stomach. The questions I want to pepper him with, but know he won't allow, are getting harder to bite back. The need to jump in the car and drop my foot like a lead weight on the gas until I'm beside him is getting tougher to resist.

"Daddy?" The word slips out in a whisper just like the lone tear that escapes and slides down my cheek.

"I'm fine, Scouty. Just fine. It's just the damn cough," he finally says when he catches his breath.

But it's so much more than that.

"What did the doctor say yesterday?" I ask, prepared for the rebuke.

"Did Sally tell you I had an appointment?" he barks.

"Someone has to." *Please. Talk to me.*

"Everything's the same. Nothing's going to change, so it's ridiculous to be worrying about me when you need to be worried about getting *the player* back up and behind the plate. It's a rarity to have a cuff tear when it's not a pitcher, so make sure you heed caution. And make sure to learn from it."

"Okay," I agree, but my mind is lost searching his voice for what he's not telling me. Did the doctor tell him he has less time left than he thought? Is that why he won't talk about it?

The notion stuns me when I've already been stunned enough over the past few months. And I'm so lost in my fear that I almost miss his soft words when he speaks them.

"I'm counting on you. I know it's a lot to ask . . . and I'd do it if I could . . ."

Words escape me as the tears slide freely down my cheeks, and my heart twists inside my chest. "Dad." It's all I can say through the onslaught of emotion I'm trying to hold back.

"We'll talk soon. Clear mind, hard heart, Scouty. Remember that and you'll be fine."

But I won't.

I'll be far from it.

And that's why I'm more determined than ever.

CHAPTER FIVE

Easton

I nod my head and lift the neck of my beer in thanks to the knock-out blonde across the bar who just sent it over.

"You need to jump all over that," Tino says with a little hum of appreciation to follow.

I smile at her—doe-eyed, legs for days, with a skirt pulled up and a shirt plunging down—and fuck, I could use a good lay right now. "Nah," I murmur, my mouth contradicting what my dick is agreeing to as I raise the bottle to my lips and look back to the guys at my table.

"Nah?" Drew sputters. "Since when do you say *nah* to a betty like that?"

Images flash through my mind. Challenging gray eyes. Muscular little body. Brown hair pulled up in a messy ponytail. A woman who isn't trying hard at all and is still sexier than the blonde baseball betty trying to add a notch to her *how many Austin Aces have I fucked* tally she most likely displays prominently on her bedpost.

"She's all yours, D. I'm sure she'd take you as a consolation," I tease as J.P. barks out in laughter at the fuck-you look Drew is trying to kill me with.

"Second is better than third," Drew replies with a direct dig at J.P., since he plays third base and Drew plays second.

"Fuck off." J.P. laughs but flips us off.

"Gladly. But I want to know why East here is passing up parting her sweet thighs when he obviously needs to get good and laid," Drew says with a lift of his chin to the blonde again.

"How do you know I need to get good and laid?"

"You've been on a permanent home stretch, which means your forearms are getting a workout, but not in the baseball sense." He demonstrates making a jacking-off motion.

"Fuck off." I roll my eyes.

"Dude, a homestretch like yours is enough to make anyone itch for some action, and since you can't get any on the field, you might as well get some between the sheets," Drew explains with perfect sense.

"Boredom makes your dick need action," Tino affirms, and I can't help but laugh at their fucked-up logic.

Fucked-up, but pretty damn accurate.

I catch Blondie's eye again, consider her, but know any chick buying me beers in Sluggers, our team's local hangout, is looking for more than a thank-you.

Could be fun.

"Ah, it all makes sense now."

J.P.'s murmur pulls me from making a mistake that I suddenly want to make . . .

"It's that fuck-hot trainer of yours that's grabbing you by the balls, isn't it?"

And knocks it out of the park, putting the image of Scout into my mind.

Not like it was very far to begin with.

"Nah," I murmur. Hell if I'll give him the satisfaction of knowing he's right.

"Bullshit. Dude, I'd let her rub me down in a second. Add in some oil . . . and we could have our own slip and Drew-slide," Drew chimes in.

"You're fucked in the head," I laugh.

"That's the hope," he muses as he raises his eyebrows, "just a different kind of head."

Over my dead body.

My own thought knocks me back a step. Forces me to suck down my free beer and reconsider Blondie's unspoken, no-strings-attached offer, but now I can't. Not when Scout is in my head, and my dick's reacting to the thought of her more than the thought of the woman down the bar.

"For some reason I don't think Scout's into screwing the starting line-up," I say with an arch of my brow. "So hands to yourself, you grabby fucker." I hope my thinly veiled threat is heard, and at the same time not heard. Them knowing I have the hots for Scout will only make life in the clubhouse worse for her.

"I agree. If she was into that, she'd be out in the locker room flirting with everyone. Sucks for you, though." J.P. taps his beer against mine.

"Depends who's doing the sucking," I say, getting a laugh for the distraction.

"Well, rumor is you're her ticket to getting the Aces' contract," Drew says.

"Really?" He has my attention now.

"I heard that Doc's worked in every clubhouse in the majors except for ours. Supposedly by fulfilling this contract and getting you back on the field, he's angling for the club to sign him to run the team's PT program. Word is, he's never had a long-term contract with a club, but after a lifetime on the road, travelling from team to team to rehab their stars . . . a la *you*," he says with a nod, "he wants to end his career this way. Getting to stay in one place for a while."

"The perfect game to close out a pennant-winning career," I

muse. Makes sense.

"Exactly."

"And how does his daughter play into all of this?"

"Not sure." Drew shrugs. "But if she's half as good as he is, it'd be more than good enough. Plus, dude, are you going to complain that you get that hot little body pressing up against you every day?"

My smile is automatic. "Not at all." I laugh.

"That's what I thought," he says as he motions to our waitress for another round. "Lucky for you, our lovely GM has given Sumo Sam his written notice. He's got ninety days and his contract is void."

"Thank Christ," I murmur, recalling the last time I let the team's lead physical therapist, Sam, touch my shoulder. At about three months post-op, my shoulder was nowhere close to where it should have been. Frustrated and feeling like I was spinning my wheels, I demanded to know why we were doing the same shit every day rather than try the new methodologies other clubhouses were using and having success with. I think back to how pissed he was that I questioned him. How he told me I wasn't healing because I wasn't putting in the time when in fact I was putting in so much time I was overdoing it. Such fucking bullshit.

"Sam doesn't know an elbow from an asshole," J.P. says.

"You're telling me."

"Yeah, Miller told me he overheard Cory tell Sam that the Aces are a forward-thinking organization and that from here on out he expects every member to subscribe to the idea or some bullshit like that. And how since Sam refused to educate himself on the newest trends—your shoulder rehab—then he was in breach of the fine print of his contract and would no longer have a position with the Aces."

"Asshole," I mutter.

"Which one? Sam or Cory?" Tino asks.

"Take your pick." I roll my eyes. "Look, I get bringing a new GM in to restructure the Aces' organization. It's always good to switch things up and trim costs after having the same people running the club for so many years. What I don't get is Cory. There's something about him I can't quite put my finger on."

"He's a bean counter." Drew shrugs. "He's a live by the contract, die by the contract, even when the words in the contract don't make any fucking sense, kind of guy. I get his job is all about dollars and cents, but this is *baseball* we're talking about here." He takes a long swig of his beer. "Then again I'm buzzed so what the fuck do I know?"

"A lot."

"I'm with you, East," Tino says. "The jury is still out on Cory. I mean . . . take Doc Dalton. The man has a legendary record of success. How fucked up is it that Cory is making him vet himself for the new long-term contract by getting an ugly fucker like Easton here back on the field?"

"Vet himself? Doc Dalton?" J.P. laughs in disbelief. "That's kind of funny."

"The man with the golden hands," I murmur, thinking of all the times I'd be on the road with my dad and watched Doc work his magic on opposing players.

"No doubt his daughter's hands . . . *and thighs*, are just as magical."

I hear the comment but my thoughts are on what Drew just said. On the fact that the club's new general manager is thinking of bringing Doc's team on board to run the club's physical therapy regimen. It's fucking great news, since I'll need the continued rehab.

But it's also daunting to have the final piece to this man's renowned career rely on whether I return to the roster within the mandated timeframe.

Nothing like adding a little more pressure or anything.

"If that's the case," I interject into the conversation that's moved on to the questionable call from the game earlier, "wouldn't Doc be here rehabbing me instead of Scout?"

Three pair of eyes angle my way. "You want man-hands on you instead of woman-hands?" Tino asks, and the table erupts into laughter.

"T, you're so hard up you'd take any hands at this point."

"At least I'm not a picky bastard like you," he replies.

"East has a point," J.P. says. "But considering I was thinking about pulling a groin tonight just so Scout could rub it out for me, my vote is to keep her around."

"Fucker," I chuckle. "You're vote's no good, though. Scout's here for me. *Only me*," I taunt. "So you're shit outta luck. Be my guest, though, and pull that muscle. I'm sure Sumo Sam would love to rub out your groin and maybe take a quick detour to find your dick while he's at it."

"Gonna need a magnifying glass for that," J.P. mocks.

Phones ding around the table and interrupt the conversation as we all move to see what's going on.

ESPN Alert: Trade rumors are swirling that Jose Santiago will likely be traded in the coming weeks.

"Fucker." My comment is repeated around the table as I stare at the name of the person responsible for my stint on the DL.

"God help whatever team he lands on," Drew says.

My phone alerts me again, and when I look at the screen, I sigh but for a completely different reason. *Not again.* "Sorry guys. Put mine on my tab. I've gotta head out."

"You good to drive, man?" Drew asks.

"Yeah. I only had two. I'm good."

Too much damn time to think.

About Santiago.

Scout.

If my arm's fucked up to the point of no return.

And only one of those thoughts on the hour drive to the outskirts of town is welcome. So, by the time I pull into the familiar gravel lot, tires crunching beneath me and the silver moonlight around me, I'm in no mood to face this. It's not like I have a choice though.

The slam of my truck door echoes as I stride up the pathway I know all too well.

"Sorry it took me so long, Marty," I say as I walk through his plume of cigarette smoke to where he's standing outside the rundown bar.

"No worries. She's not hurting anyone. Sissy called in sick tonight. I'm flying solo so I can't leave the bar to take her back to her place."

Same old song and dance. Just a different day.

The air, stale with cigarette smoke and cheap liquor, hits me the minute I open the ill-hanging wooden door and walk into the dimly lit bar. I spot her immediately. She's slumped in *her booth* with empty glasses littering the table in front of her.

"Mom."

She jumps at the sound of my voice, her eyes painted with too much makeup look up at me, and her lips, a bright red, turn up in a smile. "*Easton.*" She says my name like it's the first time she's seen me in months—excited, grateful, and hopeful.

"Hi, Momma. You've gotta stop doing this," I tell her as I fake the same level of enthusiasm, my insides fucking exhausted from this dance.

"I know, but I was so excited that you won tonight!"

"I didn't play tonight. My arm's still hurt," I explain as I help her scoot from behind the table and wrap my arm around her waist to get her out the door.

"But you were playing on the TV. I was watching it. My handsome boy. You went three for three and picked two people off base. . ."

"Good night, Marty. Thanks for calling," I say as we pass by him.

"And I was so proud of you I thought I'd go and celebrate and wait for you to join me . . . and here you are!" She throws her hands up, her happiness sincere, as I usher her inside the cab of my truck.

We drive the quarter mile to her trailer in silence, but her smile remains wide. There's nothing else I can do other than squeeze the hand she's placed in mine, so giddy that I came home to her.

"You were watching a replay of one of my games on the DVR again," I tell her gently as I push open the unlocked door of her mobile home to find the TV on and the lights blazing.

"I was?" she asks, as if it's complete news to her, and a small part of me wonders if it's the alcohol making her forget, or if something is wrong with her mind. Both options scare the shit out of me.

"Yes, you were. I wish you'd let me move you out of here, Momma." I look around the double-wide mobile home she refuses to leave. The furniture is threadbare, the new pieces I've bought her returned time and again, and the wall opposite of us is lined with stacks of boxes filled with brand new things I've given her she refused to open.

"I don't need anything. I love it here," she murmurs as she sits on the edge of her bed and I wonder if she really does or she just believes her own lies. It takes me only a minute to find the makeup wipes and remove the paint from her face.

"There's my girl." I smile when she looks up at me, face bare, lips still in a smile to match mine. "So much prettier without all that gunk."

"A lady likes gunk, East."

"I know. I know." I take her shoes off, one by one. "I could move you near me. It would be so much nicer and safer for you, and I'd be able to keep an eye on you."

"Not gonna happen. I'm not gonna leave here. He'll come back for me some day, and I want to make sure he knows where I am when he does . . . much the same way you know where to find me each time."

"Who, Momma? Who is going to come back for you?" I reiterate the same question I've asked countless times over the years.

"The love of my life." Her voice is dreamy when she says it, and the sound tugs on my heart. What is it like to hold out hope for some-one for this many years?

"And who's that?" I ask again, knowing she won't tell me, just as she never has in the past.

"Some things children aren't supposed to know," she says with a laugh. Her eyes are tired, but her smile remains. "You are always so good to me. I don't deserve you."

"You're talking nonsense now. It's time for you to get some sleep. You'll feel better in the morning."

"Are you gonna leave me?" she asks, voice wavering in panic.

"No. You know I'll never leave you. I'll be right here when you wake up."

I help to pull the covers over her, wipe her graying hair off her face, and stare at her for a few minutes as her smile slowly fades into sleep.

My sigh is heavy as I turn off the television, the lights, and then sink down on the lumpy couch she won't let me replace. Pulling the blanket she made from all my various team jerseys up to my chin, I listen for the soft rattle of her breath and wonder how many more years I'm going to allow myself to continue to do this.

"Night, Momma," I whisper like I used to when I was a little boy. And yet, this time I know no one is going to answer.

I'm the parent now.

Even when most days I still feel like the child.

CHAPTER SIX

Scout

"Faster. Faster," I shout as I watch pure male perfection move across the field.

Honed muscles ripple with pristine performance. His grunt echoes off the empty plastic seats around us. His cleats hit the base with a thump of sound.

When I click the stopwatch, I'm more than impressed with his time. "Not bad," I muse as I watch him from behind my mirrored lenses and wait for him to trot back over.

"Are you trying to kill me? What did I do to piss you off?" He pants the questions and then lifts a bottle and squeezes some water into his mouth.

"No and nothing," I answer as I hold up the stopwatch so he can see the display. "That's an impressive time."

He grunts in response as he swallows more water. "Not bad. But not my best. Are you going to explain what running bases has to do with rehabbing my arm?"

"When you run, you swing your arms without thinking about it. And swinging your arms moves your shoulder joint," I say, placing my hands on his arm to swing it and demonstrate the point. "And when you move your shoulder without tensing up, you also break up any scar tissue that might have built up in the joint. And that scar tissue is most likely what is giving you that pinching feeling when we toss the ball around."

"Huh."

"That doesn't sound like you're convinced, but I don't need you to be convinced, I just need you to not feel the pain."

"I'm still sticking with the 'you're pissed at me' theory." He angles his head and takes a step closer. "Or at the world. I just haven't decided which one you're taking out on me right now."

I bristle, hating that he can read me so easily when I've put an enormous amount of effort into trying to appear perfectly fine these past few days. But I haven't been fine. I've been far from it. I'm pissed at my dad, angry that he's shutting me out when all I need is to be closer to him. I despise that I have to hear secondhand from his caretaker, Sally, that the cold he's caught has set him back a few steps. I hate that my brother's birthday is coming up, another year gone by, making the memories even fuzzier.

So, yeah, Easton's right; I am pissed at the world. Obviously, I'm doing a shitty job of hiding it.

"C'mon, let's get you stretched out." *Conversation over.* I turn my back to him and walk to the foul line on the outfield grass. I could have stretched him perfectly fine where we were standing, and yet I needed the distraction to avoid him looking at me more closely and seeing that he's right.

"Classic avoidance. I get it."

"No, you're just *the player*." The comment slips off my tongue, more a reminder to myself than meant for him. The disdain tingeing my tone is intended for my dad, but I'm taking it out on Easton instead.

How can you be mad at a man who is dying?

"*The player*?" Easton's voice is right behind me, and I cringe. He definitely heard me.

Crap.

"Don't ask."

"No, please. I'm intrigued."

"It's just a classic Doc Dalton idiosyncrasy." I keep my back turned to him as tears burn in my eyes. Moments ago I was mentally lashing out at my dad, angry at the world, and in a matter of seconds, I'm smiling bittersweetly at the quirk so representative of my father.

I can hold it together most days, push the grief aside, not believe the prognosis, but for some reason, this week it has hit me hard.

Clear mind. Hard Heart.

Shove it away, Scout. Not here. Not now.

"Isn't that how all fathers are?"

There's a surprising bite to his tone, and yet I'm too preoccupied with my own world to delve deeper into his. I clear my throat, push the emotion away, and turn around to face him.

"How does your shoulder feel?" *Time to change topics.*

His laugh rings out across the empty field and gets lost in the vastness of the stadium. "You really don't like talking about yourself, do you?"

His smile is genuine when I meet his eyes, and I hate that it pulls on me to say more. But I can't. I won't. "No."

Without another word, I begin his routine. I work in silence— my hands on his body, his heartbeat against my palm—feeling for the bunching of muscles as I pull and push and work through the tightness in his shoulder. The hiss of his breath is my only gauge to know when I've pushed him too far.

"How does this feel?" I position myself behind him, our bodies pressed against each other's, enabling me to manipulate his larger frame.

"What's bugging you?"

I ignore his question. "Is it tight? Sore? Is that pinch still up in the top part of the cuff?"

"You're upset. That much is obvious."

"I'm fine. Can we get back to you and your shoulder? To my job." My tone is clipped. "What's hurting you?"

"I don't know. What's hurting *you*?"

I falter, trying to grasp that he's really going to push the issue, and just when I realize I've stopped moving—one hand resting atop his shoulder, the other on his bicep—he turns to face me.

Now we're body to body, my breasts brushing against his chest while his eyes search mine for the secrets I keep. And we're close, too close, but neither of us step away. It's just him and me inside a sunlit stadium with thousands of empty seats as bystanders.

His breath catches. My pulse races. I look away in a desperate attempt to avoid his question and ignore the sudden hum of desire snapping within me like a broken power line twisting in a storm.

Not desperate enough, though, to step back.

"Uh-uh." Easton's finger is on my chin, lifting my face so that my eyes scrape over the day-old growth on his chin, up to those lips, and on to the curiosity in his eyes. "What is it, Scout?"

Our gazes lock. Hold. Question without speaking. Sympathize despite not knowing what the other needs.

And it's odd because we've stood like this dozens of times over the past week. When I'm stretching him in warm-up, midway through our exercises, after we throw the ball around for a bit, and again after our routine is completed—but for some reason, this time there's an intimacy to it.

It's unnerving. It's exciting. *It can't happen.*

Seconds pass before it hits me where we are, what might be happening—*what I think I want to happen*—and I push away from him as quickly as I can. The connection is broken.

But the desire remains.

"Sorry." I shake my head, and without another word, I jog into the dugout toward the locker room, needing space from everything he makes me feel—and from making a *huge* mistake.

Stupid. Stupid. Stupid. You're in the freaking stadium, where anyone from the front office can see you, and you're standing there like a teenager begging to be kissed. Are you actually going to risk this job for a guy who will be gone and done with you before the post-season begins?

"Scout?"

"You're good for the day." Keep walking. Keep moving.

He curses behind me, and then his footsteps fall into pace with mine when I just want them to walk the other way.

Or maybe I don't want them to.

Hell if I know, because that little moment was enough to mess up my head. Sure, Easton hits all my buttons: hot, athletic, funny, and a bit of a mystery. But in this job, those buttons are pushed all the time. There are plenty of players who fit that bill. It's everything else that he just made me feel that's confusing me.

It's the fact that I wanted him to lean in and kiss me.

It's the notion that I press up against hard, male bodies all the time—so much so that I'm rarely affected by it—but right now, my body is reacting and wanting and pissed off that it *is* reacting. Easton Wylder just affected me.

It's the acknowledgement that for some reason he can see the things I think I'm hiding from the world. He sees them, and has no problem calling me out on them, either.

It's that right now I feel exposed and raw, and I hate that I am, but at the same time I feel relieved that someone sees it. That I'm not invisible, when lately, that's all I've felt as I've worked to secure this job. To succeed in getting the long-term contract. *Anything* to try and keep my dad holding on.

My footsteps echo down the concrete corridor, the clubhouse all but vacant of players since the team is traveling. I need a minute to clear my head and push away the sudden vulnerability I feel because of everything going on with my dad.

Clear mind, hard heart, Scouty.

Maybe it's the toll of my emotions, maybe not, but when I enter the empty locker room, my feet falter at the sight. It's eerie and beautiful and bittersweet all at the same time.

This is how I remember it from when I was a kid. Ford and I would tag along with my dad to work and we'd sit in the empty locker room while he got everything set up for whoever he was in charge of rehabilitating. When the team straggled in, we'd be relegated to the office with a vending machine full of candy we weren't supposed to eat but would stuff our faces with anyway. We'd giggle at the Mad Libs made naughty with words we weren't allowed to say in front of our dad—like *hell* and *damn*—and then grumble over our homework, which Ford would help me with when it was too hard. It was my dad's way of keeping us with him—our fear he'd leave us was a constant in those early years after my mom left—but making sure we didn't get in the way, or hear the cursing, or see the players as they changed.

And every once in a while, depending on how long he worked with a club, the players would come in, kid with us, give us high-fives, and make us feel like we were part of the team.

"What is it?" Easton pulls me from my thoughts. When I look his way I realize his hand is on my upper arm, his head dropped down so he can look into my eyes.

"Isn't it magical?" I whisper. *Oh my god. Did I really just say that? I'm so lame.*

His laugh is amused, but the expression on his face as he looks around us—the empty lockers, the hanging jerseys, the nameplates on them—says he has a love/hate relationship with this room. And for a guy who probably grew up here more than anywhere else, the expression, and the curiosity it raises, surprises me.

"Some days it is. Some days it isn't," he finally murmurs, confirming my assumption of his mixed feelings as his gaze lands back on mine.

And we stand like this for a few seconds, his hand on my arm, his eyes asking me what's wrong, and mine questioning why this room evokes the conflict I see hiding in his.

The clearing of a throat has me jumping back like we're two kids caught doing something we shouldn't be doing.

"Sir," Easton says with a slow nod as I meet the eyes of the giant who is standing a few feet away from us, an indecipherable look on his unmistakable face.

"Easton." He looks down to his watch and then back up, with hazel eyes that are a mirror image of his son's. "Cutting your rehab time a bit short, aren't you?"

The laugh that falls from Easton's mouth is one I haven't heard before. It's void of any humor. "This is my second session today, so no, actually, I'm not."

The man's gaze shifts from Easton's to mine as he angles his head and studies me. "We haven't officially met."

I snap to attention, suddenly cognizant of what the situation looks like—Easton and I alone in the locker room, with his hand on my arm—and stride toward him with my hand outstretched. "Scout Dalton. So nice to meet you, Mr. Wylder."

"The pleasure's mine," he says, brows drawing together as he looks me in the eye. "So *you're* the one charged with getting my boy back up to speed."

"Yes, sir," I say as resolutely as possible, a little star struck and a lot aware that Cal Wylder has a ton of pull in the front office of the Austin Aces organization. "We're making good headway."

"What seems to be holding him back?"

The question throws me. Why wouldn't he just ask his son, who is standing right beside me? He's searching, when he knows I can't tell him. Discussing Easton's status with anyone other than the GM is off-limits for me, not to mention completely unprofessional.

I glance over to Easton, who gives me no indication that he wants me to answer, and then back to Cal. Is this some kind of setup? See if the new girl can handle both confrontation and keeping her mouth shut at the same time?

"Nothing that I can tell," I say with caution, trying to feel out the situation. "Just creating a routine for stretching and strengthening, and giving Easton the time to learn what his repaired shoulder should feel like. It'll most likely have a completely different feel for him, so he needs to learn what each pinch or pain is telling him now."

"Good. Good." Cal finally looks back to Easton again. "From where I was watching in the press box, you seemed to have lost some time on your run to first. Don't let him fool you. He's faster than that, Ms. Dalton. He just has a habit of slacking a bit if no one is pushing him."

"Most players wish they had his time." I laugh, thinking Cal's joking until I notice the look on his face, eyebrows pinched as his eyes shift back toward mine. And now I'm under the impenetrable stare.

"Hmm." He doesn't say anything else, but rather lets the sound hang in the air as if he doesn't believe me.

"The stopwatch never lies."

"Well, he can do better," he says with a disapproving shake of his head quickly followed by the flash of a dazzling smile almost as if he remembers he has an audience. "But I'm glad to hear you think the shoulder hasn't slowed him down too much."

And even though the words sound sincere, I'm not sure there isn't the hard edge beneath them of a father pushing his son beyond his limits.

"Not at all, sir," I say to keep the peace and my respect in place. I glance over to Easton, noticing the strong set of his jaw, the visible tension in his shoulders, and his eyes locked on his father's, despite the tight smile on his lips.

There is suddenly a palpable tension between the two of them that grows with each passing second. I try to deflect.

"It was a pleasure to meet you, Mr. Wylder."

"Cal," he says, finally drawing his eyes away from Easton.

"Cal," I repeat. "I'll get him back on the field, but only because he's busting his ass to get there himself."

He gives me that look again, hazel eyes searching, just like his son's. "Good to know," he murmurs. "Keep up the good work."

And with that, a man I watched break every record in the book when I was a kid, turns on his heel and heads out of the locker room.

Cal may have shut the door in his departure, but the tension he brought with him still lingers.

"We need to get the fuck out of here," Easton mutters as he turns to face me. "Get changed if you want, and grab your shit. We're going for a drive."

I stand there, mouth agape. Easton takes a few steps and turns back to look at me like I've misheard him. The look in his eyes is just as demanding as his words. I want to tell him to go to hell, that I don't take orders from anyone, and yet for some reason, I do just as he asked.

This time.

CHAPTER SEVEN

Scout

We drive in silence as Easton maneuvers through the streets of downtown Austin. He's still pissed, that much I can tell, but it seems to lessen with each mile we put between us and the ball field.

Curiosity over the exchange between him and his father owns my thoughts. The picture-perfect father and son. Both uber-talented. Both a rarity in this game because they spent their careers playing for only one ball club. Both obscenely handsome.

But after the meeting in the locker room, I'm left to wonder how everyone else has failed to see what I glimpsed. The smooth and personable Cal Wylder is not so easy-going, and not so complimentary of his protégé of a son.

"Sorry about that," Easton says after some time, his voice resigned.

"'Bout what?" I turn to look at him from my seat in the front of his truck, asking my question but not really meaning it.

"My old man can be . . . a little overbearing at times. I'm sorry if it made you uncomfortable."

"I'm good. My choice of career has taught me how to handle even the most overbearing of people." I eye him up and down to let him know I'm including him in the generality. "Thanks, though."

"I've noticed." He chuckles with a glance my way before turning his attention back to the road, smile fading, and lips twisting as he loses himself back to his thoughts.

I use the time to study him. The line of his profile, the flex of his biceps as he turns the wheel, the pulse of the muscle in his jaw. He knows I'm watching, and yet he just carries on, checking his side mirror, his rearview mirror, and using his turn signals.

There are so many questions I want to ask him but don't. About the relationship with his dad and the obvious tension between them. About whatever it was that happened between us on the field earlier. If I put a voice to my curiosity, I'm only inviting his questions about my personal life in return. And while we've developed a pseudo-friendship the past two weeks, there are secrets I need to keep.

So I bite my tongue and try to quiet my head so I can enjoy the comfortable silence we've slipped into. And no sooner than I do, it hits me: I *like* Easton. And not just that lusty kind of indifferent attraction I feel occasionally with players I've worked with. The kind where, hell yes, they're hot and probably would be a willing candidate if I wanted a temporary good-time, but not good enough for me to cross that fine line of mixing my professional life with my personal life.

I've never crossed it. I have no intention to.

My studies, my softball team, graduating at the top of my class had always come first. Then I threw everything I had into working my way up the ranks to prove I'm worthy to help run Doc Dalton's business. Sure he was my dad, but I wanted to earn the position. And thankfully I did, because there's no way I could have known what the future would hold for us.

Did I have fun with men? Of course, but since I started working for my dad, no player has ever tempted me to cross that professional line like the mysterious and attractive man beside me does.

And that's a major problem.

But then again, it's not. I'm a big girl. I can handle my lusty urges. He's charming and attractive and funny and so much more than I'd assumed. Even with all of that, I think I've barely caught a glimpse of the real him. I'm intrigued, to say the least.

Wait. The truck has stopped. And I'm still staring at Easton. And he's staring back at me, smirk growing wider by the second as he waits for me to realize it.

"I'm sorry." I shake my head with a laugh, embarrassed and flustered.

"Don't be. I sure hope it's me you're thinking about that intensely." His grin is lightning quick as I try not to die a thousand deaths.

"Of course I was. Just trying to think about what to do with you next," I say with pursed lips and a shrug, and then realize that it sounds exactly like how I didn't want it to sound. I stammer to correct myself. "I mean, your rehab. On the field. For training. About your arm."

"Uh-huh." I'm certain I turn every shade of pink, all the way to red, as he just stares, and that huge grin morphs into a lopsided smile.

"Where are we?" *Smooth, Scout. Real smooth.* You're a master at changing the subject. To reinforce my attempt, I glance around to our surroundings. We're on a residential street with a park on the passenger side and a row of houses on Easton's side.

"Sorry to drag you along, but I have to do something real quick. I hope you don't mind, but feel free to turn on the radio if you want. I'll leave the keys here."

"Okay. Sure."

He turns to face me, hand pushing open the door, smile and sunglasses in place. "Hey, Scout?"

"Yeah?"

"I'm leaving now."

"Okay?" I draw the word out to let him know what he's doing is pretty self-explanatory.

"That means you can carry on thinking about whatever you were thinking about me and not get embarrassed, since I won't be sitting two feet from you."

Dear God. "I was thinking of your arm. *Your arm*," I emphasize.

He darts his tongue out to wet his bottom lip. "That's not all you were thinking about."

His laugh fills the truck before he shuts the door and leaves me with the echo of it through the open window.

I follow his very fine backside as he jogs across the grass field toward a small crowd of people. There are tables dotting the playground, with bunches of green balloons at every other one. There looks to be a group of kids seated in rows on the grass and some kind of costumed character in front of them holding up an oversize book.

I'm more than fascinated with what is going on and just what Easton is doing here. Especially after he reaches the crowd of people and shakes hands with several of them, while hugging a few of the others.

After observing for a few minutes, I conclude that this is some kind of school function, and somehow Easton is a part of it. I'm distracted momentarily from watching him when the teddy bear character throws his hands (or is it paws?) up in the air. Despite the distance, I can hear the roar as the kids shout out loud in response.

Their enthusiasm brings a smile to my lips. And when I see Easton walk up before the rows of kids, their cheers grow even wilder. Some of them jump from their seats and run to give him a hug. Despite the distance, I can see the wide smile on his face and the sincerity in his expression as he hugs them back, ruffles their hair, and then does some kind of silly routine with the bear.

The kids shift to the next activity, the next station, and yet I'm left staring into space once again, acknowledging that Easton Wylder is getting to me. That hard heart my father taught me was a necessity to get through life is slowly softening.

And I'm not quite sure how to feel or what to even do about it.

My thoughts are too loud in the confines of this truck when all I crave is some peace and quiet. I don't want to think about my dad, the stress of the contract, or how I'll be letting both Easton and my dad down if I don't succeed. Instead I just want to sit parked on the side of the road in the hometown I feel like I barely know. As a kid we were always moving on to the next city, the next injured ball player, so much so that tutors became our teachers and our beds at home felt unfamiliar.

I've missed Austin—the sights and sounds and beauty that I haven't really gotten to enjoy as an adult—and being back for this short amount of time has only reinforced the thought.

The desire to make a life here is suddenly strong. To win the contract, find a place of my own, and grow roots. I need something of my own, somewhere I can belong.

Because pretty soon . . . I'll be all alone.

The pang of grief is crippling, the swell of emotions inescapable.

Desperate to stop thinking, to stop feeling, I turn the key in the ignition and push the radio on. Music is what I need. Music will let me close my eyes, lean my head back, and get lost in the beat.

Except when the radio comes on, I'm startled when a man's voice starts talking to me. Or not me, rather, but the reader, because it sounds like he is narrating an audio book.

An audio book?

I know it's shallow, but an audio book is the last thing I ever expected to hear coming through Easton's speakers. The man keeps throwing me for loops every time I think I have him pegged.

I should turn it off so he doesn't lose his place, but there is something so soothing about the narrator's voice that I snuggle into the seat with a soft smile on my face and just lose myself in the words he speaks.

A little more than a chapter later, I'm jolted from the story when the truck door opens. Feeling like a kid caught with her hand in the cookie jar, I look over to Easton with wide eyes and cheeks flushed with embarrassment.

He doesn't say a word but just stares at me from behind the dark lenses of his sunglasses for a moment before climbing into the truck, turning the radio off, and then pulling away from the curb.

We drive in the silence that has seemed to plague us today, and I'm left to wonder why he seems embarrassed when there's nothing to be embarrassed about.

He listens to books. *How can he think I'd judge him poorly for that?*

And yet I sense his discomfort, so I try to ease it the only way I know how. "Stephen King, huh? I kind of figured you more for a romance novel kind of guy."

"Bullshit." His laughter breaks the awkward silence in the cab.

"What's wrong with romance?"

"You seriously have to ask me that?"

"What?" I mirror the posture that got me into trouble earlier: body shifted, knees angled, eyes on him. "You don't like a feel-good story? Or is it that you don't believe in true love? Maybe you just haven't found a good baseball romance to pull you in and steal your heart."

"See! That's just it. Those books give women unrealistic expectations about what a relationship is supposed to be like."

It's my laugh that fills the truck now. "Maybe our expectations are spot on, and it's the men who are unreliable." I purse my lips as he looks at me from over the frames of his sunglasses.

"That's such a crock."

"No, it's not. What are you afraid of? That you might actually like the story and maybe get a few pointers to help *better* your game?" My tone is coy, smile playful as he looks over at me.

"Are you telling me you don't think I have game?" he asks, mock offended.

"On the field? Yes. Off the field? I couldn't tell you."

"I've got game all right. No worries there, *Kitty*. Just you wait and see." His voice may sound irritated but the smile on his lips says different.

I roll my eyes while trying not to read into his comment. *Just you wait and see.* Was he saying it off the cuff? Or is he interested in me? And more importantly, do I want him to be?

"No game," he mutters under his breath and then laughs. "That's hilarious."

Twenty bucks says he's listening to a romance sooner rather than later.

A man's ego can't handle being called into question.

He'll have to find out the truth for himself.

CHAPTER EIGHT

Scout

"**S**o what was that all about back at the park?"

I glance around the hole-in-the-wall bar where we've ended up. It's downtown, somewhat near the ballpark but outside the area of the city's revitalization efforts. Texan memorabilia lines the walls, and country music plays softly on the speakers.

"It was nothing. Just an obligation I had to fulfill." He's nonchalant in his response and makes a point to avert his eyes from mine.

"Whatever, Wylder." I roll my eyes. "You don't get to act like that was nothing, because whatever it was, those kids loved that you were there, and that's pretty freaking awesome. So, 'fess up. What was that all about?"

"Why were you so upset earlier?" His eyes meet mine, searching and questioning, as he lifts the bottle of beer to his lips and takes a sip.

I shake my head. "We're not going there again."

"Then I guess you're not going to know what I was doing at the park, now, are you?"

"You're a pain in my ass, you know that?"

"It's a mighty fine pain you've got there, too, then." The words come out of a mouth turned up in a smile, but with eyes loaded with suggestion.

"Flattery doesn't make me spill my secrets."

"It wasn't flattery. It's the truth."

"Well, in that case, flattery will get you everywhere," I respond, our smiles wide but the unanswered questions still lingering between us. "You're really not going to tell me what was going on?"

He shrugs. "Seems that way, doesn't it."

"I don't think I've ever played show-me-yours-and-I'll-show-you-mine, and I doubt I'm going to start at the age of twenty-five," I say dryly.

His laugh carries over the noise of the bar. "That's a pity. You should definitely play it once in your lifetime. You never know, it might be fun." That gleam is back in his eye, highlighted by a lift of his eyebrows, and once again I'm aware of how he captivates me without even trying.

"Tell me something about you." He changes the topic, his expression daring me to refuse him.

"I never played in the major leagues."

He narrows his eyes and purses his lips. "That's the best you can do?"

I shrug and mimic his posture. "How about this," I murmur as I lean in a little closer, "you tell me what you were doing earlier, and I'll tell you something about me."

His laugh is quick but telling. "I see I've been outmaneuvered. You're a tricky one, turning that back on me, Scout Dalton, but I'll bite. God knows if I don't, your stubborn ass will have us volleying the same question back and forth all night."

"I'm so glad you have me all figured out."

"Not hardly." He shifts in his seat and looks down at the label on his beer he's playing with. "I run a literacy charity," he says softly, lifting his eyes to meet mine. "We run programs at all of the local schools to encourage reading and to make sure any kid struggling with reading, or who has dyslexia, or just needs extra help or tutoring gets it."

And there he goes, surprising me again.

"Who knew the man who's got a wicked arm and swagger for days also has such a huge heart?" I murmur, more to myself than to him, but I am thoroughly impressed. Not just because he has a charity, because a lot of players pay it forward somehow, but after watching him—his interaction with the organizers, the kids, the good mood it put him in—it is obvious this is more than just a tax write-off to him.

I love that his cheeks flush some and hate that he's embarrassed at all by it.

"I meant that as a compliment, Easton. It's nice to see someone paying the community back, and in such an important way. Don't ever be embarrassed by it. Please."

"Your turn," he says after a beat, effectively shifting the focus back on me. "Spill it."

I suck in a breath and debate how to be honest with him while keeping my promise to my father. "I have an uncle who is pretty sick. It's just hitting me harder than usual today."

"Scout." The way he says my name—apology laced with compassion—causes a lump to form in my throat. "I thought I was being so smart, tricking you into telling me something, and now I feel like a complete asshole. I'm sorry. The only thing I can say is I hope he gets better soon."

I don't know why I chuckle, but I do. The tone of it is anxious and sarcastic, and I know it's because I'm afraid if I say the words out loud, they'll come true. "Yeah, well, thank you, but he's not going to get better." I focus on shredding my cocktail napkin—anything to avoid seeing the sympathy in his eyes. I can't handle sympathy right now. I can deal with anger. I can handle disbelief. But I absolutely cannot deal with sympathy.

Sympathy will break me, when I can't break.

It will make me confess the secret I've been keeping. The one that's been eating me whole—bit by bit, day by day—because I'd give anything to talk about my dad's diagnosis. It would be so much easier if someone else knew so I could let all this bundled emotion out instead of letting it implode.

But I can't tell Easton. I promised my dad I wouldn't, so I sit in the booth across from him, staring at where I'm pushing the tiny pieces of shredded napkin around with my finger instead of looking at him.

Somehow, though, he senses that I need a connection, a something, and he reaches across the table and links his fingers through mine. I look down at our hands entwined; I study the scars on his from a lifetime of playing, and hold on to the little bit of comfort he has no idea how much I need.

"Thank you," I say after a moment to regain my composure. A huge part of me likes this—our fingers linked—but knows it's a bad idea all around. And yet, when I lean back in the booth, try to create an opportunity for him to withdraw his hand, he doesn't.

"I used to play ball," I say, feeling the need to reciprocate with something else about me, considering I wasn't completely honest with my first confession. Anything to change the topic and relieve the depressed atmosphere I unexpectedly created.

"You did?" he asks with a tone so full of warmth that it pulls on me to look up to him. There's a surprised gratitude in his eyes that tells me he wasn't expecting me to let him in any more than I did, and for that look alone, I'm glad I did.

"Yep. So, I may not have played in the majors, but I won a few collegiate championships."

"You're fucking with me now."

I laugh. "Why is that so hard to believe?"

"Because you're completely unpredictable. First a stripper and now a ball player."

"Very funny." I roll my eyes as he narrows his in thought.

"Let me guess . . . you were a second baseman."

"Uh. Please," I say in mock offense because I know he won't guess in a million years what position I played.

"C'mon. With that compact little body of yours, I bet you would've been a kick-ass second baseman."

"I like to get a little more action than second base," I say, fully knowing the innuendo that goes with it, but with the first drink down, I'm feeling a bit more daring than I normally would.

His eyes hold mine for a prolonged moment, and I know he wants to say more, but he doesn't. Instead he begins to name every position on the field while I reject them until there are only two left.

"What's left?" he asks, knowing damn well the answer.

"Pitcher and catcher."

"No fucking way," he murmurs.

"Yep." I quirk an eyebrow, and the smug smile on my lips tells him I'm enjoying the fact he's underestimated me.

"And twice in a matter of minutes you make me feel like a complete heel." He releases my fingers and drops his head into his hands, his laugh ringing out as he scrubs them through his hair. The simple mannerism makes me smile, even more so when he looks at me again, eyes intense, smile bewildered. "*Seriously?*"

"If I was gonna play, I wanted to play the best position on the field. The one that holds all the control."

"Control freak."

"Ditto." I murmur back, my smile soft, the alcohol warming me from the inside out.

"Incredible." His voice is part awe, part surprise, and it makes every part of me stand tall with pride.

"My dad used to say the best place in the park to sit was behind home plate. And so when I was about ten, I figured if I was going to play, I wanted to make sure I had the best seat in the house."

I can hear my dad's voice saying it now, the memory bittersweet.

"And my dad told me to play first base instead," he says with a shake of his head, "because catching caused too much wear and tear on your body and could shorten your career."

"So you've always rebelled against him, then?"

His laughter is quick and his smile arrogant. "That noticeable, huh?"

"There was just a touch of tension in the locker room."

"A touch? Was that all?"

Relieved he can laugh now at what upset him earlier, I put my thumb and index finger half an inch apart. "Just a smidgen."

The soft smile on his lips does nothing to ease the conflict in his eyes as he lowers his gaze to watch the condensation run down the side of his beer bottle. He collects his thoughts before he looks back up at me to explain. "He means well. He's just very particular and extremely determined that I live up to the Wylder name. He doesn't want me to disgrace the legacy he left behind, especially since I play for the club he spent his entire career playing for."

"That's a lot of pressure." I can't imagine.

"I'm sure the situation you're in is no different, living up to the legendary Doc Dalton."

I twist my lips and consider his statement. "Pressure, yes. But it's something I want to do, love to do . . . to make him proud." But I get the feeling that while Easton feels similarly about his situation, at least I had the choice whether I wanted to follow in my father's footsteps. For some reason, I don't think he did.

"Every kid wants to make their parents proud," he muses as he angles his head to the side. "But every parent holds a different standard for what exactly it is that will achieve that."

And that comment confirms my assumption that Easton feels like he's never been good enough to live up to his father, the legend. My heart hurts for him, working as hard as he does, playing a game he is more than gifted at, but living a life to earn someone's approval.

"True. That must be hard for you."

He shrugs again. Averts his eyes. Takes a swig of his beer. "When I'm playing good, it's not." He laughs, and I can tell he's uneasy with the topic of conversation.

"Tell me something else about yourself," I say, more than curious to find another piece to complete this puzzle of a man.

"You sure are full of questions," he teases.

"Please," I say drolly. "I'm sure you'd prefer to talk baseball or stats or something scintillating like that."

"Scintillating?" He laughs.

"It's a good word."

"It is," he says with a nod, "but I don't talk stats."

What? "I thought all players liked to talk about the game."

"I'm not all players, though."

"So it seems."

"First off, I'm *the* player." He quirks an eyebrow, and all I can do is smile at the reference.

"And second?"

"Second," he mimics, "I may be wrong, but I think it takes a helluva lot more to impress you than a list of above-par stats."

"True." I draw the word out while my mind is a flurry of thoughts. *Is he flirting with me? He wants to impress me? Or am I reading into the comment when he means nothing by it?*

"Stats are boring. They're my work. And while most days I live and breathe baseball, on and off the field, they're the last thing that comes to mind when I'm in the company of a beautiful woman."

That's twice. He *is* flirting with me.

"What *does* come to mind, then?"

Oh, crap. I'm flirting right back.

He flashes me a megawatt smile that lightens his dark features and brightens his eyes. And if I doubted whether we should continue this exchange or not, that smile right there pulls me in hook, line, and sinker.

"Right here? Right now?"

"Mm-hmm."

Our eyes lock as we gauge each other and try to figure out the next step in this unfamiliar dance we're moving to.

"Dance with me."

I stifle a laugh. *Is he reading my mind now?*

But my laugh is short-lived when he rises from the booth and extends his hand to me. He can't be serious.

"No way!" I laugh, batting his hand away. "I'm not letting the King of Pranks make a fool of me."

"I do love a good prank but dancing with me isn't one of them." He puts his hand out for me to take again.

"I don't know how to dance, let alone to country music."

"Neither do I. We're quite the pair, aren't we?" he asks, that boyish smile on his lips winning me over. "A pair of Texans who can't dance to country music."

"We should be ashamed of ourselves and hide in this dark corner here."

His laugh tells me he's not buying it. "No time like the present to learn."

"We'll be the only ones on the dance floor." I scramble to think of any other excuse to avoid this situation—not avoiding the limelight part of it but the dancing body-to-body with Easton part—because he's already lowered my defenses, and dancing with him might be too temptingly disastrous for me—in more ways than one. "Everyone will be staring at us."

"I live my life under the lights, baby," he teases as he grabs the hand I've refused him. "You think these dim bar lights are going to intimidate me?"

"People are going to stare."

He pulls me to my feet.

"Good."

"*Good?* We're so out of place in here."

"I've never cared what people think of me, and I sure as hell am not going to start now. Besides, there's nothing wrong with getting a little attention now and again."

He tugs on my arm for me to follow.

"Ah, you can't handle being out of the limelight now, can you?" I tease.

"I can handle it just fine. And it's not me people are going to be looking at, it's you."

"Me?" I say, but the word comes out in a whoosh of air when he stops and turns without warning, causing me to bump solidly against his chest.

"Yes. *You.*" His smile is a juxtaposition of shy and suggestive, and it tugs on so many things inside of me. Want. Need. Denial. Desire.

We're standing in the middle of the empty dance floor, and all I can think about when he looks down at me is that I need to remember to breathe.

Because chatting at a table is fine. Stretching his shoulder on the field, I can handle. But this, face-to-face on a dance floor with nothing between us, only serves to reinforce my epiphany in the truck earlier—I really like him.

And as if the universe is trying to cheer this mistake on, the music suddenly becomes louder and the lights become dimmer, prompting Easton to slide one hand against my lower back and lift my hand with his other.

Breathe, Scout.

And then he begins to move.

"Relax," he murmurs against my ear as he guides us in a mismatched array of steps that make no sense and perfect sense all at the same time. But it's not like I can concentrate on the movement with the heat of his body against mine, familiar and so very different.

It's his tutelage I'm under now. It's not me working him or stretching him. It's him guiding me. Commanding me. And the ripple of his muscles beneath his shirt is not for me to study this time around, but rather to feel. To react to. *To want.*

I'm normally one to avoid the spotlight, but Easton has just thrust me right into it. Attention shifts. Eyes observe. And there's something about knowing we're being watched that magnifies everything about the moment.

More specifically, everything about Easton.

The scent of his shampoo. The strength in his hand as it holds mine and the heat of his other splayed across my lower back. The vibration of his voice against my hair as he hums along with the Luke Bryan tune. The rhythm of his hips as they move against mine.

"You lied to me, Scout."

The heat of his breath against the side of my face.

"About what?"

The sensitivity of my nipples as they rub ever so gently against the firmness of his chest.

"You damn well do know how to dance."

I chuckle in response but don't look up to meet his eyes because I don't want him to stop whatever it is we're doing. There's something intimate about the moment that has me wanting to breathe him in a little more before it's lost.

His reaction to my laughter is to press his hand against my back and pull me closer. "I was always taught lying comes with punishment." His voice has a sing-song quality to it that only serves to draw me deeper under whatever spell he seems to be casting on my impenetrable shell.

"Punishment?" Somewhere deep down, the word awakens the parts of me curious about but inexperienced in anything of the nature, and I'm suddenly nervous.

And excited.

"Mm-hmm." His voice sounds as seductive as his body feels against mine. "Something that causes you pain."

I gulp over thoughts as my insides begin to heat up, and I'm well aware of the attention still turned our way.

And before I can take my next breath, Easton spins me out with a laugh until our arms are fully extended, fingertips barely still grasping each other, before pulling me back so I land solidly with a thud against his chest.

"See?" he says, prompting me to look up at him, the one thing I was telling myself not to do. And now that I have, I'm fully aware that our lips are only inches apart.

"*See?*" I laugh, trying to comprehend what I'm supposed to see when my body is still reeling from the feeling of our bodies colliding into each other and the mortification of being twirled in a public display.

"Being the center of attention." His voice is barely a whisper, but I hear every word. "Dancing with me isn't too painful of a punishment now, is it?"

Normally I would laugh at him—at his version of a punishment—but all I can think of is how much I want him to kiss me right now. With his lips right there. And our bodies like this.

Breathe, Scout.

"You've got a heavy hand there, Mr. Wylder." My head is so scrambled I'm not even sure how I manage to sound so witty.

And breathless.

It's in that moment that I realize we've stopped moving completely. Our feet. Our bodies. We're standing alone in the middle of the dance floor in a crowded bar, staring at each other.

"Excuse me?" At a woman's voice to our left, we shock apart like two kids getting caught for the second time today. "May I cut in?"

I look over at the attractive—and much older—bottled redhead beside us, whose smile is as evocative as the clothes she's wearing, and then back to Easton, a man no stranger to women hitting on him, I'm sure. His smile is fixed and eyes wide as he tries to figure out what to do.

"Of course. He's all yours," I say as I step back, despite every part of my body wanting to move closer. He sputters a protest, but his manners get the best of him when the woman, who must be at least thirty years his senior, has absolutely no qualms about stepping into where my shoes just were.

I twist my lips to fight my smile as he sends me a visual SOS when the woman begins to lead him around the dance floor. He's all smiles to her while shooting playful I'm-gonna-kill-you daggers across the room at me.

And as I sip my fresh drink, sent compliments of Easton's dance partner, for the first time in forever, I realize what jealousy over a man feels like.

CHAPTER NINE

Scout

"She *so* wanted you." My laugh is louder than normal, a bit giggly, and I don't care because I'm a little tipsy and a lot relaxed, and I can't remember what it feels like to be relaxed.

"Some wingman you are. Throwing me to the wolves so you can go drink all the alcohol, which could have helped to put me out of my misery."

"She was sweet, though," I explain.

"Of course you thought that. You were getting buzzed on the drinks she sent your way, while I was busy moving her hands off my ass. And I won't even get into her thoughts about the team's chances this year, or how much she kept asking if it's true that son is like father."

"If it's true that son is like father?" I look at him, wide-eyed, and cover my mouth with my hand.

"Yeah. Exactly."

"Are you telling me she's slept with your dad?"

"I have no clue, and I don't want to know," he says dryly, mock shivering.

I stifle a laugh. "And to think you were so generous with your time for her."

"What was I supposed to do? Cause a scene? I tried to escape, tried to explain I was on a date with you, but she wouldn't let me go."

"She just wanted to see if the apple fell far from the tree," I snicker, earning me a stern glare.

"Funny."

"Well, it was nice of you to stick it out." His glare is back, and I try to smother my laughter. He just walks ahead of me and shakes his head. "Look, I'm sorry. You were being very kind to her. She is probably lonely, and you just made her night."

"And that's why I wasn't rude. She just wanted to feel important."
And so you let her have that moment.

It's one surprise after another with him, and the revelation only makes me want to get to know him further. "You better watch out, or I might change my opinion of you."

"You have opinions of me? What might those be?" he asks, voice playful but eyes serious as he takes my hand to stop me. We're standing on a sidewalk in the middle of downtown Austin, his truck left in the bar's parking lot and mine a few blocks ahead in the stadium's parking lot. We decided to walk off the alcohol, but we're not walking now.

We're standing with my back to the brick wall of the building and this surprise of a man standing in front of me.

"I've been around ball players my whole life, Easton."

"And?" He says the word as if I've insulted him.

"They're *players*. They come and go on a whim. They typically need the high of the attention they get on the field to thrive. And if they can't find it, then they'll seek it out somewhere else . . . and that's never good for a relationship."

"So you've had a relationship with a ballplayer, then?" His eyes narrow.

"No. Never. It's my personal rule." And even though I said it myself, I know I'm already justifying in my head why I might make an exception for him.

"It's arrogant to brush your opinion in broad strokes across all of us players." The dark night prevents me from seeing what else his eyes are saying.

"True," I muse, "but I've heard enough locker room talk to know the truth."

"So you think that's how I am, too, then?"

"No. Yes." I tighten my ponytail and tuck the loosened strands behind my ears. "It's just . . . *they leave*. Night after night. Day after day. Game after game. And when the season is over and the limelight is gone, they seek the attention of someone new, someone who gives them that adrenaline rush. That thrill of finding someone new, or the high that comes with the risk of being caught cheating."

"Scout—"

"I've had enough people in my life leave me, Easton. I'm not walking willingly into a situation that sets me up for that hurt." And I hate that I just gave him that part of me. That glimpse into my past. I blame the alcohol for lowering my guard, but I fear it's so much more than that.

I fear it's because of him and how he makes me feel.

"You're wrong." He steps into me and out of the street's light. The shadows on his face give him an edge that's sexy, reckless, and daring. "I've played on grass my whole life, Scout. There's no need for me to see what's out there when it's green beneath my feet."

"There's turf nowadays. Everything is green," I fight back.

"If there's turf, then there's no point to your argument. No one's going to be looking for greener pastures when they're all the same color." He lowers his head so our eyes are on the same level, to reinforce what he's said.

They're just words, Scout. Declarations that have no basis. He's just a man trying to defend his own gender. His own ego.

Yet, I want to believe him.

I want to think he's not like those guys.

And God, how I want him to kiss me. Call my bluff. Because with the alcohol in my blood and the memory of his body against mine in my brain, it's all I can think about.

I spring off the wall and away from the slowly closing gap between us. "Is there a bathroom around here?" I ask the first thing that comes to mind to give me an escape, hands gesticulating animatedly, and nerves humming recklessly. "All of those drinks are catching up to me."

He steps forward under the light of the building and just stares at me. He can see through me right now—my nerves, my fear, my confused desire—and so I hold his gaze, pretend to be unaffected by him, and wait to see if he's going to let me off the hook or push the issue.

"My place is just around the corner," he says, giving me a pass, but with a look telling me we'll be revisiting this discussion where I called his character into question. "I'll take you there."

I should say no.

I should reject the offer and walk away from everything that he represents for me.

But I don't speak. Instead I fall into step next to him.

We walk through the newly revamped downtown area, past couples holding hands and hordes of college kids making their way from one bar to the next, the night still young. Our silence only feeds my insecurity and the knowledge that he's mad at me because I insulted his character. I know I should apologize, tell him that based on his actions today I can tell he doesn't fit my generalization, but I don't say a word. I can't. Because, deep down, I have a feeling that it's probably best if he stays mad at me.

It's safer.

By the time we enter the lobby of a glossy high-rise, I really do have to use the restroom. Easton laughs at me as I dance from foot to foot during the long elevator ride to the penthouse. The doors open to the foyer of his home, where a lone lamp lights the space as he ushers me to a door to my immediate left.

I take a few minutes after I use the facilities to check my mess of a reflection—hair falling from my ponytail, lipstick long gone, and eye shadow all collected in the crease of my lid. There's no way I can fix this. Not here. But I try.

I pull my ponytail out, let my dark brown hair fall, and fluff it with my fingers. And now I look like I just woke up. Shit. Is it so bad to want to look like I didn't just wake up?

I spend a few more minutes trying to look a bit more presentable, but when I check my reflection one last time—hair fluffed and cheeks pinched pink—I immediately grab my hair tie and pull my hair back up into a messy bun. This is how Easton knows me—in work mode—with my basic makeup and my hair thrown back. Anything else comes off like I'm trying too hard.

And I'm not trying too hard.

Keep telling yourself that, Scout, and maybe you'll start believing it.

When I exit the bathroom, Easton is nowhere to be found. Hesitant to overstep, but wondering where he is, I walk past the foyer and start making my way through the vast and still darkened condo. It's all hardwood floors and slate grays and blues. Or I think it is from what I can see as I move through its spacious layout. I only see that much because there is a wall of windows straight ahead of me, where I'm met with Easton's silhouette, highlighted by bright lights beyond.

Both pull at me. Tempt me to look closer. Dare me to want what they are showing me.

It's a sight—his darkness against the light—and I can't help but stare at him for a moment. Study his lines. The broad shoulders and trim waist. The wide stance and arms relaxed at his sides.

I fool myself as I take the first step toward him, past the gourmet kitchen on the left, with its white cabinets and granite slab, that I'm just here to use the restroom.

I lie to myself as I walk past the huge living room, with its over-size couches and state of the art electronics, that wanting him to kiss me was only a passing fancy that has come and gone.

I push away the notion as I pad past the massive dining table, that I'll be leaving here in a few minutes to head home and get a good night's sleep. *Alone.*

The worst part about telling yourself lies is you know the real truth.

And the truth is I want everything I just tried to convince myself I didn't.

The realization echoes in my head as I prepare myself for his ir-revocable pull, because it's pointless to pretend he doesn't affect me when my body is already humming at the sight of his silhouette.

"Your place is gorgeous. The only thing missing is a scruffy . . ." My words trail off before I can say *mutt to snuggle up with,* because when I step beside him, I'm rendered speechless by the sight before us—the source of the bright lights beyond.

"*Wow.*" It's all I can say, and I sound like a little kid seeing Santa Claus for the first time—astonished. Mesmerized. Staggered. "You're forgiven for not having a mutt," I murmur, my words barely audible as I stare.

"*A mutt?*"

"Shush and let me enjoy the view." I swat at him to reinforce my words, transfixed by a sight that's as beautiful to my eye as the man standing beside me.

Like mouth-dropping, chill-inducing incredible.

Beyond this wall of windows high above the city, the buildings dotting the darkened skyline paint a uniquely beautiful picture, but they're nothing compared to what lies directly below us: the home of the Austin Aces.

The lights are on, bringing the ballpark to life despite the fif-ty thousand vacant seats. They highlight the brilliant green of the outfield grass and its mesmerizing mowed crisscross pattern. They brighten the brown of the infield's dirt, the white of the chalk lines, and the blue uniforms of the grounds crew who seem to be working on the pitcher's mound.

He chuckles and pulls me from my trance. "I'm glad I'm forgiven when I wasn't even aware you liked dogs."

"Mutts. I prefer mutts. Preferably the no-one-else-wants-them kind of mutts. And I want one desperately, but with traveling for work and . . . *just wow* . . ." I'm rambling because my attention is engrossed elsewhere.

And for the first time tonight, it's *not* on him.

"*I know.*"

I appreciate the fact that he doesn't say anything else. That he just allows me to appreciate the view before us—the only diamond this girl has ever dreamt of. And right now I'd challenge anyone who told me this diamond doesn't sparkle as brightly as the rock you wear on your finger. With empty seats or with a sold-out crowd, this one outshines jewelry any day.

"It's your church," I whisper, not even certain I say it out loud until I glance over to Easton and find him watching me. There's a look on his face. His expression is part awe, part disbelief, and a whole lot of little boy mixed together, and it steals my heart when I had it firmly protected under lock and key.

But he's stolen it nonetheless.

"This is the place, isn't it?" I murmur like he should know what I'm referring to—the fabled house I've heard some players talk about, with its sparkling views and the private field in its depths, twenty-something floors below. And because I've never heard them say who owns the place, I thought it was a legend of sorts, a fantasy home some players aspire to have, and yet here it is.

And, of course, it's Easton's.

"It is." He nods his head, eyes intense, and I can't figure out which thing I want to look at more: the field or him.

"Is it true?"

"Mm-hmm."

"There's really a personal batting cage and mini-field beneath the building that came with your place?"

"There is." He nods again, but his eyes say so much more. I'm drawn to look closer but am afraid of what I might see because deep down I already know it might be something I won't be able to walk away from.

"Why would you need that when you have *this* in your backyard? Your office?"

He shrugs and diverts his eyes back to the stadium. It's almost as if he's embarrassed or uncertain of his answer. "Because that view, right there . . . the power of it, the strength I draw from it when I'm having that kind of game where you can feel the humming in your bones that tells you something indescribable is about to happen? This is the only place I get to have that alone. The only place where I can quiet my head and listen to what the humming is telling me without the fans or the front office or my teammates or the media watching me home in on it." He scrubs a hand through his hair and snorts. "Never mind. That just sounded completely ridiculous."

"Not in the least." I stare at him until my silence urges him to face me, meet my eyes, and see that I'm nowhere close to laughing at him. "Please. Finish what you were going to say."

"I don't know. I guess some nights I like to sit here when the lights are out, with this ghost of a stadium below me, and go to church, if you will. Think about my game." His exhale is audible and his discomfort with being so open is suddenly palpable.

"See? I knew you loved to talk about your stats."

"You and your statistics." He laughs with a shake of his head, but his discomfort is gone and his smile is genuine when he glances my way. "When they were building the new stadium, some eccentric billionaire bought this place while the building was still under construction. He was obsessed with the game and paid some stupid amount of money to build the field in the basement. The place went up for sale a few years back, and I bought it. How could I not? But I've tried to keep that it's mine on the down low. It's the one place I have that's truly mine, that's completely private and removed from everything that comes with this game."

"It's perfect."

"You haven't even seen the place with the lights on," he teases.

"These are all the lights this girl needs to know it's a perfect fit for you," I say, motioning to the ballpark's towers.

"Sometimes I'll just stand here like this after a brutal game or bad home stand, staring, thinking, and I'll suddenly get inspired to go work on what I did wrong. Sometimes I'll gear up, other times I'll head down in my pajama pants, and I'll work on it until I can't see straight and the clock reads four in the morning."

I shouldn't be surprised by his dedication, and yet I find it so refreshing to know he actually has to work at something, when he seems to be such a damn natural at everything.

"Plus, I'm super competitive so it's nice to be able to put in the extra time without anyone else knowing. Never underestimate the element of surprise."

"Never," I murmur. "And there's never a rain delay, either."

"Lately, I feel like there's been a permanent rain delay on my career." His chuckle transitions to a heavy sigh. The resignation in it tempts me to ask him more about the toll this has taken on him, but I'm startled from the thought when, without a word, he reaches over and hooks my pinky with his.

And just like I found comfort in the touch of his hand earlier, I wonder if maybe he needs the same from me right now. So I don't interrupt the moment. Instead we settle into the silence, touching and watching and trying to figure out what we are doing here.

"I'm doing my best to get you back out there," I say after a bit, letting him know I heard the frustration and defeat in his previous statement. *His permanent rain delay.*

"Is that the polite way to say you're busting my ass?"

And within seconds, we go from serious to playful, and I love that it's so easy to do with him.

"You ain't seen nothing yet, Wylder."

"Oh really?" He tugs on my pinky so that I'm forced to face him. "You've got more moves up your sleeve, Dalton?"

My smile is automatic when our eyes meet. The slow, sweet ache of want is, too. How can it not be when we're standing in the dark, he's framed by a halo of baseball stadium light, and that electric charge between us is snapping with an unfathomable current from just our pinkies touching?

There's something about Easton that makes me want when I shouldn't, need when I needn't, and desire when I know it'll be disastrous.

But damn the fallout to hell, because more than anything, I want to *feel* right now. Alive. Wanted. Desired. Like a woman.

Is that such a bad thing?

I'm sure it's not. I'm sure it's normal for most women, but not for me.

And not like this.

"I'll show you what's up my sleeve if you show me your secret baseball fort downstairs."

His laughter echoes off the glass beside us and back to my ears a second time. "Aha! So that's what it takes to impress you."

"Perhaps."

"My big bat doesn't do it for you, but my home plate downstairs does?" He shakes his head, but when our eyes meet, his laugh fades as the air between us shifts and charges with an unmistakable energy.

"Scout." All he says is my name, but in its timbre I hear so many things that I can't comprehend over my head shouting that I need to step back.

I step toward him.

Time feels like it stops.

His gasp is soft but audible.

Then starts again in slow motion.

A soft squeeze of his pinky around mine.

Then slams into fast forward.

Within a heartbeat, exactly what I both wanted and feared happens: his lips are on mine. The kiss is slow and breathtaking, with soft lips and gentle tongues and murmured sighs and guiding fingertips.

This is wrong, Scout. So wrong. But how can it be wrong when it feels like this and tastes like him?

"Easton." I tell myself to step back. To resist. To not want to kiss him.

And then our tongues meet again in a soft dance of sighs and need.

"I think we should go check out—"

His lips smother the words on mine.

"—your field—"

He nips my bottom lip.

"—your bases—"

His tongue taunts again.

"—your—"

"Will you shut up, please?" He laughs against my lips. "You've been fighting this kiss all day long, and I practiced restraint like you told me to do . . . but right now? *Right now,* I'm going to kiss you senseless, Scout, and I want to fucking enjoy it. So, for the love of God, woman, use those lips of yours on me and not on words."

His sexy-as-hell reprimand evokes a flood of emotions within me, and yet there's only one of them I can name: want.

And God how I want.

So I lean into him and take control of the kiss. I talk without sound this time. With lips and teeth and tongue, I let him know I want to enjoy the kiss just as much as he does.

I throw my concerns out the window. Tell myself to worry about them later, be mad at myself later, but for now just enjoy this virile and attractive man who wants me just as much. I slide my fingers up his chest, touching him the same way I often have to when I stretch his shoulder, but now there is no thought of anything other than how much I want to feel his weight on top of me.

He runs his hand down the line of my neck to the curve of my shoulder and then down until it rests on the small of my back, where he'd placed it earlier tonight. But this time when he pulls me in tighter against him, I don't resist. This time I welcome everything about it. The heat of his body. The flex of his hand against my back in tangible restraint. The bulge of his erection as it pushes against my lower belly.

And damn if knowing he's already hard for me doesn't add fuel to my firestorm of want.

"Scout." It's my name again, but this time I know exactly what he's asking me.

"Yes." One word. It's all I say, then that need and desire simmering between us ignites into a combustible wildfire where first-kiss-caution is consumed by unfettered lust and reckless abandon.

That hand on my back slides under my V-neck and runs up the side of my torso, thumb rubbing ever so gently over the underside of my breast on its way to help unclasp my bra.

My body burns with the expectation of his touch.

And then it lights on fire when his fingers trace their way back—skin to skin—beneath my loosened bra and over my nipples. They harden instantly as his thumbs rub circles over them—they tease and pleasure—all the while his lips and tongue launch another assault with a renewed vigor that only makes me want more.

And he gives me that *more* when he lifts my hands above my head, pulls my shirt off, and dips down and takes my nipple in his mouth. The warmth of his tongue mixed with the scrape of his stubble adds an element of contrast, soft versus rough, that twists my insides and leaves me wanting to know if he's as slow and thorough with every other part of his sexual attention.

My hands are in his hair as he teases one breast and then the other, and I'm not sure if I want him to stop and come back to kiss my lips, or if I want him to keep stoking that fire bright.

Emitting the sexiest growl I've ever heard, Easton makes the decision for me when he puts his hands on my waist and lifts me like I'm a feather. There's no hesitancy on my part, only need, when I wrap my legs around his waist, thread my fingers through his hair, and lose myself under the haze of desire his kisses are unleashing on that sensitive spot beneath my jaw.

And then he begins to walk.

His mouth is on my neck. His unshaven jaw tickles my collarbone. The cool air of the room slides over my breasts. His hips rest deliciously between my thighs.

All of those things tempt and taunt me, but it's when he lays me down on the bed, when I'm so desperate for more from him, that my own control snaps.

We reach for the waist of each other's jeans at the same time. Without any finesse, we fumble and bump hands, our laughter forcing us to come up for air, making us realize it would be so much quicker if we undress ourselves.

So in a rush of movements we strip and shimmy and step out of our clothes until we are naked, laughing in panting breaths, hungry for more and eager to have it.

But it's when I look up from where I lie on the bed to where he stands at its edge, my laughter falls off. He's watching me, wanting me, and everything about him, from his expression to his eyes to his body, is breathtaking. He's hard lines and tanned skin. He's confidence with a half-cocked grin, and he's desire restrained with the tense set of his shoulders. His fingers flick, ready to conquer and claim, and his lips part, ready to lead the assault.

But it's his eyes that command my attention.

They ask and demand and want as they slowly scrape their way up my legs, pausing at the apex of my thighs before continuing up my abdomen to my breasts. When they finally make their way back to mine, they are darkened by a desire I'm desperate to sink whole-heartedly into.

So many things about him—the look in his eye, the set of his shoulders, his impressive dick standing hard and thick between his muscular thighs, and the sexual tension snapping in the air around us—has me craving more of him and willing to beg for what comes next. The push and the pull. The give and the take. The need and the greed. The wish and the want. The climb and the release.

Lost in the haze of lust and expectation, my mouth waters. My body aches. My fingers beg to run over every dip and dent and curve of his body.

"Easton." It's his name on my lips this time. My turn to ask, to demand, *to beg.*

My knees fall apart in invitation.

His breath hitches.

My body hums, and chills chase over my skin.

He licks his lips. Steps. Stares. Admires.

And then he's on the bed, crawling over me and dipping down to take my nipple in his mouth again.

"Oh, that feels good," I murmur as my back arches and offers.

His chuckle vibrates the sensitized flesh. "I'm about to make it feel a whole lot better. Time to fuck your pretty kitty, *Kitty.*"

I manage to laugh through the sensations his skilled tongue is evoking, but it turns into a gasp of welcome pleasure when his hand slides between by thighs. His fingertips dance over my seam, taunting with a feather-light touch before slowly parting me to brush ever so slightly over my clit. Warmth. Heat. Electricity. The current of desire jolts my system, and my hips buck into his hand and beg for more.

"You like that?"

"*God, yes.*"

"I don't think God has anything to do with this, but feel free to call his name." He chuckles and looks up at me over the rise of my breasts, his eyes sharp with desire and contradicted by a cocky flash of a grin. "'Cause we're about to get biblical."

"Oh, please." I laugh, but it's lost to him as his lips claim mine and his fingers rub and tease and work my clit into a frenzy of overwhelming sensations. I writhe and lift and tense, wanting to prolong this onslaught of ecstasy and reach my climax all at the same time.

"Greedy girl," he murmurs, kissing his way down the line of my neck and up to my ear where he nips on my earlobe. "I kind of like that."

His simple praise and the soft chuckle that follows only adds to the riot of hormones racing to my every nerve as his fingers continue to work me to my brink.

"East . . ." A pant of his name is all I can manage as my hands grip tighter onto his forearms, my body edging that fine line before climax. "*East*." Another pant. Another warning that I'm going to come.

My nails score his skin. My body vibrates with tension.

And then nothing.

His fingers stop. His hand stills. My head snaps up so I can look him in the eyes. And once our eyes meet, once he knows he has my attention, he takes the pads of two fingers and slides them ever-so-tauntingly-slowly down the line of my sex. He teases me, wetting them with my arousal before just as leisurely sliding them into me.

My exhale is unsteady, nerves already strung tight and primed to snap. But it's his eyes on mine—unwavering and intense—that dare me more than anything. To come for him. To please him.

He hears every hitch of my breath. He watches the arch of my neck. He notices when I bite into my bottom lip. He feels each clench of my muscles around his finger. And it's this complete attention that creates an unexpected intimacy and encourages me to slip under that veil of pleasure.

The orgasm slams into me, hijacking my breath as the explosion of desire morphs into a flash of white-hot heat.

My hands grab the sheets. My hips buck into his hand. My lips part, but no sound escapes. My body is seared by the sensations he's just brought to life.

The bed dips as he moves, and I can just barely hear the tell-tale rip of foil over the thunder of my pulse in my ears. And before I have any chance to recover from the orgasm still pulsing through me, Easton's hands are on the back of my knees, pulling me toward the edge of the bed.

He meets my eyes as he steps between my legs and wastes no time making that first carnal connection when he runs the crest of his dick up and down my slit to prepare both of us for what comes next.

And oh, how I want it to come next. Especially if it feels this incredible already and we haven't even gotten to the good part yet.

He groans, his struggle to take this slow written all over his face. But I don't want slow. I want him. Now. And I'm desperate to have him, so in an attempt to snap that control of his and get what I want, I spread my thighs as wide as possible in invitation.

His eyes flash up to mine, a ghost of a smile on his lips that tells me he knows what I'm doing, but he holds on. Resists. And then he taunts me right back by pushing just the tip of his cock inside me so I can feel that burn that is *oh so good* before he slowly pulls back out.

I lift my hips to try and prevent him from withdrawing completely but he just steps a foot back with his cock in his hand, and smiles at me.

Smug bastard.

We wage a visual war of wills, but when he looks back down to where I'm wet and waiting for him, he caves.

But if I thought this time the wait would be over, that he was going to give me what I want—all of him—I was wrong. Because he continues to toy with me, tease me, arouse me by rubbing his tip just inside of me until I moan with want, before pulling back out.

And the best part is his expression. Not just the taut lines in his neck telling me he's struggling through the denied pleasure like I am, but the widening of his eyes and how his lips fall lax in pleasure each time he enters me.

The next time he pushes his hips forward, I prop myself up on my elbows so I can look between my thighs and see what he sees. How my arousal—visual proof of what he does to me—glistens on his shaft. How each time he pulls out, he slides a little deeper into me the next time, uses his hand to guide his cock so it rubs expertly around all of the nerves within me, and then withdraws.

Before starting the process all over again.

It's arousing. Heady. Intoxicating. To see my body accept his hard girth. To watch how I stretch around him, adjust to him, and then take him in a little more. To see how when he pulls back out, my pink flesh clings tight like I don't want him to part from me just yet. To know that, even after coming once, my body is more than willing to go again with him.

His patience is admirable. His determination to stretch me bit by bit, escalate our desire inch by inch, is frustrating and erotic and leaves me vibrating with need.

And then finally, with one final thrust he bottoms out, fully sheathed, root to tip, within me. Our mutual groans fill the room as we each allow the other to savor the moment, the feeling, our first time coming together like this.

Seconds pass. Anticipation steals our breaths. And then he reaches out, puts his hand on my shoulder, and holds me in place so he can grind his hips against mine, seating his cock even further into me.

And holy fuck does he feel incredible.

We both gasp, caught up in the slow circle he makes with his pelvis and the absolute eroticism of the moment.

And then he begins to really move.

Our foreheads are pressed against each other's. Our lips kiss and then pant and praise. Our hips move, grinding and bucking in that first-time dance as we find the friction we both need to drive us to the edge. Our hands tense and grasp and grip as Easton picks up the pace.

We crash together in a torrent of lust and lips and tongues, where wants now become needs. Where greed becomes the game, and satisfying it becomes a by-all- means-necessary type of strategy. Where bodies mesh and meet and tease and pleasure.

The room fills with sounds.

Fuck, that feels good.

Right there.

Scout.

Yes. You're incredible.

Oh god.

I can't hold back much longer.

Harder.

Good?

Faster.

Scout.

His hands grip tighter.

"Scout."

His hips buck harder.

"Scout."

A second warning. His restraint is gone.

"I'm coming." I can barely get the words out. The second orgasm that hits is ten times more intense than the first. My body, my breath, my thoughts, my sensibility is all lost as I buck and writhe and take and claim every single ounce of what he gives me while he races to claim his own.

I'm barely coherent, lost in an unforgiving sea of bliss, but when Easton's fingers dig into my thighs, I'm pulled back just in time to watch his climax slam through him. His groan is guttural. His head is thrown back. My name is on his lips. His hips grind violently against mine.

It's sexy as hell to watch him come undone. To know I did this to him. To see his muscles, taut from release, slowly relax, one by one. And when his fingers loosen their grip on me, murmurs of praise are on his lips until he leans over and fuses them to mine for one last kiss.

And then we collapse onto his downy soft bed, his weight on top of me, his dick slipping out of me, and his head resting on my chest.

Seconds turn to minutes as we catch our breath and let our heartbeats calm.

"Well, it wasn't the private field downstairs, but I guess it'll do," I tease as I lazily run my finger up and down the line of his spine.

His laughter rumbles through his chest into mine. "*It'll do?*" he asks in mock disbelief; and that alone—the scrape of his scruff and the heat of his breath from speaking—causes chills to chase over my already sated body. "I played your field all right and slid perfectly into home."

"*If you say so.*" My voice is coy and playful as I shrug and fight the smile on my lips. "This field is pretty impressive."

"I guess I'll have to try harder next time to outrank it then."

"I'm a hard girl to please."

He props himself up on his elbows and just stares at me. But there's something different about the look, the kind of different that suddenly makes me panic and feel fluttery and like I need to go but want to stay.

So I do the only thing I can think of to quiet the chaotic thoughts and prevent them from ruining the moment—I lean up and brush my lips ever so gently against his.

"A demanding woman indeed," he murmurs before giving me that tender type of kiss that reverberates to your toes and then all the way back up until it slams into your belly. *Or heart.* "Good thing I've got a big bat and know how to use it."

CHAPTER TEN

Scout

The sun is blinding. It takes me a minute to adjust to its brightness, and when I'm able to fully open my eyes, Easton's face is inches from mine, dark features half hidden in a sea of light blue pillowcase.

My first reaction is to run my fingers along the scruff on his jaw. To touch him again. To make sure he's real. And to validate every single thing I felt last night as we came together, again and again and again.

My second reaction is *oh shit*.

The buzz I had long into the early morning hours vanishes, gone with the rising of the sun. But with its disappearance comes that groggy awareness of what I allowed—what I wanted to happen—but know can't happen.

Realization hits.

Oh. My. God.

I slept with Easton Wylder.

Hot, delectable, just-as-talented-in-the-sack-as-on-the-ball-field Easton Wylder. The one lying naked beside me in bed, his tanned, sculpted body nestled beneath these pristine sheets.

The player.

A client.

My ticket to getting the Austin Aces' long-term contract. The last wish left on my dad's bucket list, to put the cherry on top of his incredible career.

The wish I just risked by breaking the rules of my ironclad contract.

My head dizzies with the possible consequences if someone were to find out.

My stomach flip-flops over the sight of him sound asleep, so peaceful, so mouthwateringly gorgeous.

Then the panic returns. Not over breeching my contract, like it should be, but rather over how last night made me feel. And man, *how I did feel.* But now that the sheets have cooled and the haze of lust is gone, I'm not sure what to make of these newfound feelings. Or what do to with them now that they still linger.

Oh crap.

What am I thinking?

There can't be feelings.

There can't be anything.

There wasn't even supposed to be sex.

There was supposed to be rehab.

There was supposed to be me getting Easton back up to par, *athletically,* so he could play again and I could tell my dad I did it. Make him proud of me. Give him something more to live for.

Staring at Easton only makes my emotions riot that much louder, but I know what I need to do.

With guilt eating at me like acid, I slide out of the bed slowly so as not to disturb him. How could I be so selfish? So reckless? I search for my clothes, all the while desperate to push these feelings away and crawl back into bed with him. Let him wrap his arms around me and kiss me again just like he did last night when we finally decided we were too exhausted to go another round.

Conflicted in heart and head, I pull on my jeans as quietly as possible and pad out into the condo to find my bra and T-shirt. They're lying on the floor, a scarlet letter of shame to slide on as a reminder of what I'm about to do: leave as silently as possible.

The elevator ride down feels like it takes forever.

It gives me too much time to think. To regret. To realize Easton lifted me up last night. *And I let him do it,* when I definitely weigh more than he should lift with his shoulder. Did he hurt it? Did he reinjure anything?

No. He's fine. It's my panic talking.

Because there was no pain in that moment. There was only want and greed and need and selfishness and selflessness. Definitely not pain. That sexy growl of his fills my head and begs me to stop the elevator right now and press *penthouse* instead of *lobby.*

Go back.

I can't.

Go back.

I press my hand to the row of buttons illuminating five random floors. The elevator stops abruptly at the next floor, its doors open to an empty hallway lined with expensive carpet and doors to other condos.

I stare at the emptiness as my heart fights against my mind.

Duty wars against desire.

Promises made battle against personal wants.

Responsibility clashes against recklessness.

Selflessness is pitted against selfishness.

The doors slide shut, and I close my eyes then press **L** for lobby.

When the doors open, my composure is held together by a thread. I need to get out of here, need time and space to think. Blinded by emotions I can't process just yet, I accidentally run straight into a young coed, knocking her binder to the ground. I scramble to help her pick up the papers that have fallen out, focusing on the words on the pages—teaching credential requirements and adult development something or other—because it's so much easier than meeting her eyes. Embarrassed, frazzled, and moments away from crying, I mumble an apology to the polka-dotted sorority letters printed on the front of her sweatshirt.

"Sorry," I mutter, trying to sound sympathetic when all I feel is responsibility heavier than the weight of my world.

To my dad.

To the Aces.

To Easton.

And as I push open the doors to the street and suck in a huge breath of morning air, the first tear slips down my cheek.

I hate myself for it.

But I hate myself more when my phone vibrates in my purse. The panic I felt upstairs pales in comparison to how I feel when I look at the screen of my phone.

And in an instant, every reason I had for sneaking out and leaving Easton upstairs becomes validated.

The ring through my Bluetooth swallows the silence of my car. I startle at its sound, then cringe, because without even looking at it, I know who's calling.

I ignore it.

He calls back.

I ignore it again.

He calls back again.

After three more rounds of *ring, ignore, repeat,* I'm more aware than ever that sneaking out was total chickenshit. And as much as I'd like to push ignore again, I can't. I have to face him, I have to try and smooth this over without damaging our working relationship, so I bite the bullet and answer.

"Hello?"

"Where the hell are you?" Easton's voice fills the line. Its confusion laced with disbelief mixed with anger and a touch of rejection.

"Good morning." Keep it professional, Scout.

"It would have been an even better morning if you were still here. But you're not. And I'm a little confused as to why."

"Easton." His name is a sigh. An olive branch. It's anything to explain what verbally I can't.

"Don't 'Easton' me, Scout. Where are you? Because you sure as hell aren't in my bed."

My dad's sick. Sally texted five times while I was lying in your bed, trying to tell me he was having a hard time breathing. Asking me if I could come home and visit with him, not only to brighten his mood, but to remind him why he needs to fight harder to get over the funk he's in.

"I had some errands to run," I lie.

I'd rather be with you, too. I'd rather have met you under different circumstances. That would have made all of this ten times easier.

"Errands? Wow. That's a way to make a guy feel confident in his abilities. 'Hey Easton, it was so great last night, but I'd rather go to the store to pick up some toilet paper than have sleepy morning sex with you,'" he says, but his attempt to sound like me does nothing to hide the irritation lacing its edges.

I glance over my shoulder then change lanes as I work up the courage to say the words I need to say but don't really want to say. "Last night was a mistake," I whisper as if I don't want him to hear. Because I don't.

It's a lie.

"Come again?"

"We can't do this."

"Well, we did do this, and it was fucking incredible, so tell me something I'm actually going to believe."

I'm afraid of what I'm going to find when I see my dad for the first time in a month.

I clear my throat but lose the battle against tears for the second time this morning, and it takes everything to sound unaffected when I speak. "If Cory were to find out, he'd fire me."

"Bullshit." He says the word, but we both know it's true—the silence hanging on the line tells me, so I take advantage of the moment to try and reason with him.

"I'm contracted by your employers, Easton. I *have* to remain unbiased . . . and I sure as hell don't look unbiased if I'm sleeping with you one minute and telling them to reinstate you the next. Call me crazy, but they'd second-guess every opinion I have when it comes to you. My credibility would be shot to hell when it's a vital, necessary part of my job."

"Credibility is one thing, Scout. Sleeping with me is another. Now find another way to spin this so you can avoid having to explain why you tip-toed out like you were some one-night stand. *I'll wait.*"

I hate that his words make every part of me sag in relief and in sadness. But they do, because he didn't consider me a one-night stand and because I know it can't happen again.

"I just can't right now. If someone found out, then . . ."

"No one's going to find out. Are you going to tell someone? Because I'm not. Who else knows about last night and is going to say something?"

My mind scrambles for an explanation, a validation. "What if someone recognizes me leaving your place? Another player? The media? The damn girl in the lobby? And they go and tell the press?"

"Girl in the lobby? What are you talking about?"

"Nothing. No one." I shake my head and grip the steering wheel harder, knowing I sound schizophrenic but unable to stop. "Just never mind."

"There's something you're not telling me."

"No." My voice breaks, and I clear my throat. "There's nothing.

It's just . . ."

"It's just? That's all you're going to give me?"

"I've gotta go."

"This discussion isn't over, Scout."

Yes, it is.

I hang up the phone just before the sob breaks free. I know I'm being overly emotional. I know that everything with my dad is making me sensitive. But I also know that there's something about Easton that I can't let go of just yet, but I have to.

Is he the type who'd leave?

Of course he would. *All men leave, Scout.* All people leave. That's what they do.

But what about last night? What about how he made me feel? And not just the sex—because that was pretty damn incredible—but all of the other feelings I went to bed high on and woke up still swimming in. Do they mean anything? And more importantly, do I want to *let* them mean something?

I fight the urge to call him back. To ask him if we could table this for another place and time. Tell him that my dad's sick, explain why this contract is so important, and let him know I'm scared, because if I feel this much after spending only one night with him, how would I feel if we were to spend more together?

But I can't call him back.

Because it all comes back to my dad.

To the promise I made him.

To the fact that anyone I've ever truly loved in my life has left me.

And the one I've loved most will be gone soon, too.

CHAPTER ELEVEN

Scout

"He's going to be pissed that you took the time to drive all the way out here, Scout."

The lines of worry etched on Sally's face warm my heart. "I know he will, but two hours isn't that long of a drive. Besides, I'm sick of him being the one to dictate the visitation terms. And don't worry, I won't tell him you called." I pull her into me for a hug and then chuckle. "Why, I just needed to take a drive to clear my head, Sally, and lo and behold I ended up here." I bat my lashes and smile to reinforce the lie.

She smiles, but it does nothing to ease the weariness in her eyes. "He doesn't want you to see him like this," she whispers. "He's got a lot of pride, and it's hard for him to know you see him as weak."

I sigh. "He's the strongest man I've ever known. Even now. How can he—"

"Who are you talking to Sally?" My dad's voice booms through into the kitchen where we stand.

My smile is as automatic as the drop of my heart into my stomach as I prepare myself for the unknown. What will he look like?

Weaker? Bedridden? Gaunt? Has he gone downhill quicker than expected so that I'll be shocked at the sight of him?

With a fortifying breath I walk into the living room where his hospital bed has been set up to make it easier for him to get around, for Sally to tend to him, and because it allows him to stare at one of his favorite places in the world, the endless fields of tall grass that stretch to the horizon.

Relief overwhelms me when I see him out of his bed, sitting in his favorite chair by the window. "She's talking to me."

"Scouty?" Love floods into his voice as he turns and sees me standing there, but it's quickly replaced with upset. "Why are you here?"

"Because I needed to see you." I've never spoken truer words. And while he doesn't look any feebler than the last time I saw him, I know from Sally that he is. The cold he can't shake has knocked him on his ass and taken its toll on his already weakened immune system.

"Nonsense." Irritation litters the edges of his voice. "I told you that you could come to see me once you've won the Aces' contract."

I grit my teeth and bite back the hurt his disregard causes. "Well, you may want to shut me out, Dad, but you don't get to control me." My tone is no-nonsense while my heart aches. He must know that Sally called me, updated me on his rough week, but I refuse to let her take the blame. "I wanted to take a drive today. Clear my head, think about some things. So I ended up here. What are you going to do, kick me out?"

I hold his glare and tempt him to do just that, and I hate that for a minute I wonder if he actually will. He's been so stubborn and difficult in the past six months that a part of me wouldn't put it past him.

"You're not going to prevent me from seeing you. If you try, I'll let *the player* figure out his recovery on his own and take up residence here in my old room."

"Your old room's full of stuff."

"I'm a big girl, I know how to throw *stuff* out." And I know that will get him, break through his obstinacy—the fear that I'll sneak in here with black trash bags and clean out his clutter of memories stacked in boxes in my old room. Newspaper clippings on giants of the sport he helped rehab. Articles highlighting Ford's pitching stats and my softball career. Trophies and jerseys for the teams he's worked for. It's a treasure trove of memorabilia any baseball collector would die for.

He eyes me again, but I can see his lips fighting the smile I know he wants to give me for doing just what he taught me: giving as good as I'm getting. "You can stay for a bit, but one sign of waterworks and I'm kicking you out."

I nod, understanding the hard-ass is giving me a mulligan so long as I don't cry. Stepping beside him, I place my hand on his shoulder and squeeze, needing to touch him. And when he lifts a hand to place on top of mine, I'd give anything to be a little girl again. Then I could crawl into his lap like I used to do and listen to the rumble of his voice as he told me stories about a mom I never really knew, but who he swore loved me. The stories I now know to be lies, because a mom who walks out on her two children getting ready for bed while her husband's washing the dishes without ever looking back never really loved them at all.

This house holds too many memories for me, good and bad, and I wonder if maybe that's why my dad's forcing me to distance myself from it.

"Tell me about how Easton is coming along."

The pang in my chest is real at the mention of his name. The images of him last night—his smile when he was dancing with me, the adoration on his face highlighted by the bright lights of the stadium beyond, and the moonlight across his face as he sank into me—all flash through my mind and force me to act like none of it mattered when every single thing did.

Forced to switch mental gears, I try to care about work right now.

A safe middle ground for us. Well, safe for my dad, but not so much for me.

"The player is doing well," I murmur, knowing damn well Easton's cologne still lingers on my skin as I go into the details of his therapy, what still pains him, what I think he's hiding, before I listen to the master of the trade tell me what he thinks I need to do differently or add to my regimen to help. "What I don't get, besides the obvious—that the team needs him on the field because he's just that good—is why rush it? Why give a timeframe for recovery on a franchise player?"

My dad angles his head as he contemplates the question. "Beats me, Scout. I learned a long time ago that front offices rarely do things that seem reasonable to the public, but in the long run make perfect sense."

"Yeah, well, how about they make common sense instead of aiming for perfect sense," I grumble in defense of Easton when there's no need to defend him.

And it's the look in my dad's eye that unnerves me. The one that tells me he's reading my thoughts when I sure as hell don't want him to. "You like him, don't you?"

"Yeah, I do. He's nice, easy to work with, and wants to recover. What's not to like about that in a player?" I figure that's as safe as anything.

"True." He nods his head again and chews the inside of his lip. "Is this going to be a problem?"

There are so many ways I can take his question, so many ways I can answer it, and so I don't say anything. Does he mean am I going to be able to get Easton back on the field in the allotted time? Does he mean that he can see right through me, knows something happened between Easton and me, and is wondering if it will jeopardize my standing with the club?

When he chuckles at my lack of response, it's music to my ears. *He's let me off the hook without answering.*

"How is it you can have two kids, raise them exactly the same, and they turn out so completely different?" he asks, and I know now that he didn't let me off the hook at all. His chuckle was just prepping me for the schooling he's about to give. "You were always pushing boundaries while Ford was . . . he was always so concerned with making everyone happy. You were always willing to take risks, and he was always the one who would stay the course. You were always so hard to read, and he was the open book. You were opposites in so many ways, and yet so very much alike it scared me some days."

I watch him. The lines in his face may have changed over time, with age and illness, but he still looks the same, still seems the same, and it's hard to believe he's really that sick. That he's mortal and not the invincible man the little girl in me still sees.

"But you changed, Scouty girl. After Ford died, I know you tried to be both for me. That you stepped into his shoes—tried to give me pieces of both of you—even though some days I know it killed you to be someone you weren't . . . but you did it for me. So, thank you. I wanted you to know I appreciate that."

"Dad . . ." I fight back the emotions his acknowledgement churns up. Hearing he knew how hard I'd worked to try and fill the hole Ford's death left in our family—and in his heart—means more to me than he'll ever know.

And at the same time, I hate hearing it. I hate wondering if he's slowly checking items off his mental list of things left to say, and that this is the slow, winding path of him starting to say good-bye.

"You promised you wouldn't cry."

"I'm not." I sniffle and swallow what feels like a boulder in my throat. "I just don't understand why you insist on not letting me—"

"I have my reasons," he barks, and stuns me into wondering what the hell just upset him so much.

I stare at him, wanting to question him, to finish my thought. But I shift my gaze to the field outside again, to the good memories of playing hide and seek with Ford for hours, to try and abate the tears sobbing silently within me.

"He'd be thirty, this month, you know."

"I know." The silence stretches between us, interrupted only by the rattle of his breath. "No father should have to bury his son," I whisper, not sure if it's to remind me or to reassure him.

"And no daughter should be left all alone to bury her father."

CHAPTER TWELVE

Easton

A fucking *text*?

That's how she's going to play this bullshit game with me? Leave me to do my rehab by myself because she can't face me or the fact that the other night was incredible and she left without a word?

"I just can't." Seriously? Those three words were all she could give me before hanging up, followed by a text detailing my rehab routine for the day? Four reps of weighted arm swings and the rest of the regimen?

Total bullshit.

Fucking women.

But I should be happy about this, right? She's not Doc. She's nowhere near as skilled, experienced, or knowledgeable as him. So maybe if I bitch about her, tell the GM, then they'll demand Doc come here instead. He's the best after all.

If that's the case, then why do I want her? How come I keep thinking about that look in her eyes and the feel of her body and the sound of her laugh?

She's frustrating.

And sexy.

She's stubborn and unrelenting.

And goddamn beautiful.

She's fucking irritating is what she is.

She doesn't want to pick up the phone? Then fine. I've got this. I'll bust my ass on my own. I don't need her. I knew that the first day I met her.

But I like her.

Fuck if that isn't perfect. And fitting. Wanting a woman I can't have.

Wanting a woman who could cause trouble if others found out.

Wanting a woman who made it clear she doesn't want me back.

Scratch that. There's nothing clear about it. She's about as clear as mud, because she wants me. A marathon of sex is about as good a validation as any.

Now I just need to figure out how to make her admit it.

Damn woman.

I grit my teeth as I prepare for the pain that typically begins with the fourth set of repetitions, and then startle when it doesn't.

There's no pinch. No burn. There's fucking nothing.

I repeat the movement. I lift and twist and turn a few extra times.

And still nothing.

I try one more time, push my shoulder farther than I should, until I feel a faint pinch before dropping the weight. And when I look in the mirror, I have a stupid grin on my face. It's been so long that I forgot what it even feels like to not hurt.

And, of course, I immediately want to call Scout and tell her so she can celebrate with me over this tiny fucking milestone that shouldn't feel like a victory but does.

But I can't. Because she won't pick up. And I know this because

I've called and texted—enough times that I lost count—without getting a return response.

Someone did a number on her. That much I can tell from all her talk about players moving on and leaving her behind, but fuck if I can figure out who it was. No one I've talked to can remember her ever dating anyone. Her social media accounts show shit other than pictures of her in other team clubhouses posing for the camera with various players, arms hanging casually over her shoulders.

Fucking lovely. Isn't that her term? Lovely? Well, that's the first thing that came to mind when I saw the picture of her sandwiched in between Rizzo and Bryant after she worked with the Cubs last year. Or of a shirtless Posey laughing with her in the Giant's clubhouse.

Not a single personal picture. No mutts. No weekend out boozing it up with girlfriends. No inspirational sayings that you want to roll your eyes at and scroll past. *Nothing.*

But she can go out dancing with me. She can stare at my stadium from the darkness of my condo and put into words everything that the sight of it makes me feel. A woman who can understand that shit is not normal.

And now she won't talk to me? Can't face me?

The other night was not a mistake. No way. No how.

"Where's Ms. Dalton?" The voice of the club's GM startles me from the other side of the training room. "Are you on her clock or are you putting extra time in on your own?"

I'm not sure why I hesitate to respond, but I do. He's hard to get a read on, and so caution is the name of the game until I can.

"Hey, Cory. How's it going?" Wiping the sweat from my face with a towel, I walk toward him.

When he steps into the room, I'm surprised to see my father right behind him. *The best-buddy squad. Great.*

"Good. And you? How's the arm?"

"I'm feeling great. The shoulder's feeling the best it has since surgery. I'm anxious to get back out there."

"I'm sure you are. Is Scout around?"

"She caught a bug. I told her to stay home, but we've talked and gone over my regimen so I can stay on task." The lie comes out smoothly, but I can't for the life of me figure out why I feel the need to cover for her at all.

And yet I did, the need to protect her unexpected, but there nonetheless.

"I'm impressed that you came in on your own to get it done," my dad interjects.

I stare at him, trying to comprehend why he'd think it was anywhere near okay for him to say that. And around my boss, no less. I'm not a child. This is my job, and I'm damn good at it, so he needs to leave me the fuck alone. The thought manifests into words, but I bite my tongue so hard it hurts.

It's not worth it. Besides, Cory's expression is guarded, making it nearly impossible to gauge his thoughts. And since professionalism is always the best route, I play the part they expect me to play.

"Like I said, I'm anxious to get back on the field. I miss contributing to the team." I spout the company line, and even though they smile in response, there's something off here. Something I can't put my finger on but can sense nonetheless.

"The guys miss you, too. The Aces don't quite feel right without a Wylder on the field."

My dad laughs and slaps me on my good shoulder. "Keep up the good work, son. I have no doubt you'll be back to fighting form soon enough."

"Neither do I," I say.

"Make sure to tell Ms. Dalton that I'd like a report in the next day or two on your progress."

"Will do."

I watch them leave and blow out a breath as I try to figure out what the little visit was all about. I don't want to care but have to. He's my boss.

"Everything good in here, Easy E?"

My smile is automatic, the irritation vanishing in a heartbeat at the voice I've known since I was eight years old. I turn to find the familiar face of our clubhouse manager, the man who used to entertain me with stories and jokes when my dad was too busy being the public persona.

"Hey, Manny-Man," I say in the same exchange of nicknames we've done for over twenty years. "How're you doing today? You staying to watch the game tonight?"

"Pretty damn good. And nope. You know me. I only stick around when the greats play."

"Are there no greats playing today?" I ask with a shake of my head.

"Greats are few and far between, son," he finishes his typical retort and surprises me when he continues. "I've watched enough baseball in my life to hold off watching another game until it's someone who's going to dazzle me with his talent."

"Picky. Picky."

His grin just widens, and I love that even though I'm injured, he's still Manny-Man.

"I see the old man is still as hard on you as ever," he says with a knowing nod, just like he used to do when he'd find me alone in the locker room, sniffling away tears in secret after I was hurt by something my father would say.

"Yeah, well. Why change now, right?"

He just nods, never one to be disrespectful, but a man I'm glad to have on my side.

"True." He laughs, contrary to the gravity in his eyes as he searches to make sure I'm okay. "Look at me—forty years, and I'm still doing the same goddamn thing."

"Taking care of us pretty boys?" I tease.

"There's nothing pretty about you, son." I bark out a laugh at the good-humored dig. "But that tough cookie who's been working you over? Hoowee. Now, she? She's definitely pretty."

"She sure is," I murmur before I catch myself, and wonder why nearly every conversation of late seems to come back to her.

Because she's the one in charge of the decisions.

And the one currently clouding up and fucking with my head.

CHAPTER THIRTEEN

Scout

My lungs burn.

My legs ache.

And all I can think is one more side of the stadium before my nerves are calm and emotions dulled enough to be able to face Easton today.

Because how do I keep things professional when every time I have to touch him, I'm going to be reminded of the other night?

So, running the stadium steps I go. Up one section. Lower loge to loge to upper loge, across the top row of empty seats, then down the other side.

I replay my meeting with Cory. His insistence that I answer whether I think Easton will be up to speed by mid-August. His pressure on me to say if he'll be back to one hundred percent, or if he will slowly slide down the slope of injured and irreparable that sometimes happens despite all rehab efforts.

Frustrated with their businesslike attitude when it comes to a human being—to tendons and muscles and soft tissue you just can't superglue back together—I push myself harder. To the next section, to the upper loge, to the loge, to lower loge, and then to the next.

Forget about it, Scout. It's his job to get good players on the field and win pennants. Players are commodities.

I sprint across a row of seats.

Screw that. Players are people.

My lungs burn, but I need more.

Martinez hits a ball over the left field wall in his early morning batting session on the diamond below, but the crack of his bat is silenced by my ear buds. And I need it to be. I may be in the stadium, but I need to forget about baseball for a few more flights. And, in particular, a specific baseball player.

So, I continue to push myself. To use the physicality to burn my mind and ease my soul. To eat away at my anger. To calm me the hell down when all I feel is uncertainty.

When all I want is something I can't have.

So, I climb. Section by section. Step by step. Trying to shed the burden of my emotions with the sweat that drips off my body.

But the clearer my mind becomes, the more room I have to think, and of course I veer to where I shouldn't. To Easton and everything about him. The contrasts. The unexpected. The disarming smile and the intense eyes. His soft groans in the dark and his baseball-bat-roughened hands on my skin. The vulnerability he pulls out of me, when I'm tough with everyone else.

This is not a good sign—me thinking about him.

Not at all.

And, of course, when I turn to run down the next section of seats, he's right there, running behind me. Matching me step for step.

I ignore him.

I still get thirty more minutes to myself before I have to deal with him.

I still need thirty more minutes to figure out how to look at him and not want to feel how I feel.

I still want thirty more minutes to calm the flutter in my belly just from knowing he's near me.

So, I run faster. I take the steps two at a time.

He does the same and double-times it so that he's now running beside me instead of behind me.

I push harder. Irritated. Competitive. Not wanting him to think I'm weaker or less than or both, even though he's never made me feel that way in the first place.

But having feelings for him does, and so that makes it his fault. All of it.

And so, I run. But this time, instead of turning to cross over to the next section, I run straight through the exit to the concourse beyond.

One of my earbuds has fallen out, and my shoes squeak on the concrete as I run in an all-out sprint down the empty corridor, past the vacant concessions stands and team merchandise kiosks.

His shoes slap the concrete behind me, and his labored breathing echoes through the space.

I know he's fast. Having clocked his time, I'm well aware he could be ten steps ahead of me in seconds if he really wanted to be, and the fact that he's not grates on my already irritated nerves.

And at the same time, I'm out of gas—my legs, my lungs, my everything—and so I have no choice but to stop when I'd rather keep running right on out of the stadium instead of having to face Easton.

"Scout."

Keep running.

"Scout."

I can't even breathe, let alone talk.

"Hey."

I can't do it anymore. I can't run another step, and so I stop, knowing I'm going to have to face him—right here, right now—with a mind and body so exhausted it's going to be tough to keep my guard up.

With my hands on my knees, sweat stinging my eyes and lungs

heaving harshly, I glance over at Easton, strangely satisfied to see he's just as winded as I am. Hands braced behind his head, elbows out, he walks around this mecca of gray concrete to cool down.

"It's not your time yet. Go away." I know I'm being mean. I know he doesn't deserve it. And yet I need to catch my breath so I can think straight.

"I have just as much of a right to be in this stadium as you do, *Kitty*." The nickname is a taunt I try to ignore. He has a way of pushing my buttons, and that damn name is just one of them.

Especially when I remember how he was pleasing my body the last time he called me that.

And that pisses me off more. I hate that I'm supposed to feel like I don't care when all I want to do is care.

"I'm not on the clock yet, so this is my time."

"Like hell it is."

If he was looking for my full attention, he just got it. And not only that, but my temper to go along with it.

"Excuse me?" I stand to my full height and look at him for the first time. And when I do, every part of my body wants to move toward him instead of rail against him.

"You heard me," he says, meeting me glare for glare as he takes a few steps toward me. "I never figured you to be the love 'em and leave 'em type, but hey, you've already underestimated me . . . so I guess we're even. Right?"

There's a bite to his tone. A defiant rejection edged with bruised ego. And all of that and more is reflected in his eyes as he takes another step closer while I glance around frantically to see if anyone is within listening distance.

"No one's close enough to hear me, Scout. Or to save you from having this conversation."

"We're not having this conversation, so it's a moot point." I begin to walk away, and he sidesteps to block me. I'm forced to stop, or else I'll end up face first in his chest, and touching him right now is not exactly the smartest thing.

"We are having it because there're a few things that we need to get straight. First one: I've had plenty of fun in my life, in and out of the sheets. But not once have I ever snuck off in the early morning and not faced what I did or didn't do the night before. I'm a bigger man than that, and something tells me you are, too. So, you want to tell me what's going on?"

His dig is real. His hurt breaks through the spite in his tone. I hate that my immediate urge is to apologize and explain . . . but I can't. I must stand my ground with him. I have no other option.

"Like I said, I'm not on the clock."

"You're damn right you're not. But I'm not your clock, sweetheart."

"Leave me alone." The comment is quick off my lips, my temper flaring and body on fire from his words. The ones that make me want to step into him and let him taste the anger on my lips.

"What? I thought you weren't on the clock. Remember? So, that means you don't get to tell me what to do for about . . ." He looks at his watch then back up to me with amusement in his eyes. "Fifteen more minutes."

That grin of his is maddening. And sexy as hell.

"Exactly. So, if you'll excuse me."

His hand is on my arm in a flash, and now my back is against the corner of two walls, and he is directly in front of me.

"You're determined. I'll give you that." He nods and squeezes my arm ever so slightly as he steps farther into my personal space. And now when I breathe in, it's him I smell. His shampoo. His cologne. His fabric softener. *Him.* "But I'm wondering where that fast-talking, loud-laughing, carefree girl I was dancing with the other night went because, while you're still goddamn gorgeous, all the rest of her is nowhere to be seen."

"Everyone makes mistakes, Easton."

His chuckle is a low rumble that fills my ears and echoes in my head as he moves so that our bodies are merely a whisper away. Heat. Want. Need. All three dance a troublesome tango inside of me as he leans in so his lips are by my ear when he whispers, "It wasn't a mistake. You know what I think? I think I got to you. I think when you close your eyes, you think about me. I think you don't want to, but you do, because God knows I think about you, Scout. About what we did. About how I want more of it. With you. And you can give me the company line all you want, about how you are under contract and so we can't pursue this, but fuck that. I don't like to play by the rules. A contract is business, Scout. But this? You. Me? This is pleasure."

His words ignite every ember of desire within me. "You don't understand."

"Then try me." The honesty in his words combats the promises I've made outside of this. When I refuse to meet his eyes, he provokes me. "I never figured you for a coward, Scout."

"You know what? You're right," I state with an enthusiastic nod and a shrug of my shoulders. A ruse to mask the truth. "The other night was fun. Incredible. The best sex I've had in a while, but that's all it was—sex. A little fun to let off some steam, and now that we've got each other out of our systems, we can forget about it. As you can tell by the way I left, I don't do commitment. I don't do more than what we did. So, thanks for the good time. Now let's get to work."

I try to dart past him, and end up with his hand back on my upper arm, refusing to let me run again.

"Thanks for the good time?"

"Yep. *Thanks.*"

His hazel eyes narrow, the edges tinged with green today as he squeezes my arm. "You're scared." And he makes the statement so matter-of-factly that my denial is automatic.

"No."

"How did I not see it before? Why do I scare you?"

Mayday. Mayday. I avert my eyes. Shift my feet. "That's such bullshit. Make sure to flatter yourself while you're at it."

"It's not flattery if it's the truth," he quips, trying to get a smile out of me, but it's kind of hard to smile when your heart feels like it's beating out of your chest and your first instinct is to sprint but your feet refuse to move. "Besides, there was no need for you to run unless you were spooked."

"What, so now a woman can't have a one-night stand without a reason?"

"Nice play, but no dice. You knew this wasn't a one-night stand, Scout. You knew we were going to have to see each other for the next few weeks. So you can try to convince yourself, but I'm not buying it."

My thoughts fly out of control, and none of them manifest into words, so I just stand there looking at him, mouth opening and closing, like more of an idiot than I already feel.

"Then why push the issue? If you don't believe what I'm saying, then why don't you walk away?" There. I said something.

And yet I feel everything.

He chuckles, but it is anything but amused. "Because talk is cheap, Scout. Your lips are saying one thing, but your body and eyes are telling me something completely different. Did you already forget how incredible the other night was? How good I made you feel?" His eyes pin me motionless with a dare to refute him. "So go ahead and lie to yourself—stand by your one-night stand excuse—but just know I don't buy it for one minute. I was there. I know the truth."

"Maybe I'm just a girl who likes to see how many major leaguer notches I can add to my belt." *Deflect. Divert. Distract.*

"You're full of funny today, aren't you? Do you think the other night would have happened if I thought that you were a baseball betty trying to charm me into the diamond between your thighs?"

"Then why *did* it happen?" The question is out before I can stop it, and I know it's surprised him because I can feel his fingers stiffen on my arm. I immediately want to know and don't want to know the answer.

"Because you're incredible? Is that a good enough answer?" He angles his head and just stares at me for a beat in a way that has heat spreading from my center out to my toes and back in. "Because we had a day."

"A day?"

"Yes. It wasn't good. It wasn't bad. It was just a day filled with a little bit of everything, and you don't share *a day* with someone you don't like." His reasoning is simple enough, and sounds so sweet coming from this gruff baseball player who is a mixture of so many things. "And because we danced. We drank. We sulked. You stood in my apartment and looked at a symbol representing my whole life and summed up how I feel but can never put into words. You got me. And then *you seduced me.*"

"I what?" I cough the words out as that soft smile of his turns big and bright.

"You seduced me. A beautiful woman with a sharp tongue, a sharper mind, and a look in her eye that said she was scared and confident, haloed by the light of a baseball stadium . . . I mean, a man only has so much restraint when it comes to that kind of perfection."

And I'm a puddle. A big, messy puddle of feelings that are so foreign I'm not sure what to do or say or how to act other than to reject the words. But for some reason nothing comes from my lips because . . . because, look at him. Complete virility mixed with sincerity. Everything a normal woman would fall into the arms of when all I can think of is running away.

But my feet don't move. They don't listen to my head because they are too busy listening to Easton. They are too busy letting his words break them down and give them an ounce of hope when hope was supposed to be lost.

All I can do is stare at him—wage a war with everything I've conditioned myself to believe—and try to trust what he's saying.

"Or maybe you were just using me so you could see my private baseball field." He delivers the joke with a soft smile, but his eyes tell me he knows I'm freaking out inside and is trying to add some levity to calm me.

"Perhaps." I give him an inch and secretly wonder if I do so because I want him to take the mile.

"See?" He shakes his finger at me as his smile grows. "You forget I can read you. And you like me, Scout Dalton. So, pretend all you want that you don't. Tell me the other night was a mistake. But I'll be over here chipping away at whatever is preventing you from admitting it, because that night was incredible. And not just the sex. That was phenomenal, too. But you . . . . You *get* me. In a world of people wanting the throwback baller they see on the field, you understand there is more to me than just *him*. For some reason you seem to understand the things no one else does, the parts of me I'm not sure I even get, and yet you're able to put words to it. So, yeah . . . the sex was great. You can stick to your guns, tell me it wasn't, tell me it was a mistake, tell me you don't feel a damn thing when we touch . . . but I do. And I want to go out again."

He leans forward and kisses me. I'd like to say it's against my will, but I'm all in, despite trying not to show it. Because we're here. At the stadium. And I can't kiss him.

But I do. With lips and tongue and heart, while his hands hold my shoulders still and my body motionless.

I missed him.

The single thought runs wild in my head over the few seconds I allow myself to be kissed senseless and reminded of how incredible he tastes.

And how amazing our chemistry is.

I want. And don't want.

I know we should stop. But I can't make myself step back.

Sensing my sudden hesitation, he does it for me. He tears his lips from mine and stares at me with a vigor I've not seen from him before.

"Easton—"

"You can refuse me all you want . . ." He laughs, stopping the rebuff on my lips. "But I should warn you, I'm a determined man. I'll win, Scout. I'm a gamer, remember? So I'll get that date. That next kiss. Earn them from you, including the halo of stadium light in your hair. And I'll wear you down until you figure out there's no need to be scared of me."

He lets go of my arms and steps back as the arrogance returns to his grin. "It's going to be a bitch, isn't it? To have to stretch me. Body to body. To have your hands on me. To have to watch me get hot and sweaty. To hear me groan when I lift weights and not remember that's the same sound I made when I came. To rub me out—nice and slow. To be around me so much you're sick of me, all the while denying there's something here worth figuring out." He takes another step back, adjusts his baseball hat and lowers the sunglasses resting on its bill to his eyes. "Have fun with that. I know I will. You've got five minutes before I'm on your clock. Tick. Tock."

And with one last flash of a grin, Easton turns on his heel and jogs down the corridor like we didn't just run a race.

Or he didn't kiss me senseless and then leave me speechless.

I'm breathless.

I'm stunned.

God, I'm fucked.

CHAPTER FOURTEEN

Scout

"Hey, Scout?"

"Hmm?" I murmur as I busy myself pulling my glove out of my bag, anything to keep my distance from him.

"I need to be stretched." His sing-song tone, laced with the promise of his words from the corridor, floats from where he's sitting on the right field turf and hits me squarely in the gut.

"Start your warm-up."

"I already warmed up," he says, prompting me to turn his way and see his grin in full effect and aimed whole-heartedly at me.

"Lovely," I mutter as I make my way over to him, more than aware of the trio of players working out in left field with their conditioning coach. No rest for the weary, even on an off-day in their insane schedule.

"What was that?" he asks, cheer infused into his voice because I know he's pushing those buttons he mentioned upstairs.

"Nothing." I put my hands on my hips and stare down at him where he sits on the turf. He's changed into his baseball pants, cleats, team T-shirt, and a new baseball hat. Add to the mix that grin on his face and he's irresistible, but hell if I'm going to let him know I think that.

"How do you want me?" he asks, and I know he's trying to pull me back to that first time we met. We're around each other so much it feels like that was months ago, but in reality, it has only been weeks.

I don't give him the satisfaction of an answer, but rather motion for him to stand up. Stepping behind him, I begin our routine—stretching, working through the stiffness, and feeling for any click in his shoulder.

I work in silence, trying to listen to his body and ignore it all at the same time. His taunts from earlier replay in my mind, challenging me to disregard them, despite the ripple of his muscles and heat of his skin beneath my fingertips that only validate them. Because with each touch of his arm, each rotation of his shoulder, all I can think of is what his biceps looked like when he braced his body over me. When he sunk into me. When he made me come.

"Can you do that one again?" he asks softly.

So focused on his shoulder, I repeat the stretch without skipping a beat. And when I press his arm up, I'm met with Easton's waiting eyes and knowing smile.

"Seriously?" I say, dropping his arm instantly, pissed that I just willingly walked right into his *extra stretch* so he could maneuver me closer to him without questioning it or him.

He blinks his eyes a few times and feigns innocence. "It's gonna be a bitch, isn't it?"

"You're a pain in my ass." I laugh, wanting to maintain a hard line but unable to because I know he's right. I step into him, jab my finger into his chest, and try to discipline myself anyway. "If *this* is contract, and *that* is pleasure, then let's keep it that way. Don't bring it on the field. This is my job. *You're* my job. So, suck it up, Hot Shot, get your gear on, and meet me behind home plate," I say the words that I know will stop him from saying anything else.

"What?" His excitement is heartwarming.

"You're throwing down."

"What did you just say?" I can hear the hope in his voice as he jogs up beside me, and it tugs on every heartstring that he hasn't already tugged on.

"You heard me."

"I know you didn't just say that to distract me from the conversation and not plan on following through."

"I wouldn't do that. Not when it comes to your arm. This is contract, remember?"

"Then say it again." His grin is contagious, and I smile at his reaction, my bipolar emotions on overdrive.

"Please don't tell me you forgot what throwing down is." I toy with him, speaking to him like a teacher does to a child, fingers pointing to each location as I explain. "I know it's been a few months, so I'll explain. Throwing down is when the catcher, *that's you*, sits behind home plate—that's the white thing over there behind the batter's box. And when the pitcher—that's the person on the mound—throws the ball to you, you throw the ball down to second base—that white square *way* out there—to try and get the runner out who's trying to steal."

"Thanks," he says drolly as he gestures to the glove in my hand and then stops when he notices his gear already laid out in the dugout. Thankfully Manny was around and helped me get that part done. "You're serious, aren't you?"

"As a heart attack."

The look on his face will forever be etched in my mind as one of those times my job is incredible. Reverence. Awe. Gratitude. Relief. All of them are reflected as he slides on his armor. The barely visible inscription *Thou shall not steal* written in black sharpie around the edge of his chest protector makes me smile.

I'm reminded of the times I've watched a game on TV, stared

at his inscription, and wondered what kind of cocky asshole would taunt a runner by wearing that. But then within a few pitches he'd pick the runner off the base with such ease, I'd know that if anyone could pull off wearing that chest protector, Easton Wylder could.

Waiting for him at home plate, I give him a moment to enjoy feeling semi-normal again, putting his gear back on for the first time in months. It's a milestone—physically and mentally. And I love that when he walks out of the dugout, he's greeted by hoots and hollers from his teammates still in left field.

"'Bout fucking time, Wylder!" one of them yells, which earns him a middle finger from Easton, but his huge grin doesn't lie about how this makes him feel.

"So, here's the deal . . . we'll start off slow. We'll warm up tossing the ball, and then once you're warm enough, I'll take a few steps back—we'll throw some at that distance—and then I'll step back farther, keep going until you feel any pain or discomfort."

"Sounds good, but why the gear?"

"Because you throw different with your gear on. You might not think so, but you do. Slow and steady wins the race here, Easton. There's no prize for coming out hard."

"Fitting." His laughter is loud and rich and hits me about the same time I realize the innuendo in my words. All I can do is shake my head and step down the first base line. "I know all about slow and steady, Kitty. Don't you worry there."

I turn to glare a warning at him. "This is contract, Hot Shot," I say knowing damn well he's enjoying this. "We'll start working our way to first base, and then, depending on how you're feeling, we can move on to second."

Thankfully, he lets that innuendo slide with only a snicker as I lift my glove and motion for him to throw the ball.

"How is it feeling?" It's been about thirty minutes since we started, but the grin on his face tells me all I need to know.

I think.

"Good. Better with each throw."

"That's good." My hands go automatically to his shoulder, pressing, kneading, feeling. "Was there any tightness or pinching or—"

"A little tightness, but this is the most I've done in months, so it feels good."

"Mm." I stare at him, wishing he'd take off his sunglasses so I could see his eyes and know if he's being truthful or not. But this is where I have to trust him. He knows his body best, after all.

"So, do I get to play with second base?" he asks, hopeful that I'm going to let him throw the full distance.

"Wouldn't you like to know." I laugh because all of this—his lack of pain, how good his arm looks and feels, our flirty banter—has put me in a good mood. Add to that working with Easton out in the sunshine and making progress has given me time to think.

"You're looking good," Drew Minski says as he jogs over on his way to the dugout from the outfield.

"Feels fucking great to have leather and laces in my hands again," Easton says.

"Hi, Drew." I greet him when he nods my way. "Great at-bat last night."

"Thanks." He glances over to Easton and then back to me. "Hey, man, some of us are thinking about going out tonight if you want to hang with us."

"Thanks, but I have plans," Easton says, and I hate that regardless of how much I've pushed him away, a little part of me is jealous of whoever he has plans with.

"Your loss. I know it's your thing to keep them all strung on a line, but that pretty little blonde keeps asking for you." He chuckles in that way that says, *go for it*. I've been in enough clubhouses to know the sound of encouragement when I hear it.

And the sound of it pisses me off.

He's got plans with one woman, is stringing the blonde along, all the while making promises to me. Done with the conversation, and not wanting for him to read the emotions I can't seem to hide from him, I turn without saying another word and head over to grab my bag.

I try to be rational. I try to not care, and I hate that I've lowered my guard enough, let myself hope enough, that I thought he really liked me. Believed he was different. Not a player.

And the idea of other women liking him irritates me because I know thousands of women would way more than just like him; they'd hop in bed with him without a second thought.

"Scout?"

"You're done for the day." I try to hide the hurt, try to hide the fact that I might be overreacting, because I should know better. Hope is a dangerous thing, especially when you're pinning it on someone else.

One step forward and five steps back in the *How Fucked-up Is Scout's Head* game.

CHAPTER FIFTEEN

Easton

Cool down like normal. Ice for twenty minutes on, twenty minutes off. Text me if you have any problems.

    -Scout

    A note?

    She left me a fucking note?

    Whoever did a number on her is a fucker. Grade A asshole. But I don't have time to worry about him because I need to find her. Talk to her. Wear her down. Figure out what the fuck spooked her again.

    I run out of the locker room—cleats still on—and see Manny. "Hey, Man. Did you see which way Scout went?" A grin spreads slowly on his lips, and I know he's assumed I'm looking for her for more than just my cool down instructions. "Save the lecture, old man."

    His grin grows wider, and he points down the tunnel that leads out to the parking lot. "No lecture at all."

    His laugh echoes after me as I hustle down the corridor and out the side entrance of the ballpark. It only takes me a few seconds to spot Scout and jog after her.

"A note, Scout?"

She freezes midstride for a split second before she begins walking again. "Yep. A note. You worked out. You can cool down with my instructions. I'm your trainer, and—"

"If you're my trainer, then do your goddamn job!" I shout at her, frustrated in every way imaginable by this woman who continues to test me, push me away, run away, when I can see in her eyes that she wants me just as much as I want her.

"I was. You got your instructions. You know what to do. Didn't know I had to hold your hand, Wylder."

"I know what to do, all right," I mutter as I glance around to make sure no one from the team is around. *Throw you over my shoulder and take you up to my place so we can figure this the fuck out. And then I can lay you down and we can make this all better.*

"Once a player always a player, *right*?" she sneers.

"Drew." His name is all I have to say to know what she's pissed about. I'm a dumbass for not putting two and two together.

"String 'em along? Is that what you're doing to me, so you can keep a woman in every city, ready and waiting for when you pass through town?" The hurt in her eyes is undeniable, and I hate that I put it there.

"What the fuck did he do to you to make you think so highly of men, Scout?"

Emotions flicker through her eyes before she can clear them and avert her gaze. "Never mind. Forget I said anything."

I jog after her, pissed at myself for chasing her, and at the same time wanting to figure out what exactly is going on. "The blonde is no one."

"Mm-hmm." She keeps her eyes focused straight ahead and refuses to look my way.

"Seriously. You want to keep this all secretive—"

"There is no *this*."

"And Drew is part of the club," I explain, completely ignoring her remark. "What did you want me to do? Correct him? Tell him to shut up when normally I just laugh at all the guys' ribbing over the women in bars? Then he'd really know there was something going on between us. And there *is* something going on between us," I say, cutting her off before she can argue with me again. "So save yourself the argument."

"You're an arrogant asshole, you know that?" she spits out as she turns toward me, arms folded across her chest as if that will protect her from the truth she can't seem to face.

"Maybe, but you're fucking adorable when you're angry at me."

There's a slight crack in her anger. A bit of a smile.

"And I kind of like that you were jealous."

"I was not."

"Ah, Kitty, but you were." Another crack in her smile. "A woman only storms out when she's jealous, and while the sight of your ass swaying as you stalked away was almost enough to let you keep being pissed, you needed to know the truth. There is no blonde in the bar waiting just for me, because she waits for anyone. There are no strings of women. There is no one else in another city."

She stares at me. Searches to see if she believes me, and fuck . . . not only can the woman stand her ground, but she can take care of herself too. Tell me that's not sexy as hell.

And frustrating all at the same time.

"Tell me what you're thinking, Scout." There's too much silence. Too much time for her to doubt and poke holes in what I said and bend it to match whatever insecurities are banging around inside of her.

"I just . . . you're just . . ."

"I think you're thinking how much you want to kiss me right now."

"Too much," she says at the same time I speak, and we both smile softly as it feels like the explosive wave of her temper may have just blown over.

"So you want to kiss me *too much*?" I say, combining our comments and garnering a huff from her.

"I don't know what to do about you," she finally says, softly and full of trepidation.

"Nothing, Scout. There's nothing *to do*. There's just *us* going out to have a good time. There's just *us* figuring out if there's anything here. There are no commitments. There's no need for anyone to know anything. It's just us getting to know each other and enjoying each other's company."

"What if I don't want that?"

There's that doubt again. The insecurity I don't understand.

"You want this."

It takes everything I have not to lean in and taste those bee-stung lips that tempt me every single time I look at them. Not to lean in and remind her of how it felt earlier when we'd kissed.

There's just something about her I can't let go, and I don't even know her that well yet.

Because there are women who are good for a quick fuck. There are women you would fuck, but are better in the friend zone. And then there are women like Scout. They make you wonder, make you crave them, and drive you absolutely fucking crazy because you want them when you shouldn't. They're an enigma. Confusing, alluring, tempting, and fucking perfection.

I stare at her, with her ponytail whipping around her face on the downtown sidewalk, and have never wanted so badly to pull a woman against me and soothe the trouble in her eyes as I wait to hear her response.

You want this.

"Easton. The contract. My dad. It's just—"

I look around for space. For privacy. For what I need to prove a point that she needs to feel, not just hear.

"Complicated? Messy? Welcome to life, Scout. Mine's all of those and then some, and you don't even know the half of it."

Her smile tugs at me. Makes me want to take care of her when I've never wanted to take care of anyone in my life other than my mom.

"Easton."

"You keep saying my name like that and I'm going to think you like me."

She laughs. The darkness clears from her eyes some, and I know I've made an inroad.

And at the same time, we pass a little alleyway behind the stadium, out of view of the public, and I push her backward into it. Before we even clear the sidewalk, I have my lips on hers.

God. Damn.

She's fucking addictive.

I want her.

Her taste.

Must have her.

The scent of her perfume.

Say yes to this, Scout.

The softness of her lips.

Say yes to me.

The tentativeness of her tongue as she fights her will to dive right in.

Let me the fuck in.

Even her temper turns me on.

And so I take what I want from her. What I need from her. My dick hardens from the kiss. From the way her fingers twist in my shirt. From the feel of her tits rubbing against my chest. From the goddamn moan that sounds like the white flag waving as she surrenders herself to me.

I don't want this to end. But my dick is hard and I still have my cup on, and fuck, that's a miserable feeling. Plus, we're on the street. Near the stadium. And while I'd love to relieve the ache in my balls by doing a variety of things with her—right here, right now—it pains me to have to end the kiss.

To pull back and try to hold tight to my control that's hanging by a thread.

But I don't release her from my grasp when I lean back and look in her eyes. I try to catch my breath, try to quiet the caveman side of me, and then she speaks.

"Well, I guess that's getting to know each other as good as any other way."

The smile is there, but it takes a few seconds before the cautious look in her eyes reflects the same confidence reflected in her voice.

But fuck. I'll take it.

I'm putting myself out on a limb for a woman who wants to run, when for the life of me, I've never been one to stay.

But I'm not going anywhere.

CHAPTER SIXTEEN

Scout

Nerves rattle around within me when they shouldn't.

"This is . . . unbelievable." I look around the facility. There's a state of the art batting cage with a multi-pitch batting machine set up on one end, and a sloped floor to collect the balls and refeed the machine. The turf beyond houses a complete infield. The walls are littered with sports memorabilia from some of the greats—signed jerseys, bats, and balls from Mickey Mantle, Babe Ruth, Jackie Robinson, Hank Aaron, Ted Williams . . . and a few from Cal Wylder.

I walk along the walls, stare at the living history lining them, and am in awe of the mini-museum of men I grew up hearing my father talk about.

"It's my wall," he muses quietly, allowing me to take it all in as I turn from the legends beside me to face one that I feel has equal potential.

"It's a good wall," I muse, heading over to the rack of bats all sized and weighted to match his preferences. "I've never seen anything like it."

"Yeah, well . . ." He shrugs and blushes and it's rather adorable.

"The machine is having issues, or else I'd tell you to hit a few."

"I haven't touched a bat in what feels like years." I run my fingers over the butts of them and then continue to explore the space. We both fall silent, but I know he's watching me, and I'm not quite sure what to do about it.

I asked to see the field because it was safer than going into his condo where I will be reminded of the other night when I need to still process the events of the day and how I feel about them. How I let him wear me down, kiss me senseless twice, and then manage to get me to admit that maybe I want to see where all of this leads us because me agreeing to come here means it is, in fact, going somewhere.

And that scares the hell out of me.

There's a wall to the left of a bathroom. It's lined with framed jerseys in different colors and sizes, and it takes me a minute to figure out what they are. "These are all of your Little League jerseys, aren't they?"

I stare at the simple idea and can't believe how touched I am by the sight of them. The history he has with each one. The memories from then that made the man he is now.

"Yes. My parents kept them all." He says nothing more, and the silence prompts me to wonder more about him, his family, but I have a feeling it's an off-limits topic.

"Have you always wanted to play baseball?" It's a simple question, one I expected him to answer immediately, and his pause piques my curiosity.

I turn to look at him while he's looking at his history on the wall. I take in his profile—the bill of the baseball hat shadowing his face, his thick lashes, straight nose, and full lips. His scruff is longer today than normal, and there's something about it that's incredibly sexy.

"It was what was expected of me." The honesty in his voice is haunting. His exhale is uneven. "I mean, I'm Cal Wylder's son."

There's an unreadable emotion in his tone, and I sense there is so much more beneath the surface, but I'm afraid to pry, even though I want to.

"Were you always good at it? You're such a natural, but I'm sure it had to be hard living in the shadow of your dad."

He chews the inside of his cheek as he continues to stare at the wall. He points to one of the smallest jerseys up there. It's a faded dark green with the number ten on its back. "That was my first year playing. I remember I got in a fistfight with Joey Jones. He told me I had to have been adopted, because there was no way Cal Wylder's son could be so horrible at playing baseball. I cried for days. My dad was on a road stretch and I dodged his phone calls, too embarrassed to tell him what had happened. I knew he was going to be so disappointed in me—not because of the fight, but because of how bad I was. I spent days sick to my stomach and worried about what he was going to say when he came home and saw for himself."

I want to walk over to him and hold his hand. I want to tell him I'm sorry. Tell him I understand about living in shadows of giants and the weight those shadows bear. I want to do anything but hear the sadness in his voice. Yes, he has the last laugh now, being as successful as he is, but even success can't erase the scars of childhood memories.

"That must have been hard."

He nods, shifts his feet, and then points three jerseys down to a dark blue one with the same number on it. "That was the year everything clicked for me. I was eight. My hand-eye coordination suddenly matured, and I learned to read a ball out of a pitcher's hand. All of a sudden I went from zero to hero. And, of course, that meant my dad came to more games when he could. Suddenly I was Mr. Popular. Kids who wouldn't give me the time of day before now wanted to be my friend in the hope that they'd get some pointers from a major leaguer when he showed up."

I close the distance between us and step up beside him, our arms touching, and let him get lost in his thoughts.

He points to the next frame over, a red and white jersey; this time the number on the back is eighteen. "That's the year my parents divorced. I lived at the field that season. It was so much easier than being at home where my mom cried nonstop, or being with my dad when he was in town and feeling guilty for leaving my mom home alone. Baseball became my escape that year. I put everything I had into it. It was the first time I really fell in love with the game."

"So, back then you played to escape. Why do you play now?"

He laughs. "Because I make a shit ton of money, and who wouldn't want to play baseball for a living?"

"True." I nod, but can sense the unspoken words and the underlying hint of sarcasm. "Do you still love it?"

"Some days."

"If you have a shit ton of money, then why do you still play?" I know I'm pushing, but I'm intrigued how a man who is so incredibly talented and oozes respect for the game has misgivings about saying he loves it.

"For my dad."

"For your dad?" His answer surprises me. "Not for you?"

"No."

"Do you love it?" I ask the question again, forgetting that I already have, and before I can tell him to disregard it, he responds.

"Yes. No. Fuck, Scout, most days I don't know." He turns to face me for the first time, and I can see the conflict in his eyes, the uncertainty in his expression, and the tension in the set of his shoulders. "It's all I've ever known. All that's ever been expected of me. It's hard to explain without sounding ungrateful because I'm extremely blessed in talent and luck when I know there are a million others who would kill to fill my shoes. It's just complicated. I have a love-hate relationship with the game just like I guess I do with my father."

Reaching out, I link my fingers with his. I don't say a word. I try not to judge. All I do is just listen, because the pain in his expression says that's exactly what he needs from me.

His laugh is unexpected and loaded with sarcasm. "Fuck," he says as he lifts his hat, runs a hand through his hair, and then sets it back down. "When I said we needed to get to know more about each other, I sure as hell didn't mean this. We're a far way off from learning if the other likes sushi."

I smile and squeeze his hand. For a man who seems pretty open, I can tell he's a bit exposed and uncomfortable. "Sushi? It's all right, if you count California Rolls as legitimate," I say to try to get a laugh from him. "I'm not very adventurous with it. And this conversation is okay. This is real, Easton. I assure you, I have more *real* than I care to think about in my own life right now, so this is okay."

"Yeah. Thanks." He looks down at our joined hands and shakes his head as if he's trying to convince himself of something I can't understand.

"It's admirable to play for your dad, but have you ever wanted to do anything else? For yourself?" I leave the unspoken question hanging out there. The one I think I know the answer to: do you think your dad won't love you if you don't play?

"I'm good at this, though." He lets go of my hand and paces to the other side of the batting cage to stare at a picture of him and his dad on the wall. "I sound like such a pussy saying that. Like I don't have a backbone, or I don't like to play, but I assure you, I do . . . there's just a history that . . .. My dad is fucking Cal Wylder. He's perfect in every way. The Iron Giant of baseball who broke records and is still the public darling of the club. He's never had a blemish on his career. In fact, the only mark he's ever had against him in his perfect life has been his divorce from my mom."

"Nobody's that perfect, Easton."

"He is." There's bitterness in his tone.

"We all look at our parents through rose-colored glasses. Those lenses make you miss their flaws, overlook their shortcomings . . . and still be able to love them unconditionally." He turns to look at me and narrows his eyes in thought. "God knows my dad is far from perfect, and yet when I see him, I see the person I want to be when I'm his age. I overlook his grumpiness and stubbornness and his need to have opinions about everything, even when I don't ask for them. So I'm sure your dad is not perfect."

"He's pretty damn close to it, Scout. And even if he's not, he demands it from me."

I have no comeback for him because I saw it for myself the other day in the locker room. I wonder if Cal Wylder has always been that hard on his only child.

And I hate that I think I already know the answer.

CHAPTER SEVENTEEN

Scout

"I'm sorry I don't have a place to invite you to," I apologize as I take a seat at the large island and watch Easton move with ease around the kitchen.

"Did you just move here?"

"I've kind of been on the move since I graduated college, shifting from clubhouse to clubhouse with my dad over the past three years. Learning from him so I could finally make sense of the things I watched over and over as a kid but didn't understand. So, I'm currently living a few blocks over, on the other side of the stadium, in a furnished apartment until I figure out what comes next."

Easton looks at me for a beat—something fleeting in his eyes I can't quite pinpoint—before uncorking the bottle of wine and pouring two glasses in silence. He slides one across the counter to me and then meets my eyes. "What is next, Scout?"

"I get you rehabbed, get your arm to one hundred percent, and get you off the disabled list, for a start."

"You think that's going to happen?"

"Yes." I nod my head for emphasis. "Today was a huge start. How does your shoulder feel? You really should have some ice on it."

He laughs as he turns and grabs a medical ice pack from the freezer and presses it to his shoulder. Then, with a skill that tells me he's done this more times than he can count in his career, he begins to expertly wrap an ACE bandage around the pack to hold it in place.

"So rehab me, and then what's after that? Are you off to another club? Another city? Moving on?"

A part of me hates the lump that suddenly forms in my throat when I realize what he's asking. The woman who's afraid of getting too close to someone because everyone leaves her is now being asked if she's going to leave. And the other part of me breathes in the feeling of having someone care enough to ask. Someone I want to care.

I take a sip of my wine and meet his eyes above the rim of the glass. I'm afraid to respond, uncertain of this next step between us. Downstairs was easy. We talked baseball, we talked about him, and we avoided the topics that had ruled our afternoon so far.

But now, the tables have turned. Now, the spotlight is on me, and I wish I could answer him, but I'm not sure what that answer is just yet. Or if I want to even have one, in case I get spooked again and need to leave.

"I'm not sure." My voice is barely a whisper when I finally find it to speak.

"Rumor has it Doc is vying to get the permanent contract with the clubhouse for the team's physical training. Is that true?"

I nod. "Yes. It is. It's the only clubhouse he hasn't held any sort of contract with over his career."

"And so that's why he wants it? Just because?"

"He's kicking around the idea of retiring," I lie, repeating the story he's asked me to tell.

"Retiring? I don't see him as one who'd want to retire."

"Yeah, well . . . there are a lot of things about my dad that I don't understand, so your guess is as good as mine."

"What I don't understand is . . . hasn't he already fulfilled that goal then? I mean, technically he already has a contract with the Aces, since you're here for me. So, once you're done with me, you can move on to the next clubhouse? The next team? The next injured player?"

He doesn't relent. Not the intensity in his eyes . . . or the searching questions . . . or the unspoken ones. The ones that say: tell me if you're leaving.

"That's the typical MO, but this time around, he's looking for a term contract for the season and beyond. A multi-year agreement."

"Hmm."

"What does that mean?" I wish he'd just come out and ask me what he wants, because I feel like he's leading me somewhere.

"Well, if Doc has done things one way for all these years . . . why change now?"

"Because of me." The answer is automatic, and I realize that I've given him the truth, but can't give him the reasons why.

"You?"

"Yeah. He lived this life. He knows how hard it is to feel settled when you aren't anywhere long enough to let roots grow, let alone have a family . . . and he doesn't want that life for me, so he figured if he got a contract for a team as a whole, then that would give me a place to settle for the first time since I graduated from college."

And because he knows I'd rather quit than not be near him in these last months.

"So you'd be the one to stay then?" He leans a hip on the kitchen island and digs deeper. I nod slowly and concentrate on tracing the lines in the granite on the countertop.

"You wouldn't move on to another team?"

"Not if I get the contract."

He's quiet for a beat. "Is that what you want, or are you just doing what your Dad wants?"

The irony in his words is not lost on me. He's turning my questions back on me. I lift my gaze to meet his, suddenly very aware of how similar our situations are.

"It's what I want," I say softly.

"And it's dependent on me, right?"

I stare at him, see the curiosity in his eyes, and wonder if, when it comes to why I want to stay in town, we are speaking about my career, or about whatever this is between us.

"In a sense." I chew on the words, not wanting to put pressure on him to heal quicker to get me the job when I've already seen the amount of pressure his dad puts on him.

He nods and then swallows the rest of his glass of wine without saying a word, leaving me wondering what he's thinking. The mood between us suddenly turns uneasy, both of us with questions to ask but unsure how to ask them.

If I were to stay, how would this change the dynamic between us when I'm no longer just in town for a few months?

"What does your mom think about all of this?" he asks, throwing me for a loop.

I stutter to answer as a part of me hides in shame over my own mother not wanting me. Then again, he's shared so much with me tonight, been so open, how can I not be honest about the one thing I can?

"I don't know. I haven't seen her since I was five."

"Scout . . ." His voice trails off like most people's do when they hear that news, uncertain what to say.

"Hey, it's not sushi, but that's my bet-you-didn't-know-about-Scout fact of the day," I joke, trying to quell my immediate defense to shut down after letting someone in.

It's my thing. It's what I do. And every part of me revolts at my need to avert my eyes and change the topic.

And so, when I lift my gaze and meet his, I see compassion there. Understanding. Acceptance. All of them cause a flutter of anxiety to fly in my belly, and yet the feeling is a far cry from the all-out panic that usually consumes me.

Once again, Easton is making me feel instead of shutting down, and I'm not quite sure what to say now.

"Did you say sushi? I think that's exactly what we need." He smiles softly, giving me the reprieve he somehow knows I need. "I'm starving. Want to order some takeout? I know a great place that delivers."

Saved by sushi.

"Perfect."

"Can you grab that?" Easton calls from his bedroom when the buzzer on the elevator rings.

"Sure." My stomach rumbles at the thought of food being on the other side of the sliding doors.

I hit the button to open the elevator and am startled when I'm met with the hazel eyes and curious expression of Cal Wylder.

"Ms. Dalton?" He says, as calm as can be, all the while subtly looking me over—for what, I don't know. Probably wondering why Easton's trainer is making house calls.

"You're not sushi." The words fall from my mouth as the panic I had averted earlier comes full circle and slams back into me. And then I realize what I just said to him. To Easton's dad. To the club's liaison. The man who now is probably putting two and two together when he can't. That I'm here. Off the clock. What if he tells Cory? *Fuck.* "I mean food. You're not food. Chinese food. I mean Japanese food. You were . . . it was supposed to be delivery."

Someone please kill me now before I make an even bigger ass of myself.

"Dad?" Easton walks out to the foyer, and the sound of his voice helps to calm my rioting nerves. But when I turn to look his way, I want to die. He's wet from a shower I didn't even know he was taking, wearing gym pants slung low on his hips, and he's running a towel through his dripping hair.

"Well, now that I know your shoulder's feeling good and iced, I should get going," I say and scurry from the room like the petrified mouse I am.

"Scout," Easton calls after me, resignation and agitation mixed in his voice.

"Typical, Easton." Cal's voice, followed by a heavy sigh, stops me dead in my tracks just as I step into the kitchen area and out of their line of sight. "I should've known."

"Should have known what, Dad?"

"Always playing the women, getting distracted by a piece of ass, instead of playing the field like you should be."

I straighten my spine where I stand, needing to leave but knowing damn well that would mean having to walk right past them. Every part of me bucks the idea of giving Cal Wylder the satisfaction of my running away, tail tucked between my legs.

"A piece of ass? Really, Dad? What I do off the field is none of your business or the club's. Not if I have a friend over for some dinner and a movie. Not if I have a woman over and she's more than a friend. Not if my fucking trainer stops by to check my shoulder and make sure I've iced it, since I was throwing down to bases today for the first time since my surgery and she was concerned about how it was doing. So, don't you fucking dare walk into my house and judge a situation when you have no clue which of the three it is."

There's a tense silence I can feel all the way in the kitchen, and I realize I'm holding my breath.

"You have a habit of getting distracted."

"Distracted? Really? I put in six hours today between the gym, conditioning, and rehab. And I put another two in first thing this morning at Children's Hospital visiting sick kids . . . so please, tell me what else I was supposed to be doing when I'm on the damn DL?"

"Easton." There's a pause, and my mind runs through the image of them standing face to face, mirror images separated by twenty-five years. There's a sigh, and I can imagine Cal looking just like Easton does when he runs a hand through his hair and tries to figure out what he's going to say next. "You're right. I'm sorry. I just want the best for you, son. I want you back on the field showing everyone you're good as new and one hundred percent."

"Fucking Santiago," Easton mutters with vitriol.

"There's always going to be a Santiago in your career, son. Always." There's a sadness to his voice that pulls on me and makes me wish I could see his expression. "Another player who's jealous of your success or pissed at a pitch you called against him and is going to try to bring you down."

I wish I could hear Easton's response, but he speaks it quietly.

"So you threw today? How'd it feel? What did Scout say about it?"

"It felt so damn good to be back in my gear." I can hear the smile in his voice, and, silly or not, I love knowing that I helped to put it there. "And it feels good. A little stiff, and I'm sure it will be sore tomorrow, but right now, I can't complain."

"And Scout?"

Even though there has been a mood shift in the conversation, I sense a hesitation in Easton to respond. I can't deny that I breathe a little easier knowing he's just as cautious about others knowing I'm here—that there is, in fact, something going on between us—as I am.

And it takes this moment to hit me square in the solar plexus and knock the wind out of me. *I want to stay in town.* I want to get to know Easton better. I want to know what it feels like to wake up next to someone in the morning without freaking out that I'm too close, too attached, and I need to create some space to protect myself for when he leaves.

I reach for the glass of wine I left on the counter and finish it off, stunned by the realization but liking the good kind of flutter it puts in my belly. The same kind of flutter I get when Easton cocks his head and stares at me with that knowing smile on his lips.

And now cue the fear. The worry that we both work in a volatile business where there are no guarantees where you'll be from one year to the next, and that means he could still leave me. He could still move on.

I could still be left behind.

Take it day by day, Scout. Enjoy the time; don't think about tomorrow. But, I want tomorrows with someone. I want yesterdays, tomorrows, and next years with someone because I've never gotten that chance before.

And that's why I can enjoy Easton, but can't get attached to him.

"Why are you pushing me so hard to get back on the field?" Easton's irritation breaks through my thoughts, pulls my attention away from my fear and back to his conversation.

"Because nothing is guaranteed," Cal says and unknowingly confirms my resolve. "Contracts are contracts, son. When you sign on their dotted line, you become a commodity."

"Meaning?" Frustration resurfaces in Easton's voice.

"Meaning this is a business. While you may play for the love of the game, the team is in it to make a profit. And you not on the field is not helping their bottom line."

"Do you know something I don't know, Dad?" His voice escalates, disbelief vibrating in its timbre.

"No. Not at all. I just know how clubs operate. Four months is a long time to be out."

"Yeah, well, it's not like I'm a pitcher, coming in for one game, and then getting five days off. I play every day. My arm returns almost every pitch, so I'm not being a pussy here. I've played through the pain before. A cortisone shot and some oxy and I'm good to go for a big game . . . but this isn't just a strain, and for some reason I don't think you get that."

The physical therapist in me wants to give him a standing ovation for understanding the seriousness of his injury, while the child in me understands Easton's plight in wanting his father to comprehend where he's coming from.

"I know you're not. It's just . . . I can't quite get a read on Cory yet. And while I may be the face of the club, first and foremost I worry about you as my son."

"I know you do."

The elevator dings and the forgotten Chinese food delivery arrives. When Easton walks into the kitchen with the bags in his hand, his father is not behind him.

He doesn't say anything at first—just sets the food on the island as he gathers plates and silverware from drawers I'm not familiar with. I watch him, wondering if I should leave and let him have time alone with his thoughts, when he surprises the hell out of me by grabbing my waist and pulling me against him.

Strong arms wrap around me, and his chin finds its way onto the top of my head. My arms snake under his and around his torso, unsure what else to do other than be here for whatever it is he needs right now.

I can feel him breathe in deeply, can feel him clench and unclench his jaw, can hear his heart beneath my ear where it rests against his chest. The stirring of desire that is always a constant when he's around smolders to life, but I know this is so much more than that, so I hang on and let the moment be.

"It's been a day," I murmur, drawing a rumble of a laugh from him.

"Yes, it has," he sighs. "Let's eat."

CHAPTER EIGHTEEN

Scout

"You will be hungry again in one hour." Easton laughs when I read my fortune. "Very cheeky, but probably true. What does yours say?"

I glance over at him reading his, and he hands the little strip with his fortune to me. "Here."

"*The fortune you seek is in another cookie.*" I roll my eyes. "These are funny. Someone was definitely in a mood when they made these."

"Seems like it."

I'm sitting in the corner of the couch, my back against the armrest and my arm propped up on the back. He's beside me, leaning forward with his elbows on his knees, turning the uneaten fortune cookie over in his hand. He's here, but still a million miles away. My eyes wander over the definition of his torso, admiring the obvious work he's put into his physique, and my fingers itch to reach out and touch him.

"You've been quiet. You okay?"

"Yeah, just thinking," he says with a sigh as he tosses the cookie onto its bag and leans back beside me. He rests his head against the couch pillows, then turns it to the side so he can meet my eyes.

"Care to share?"

"A lot of things."

"Mr. Forthcoming," I tease.

"You want a rundown, then?" His smile is wide, and I can sense his playful side emerging.

"A rundown?"

"Yep," he says with a nod.

"I'm a 'list girl' so you're talking to my heart right now."

He shakes his head and rolls his eyes. "You want a list?"

"Only if you want."

"She wants a list," he teases as he reaches out and squeezes my knee like it's the most natural thing in the world. The casualness of it causes a welcome discord. "Let's see. The first thing is how you definitely like more than California rolls, but I have to lie and tell you it's shrimp in order to get you to try it."

"Oh, God. What did I eat?" His smile is contagious, and even though I'm suddenly alarmed that I ate something off-the-charts odd, I can't help but smile with him.

"Just a little of this and a little of that."

"I'm not liking the sound of this."

"Sometimes the less you know the better," he muses, and I try not to read into the comment too much. "What else? Hmm. I wondered what you used to be like as a catcher. If you were the quiet but commanding type or the smack talker who annoyed the hell out of the batters."

"A little of both." I blush but allow a smirk to play on my lips.

"Ah, so you *were* a smack talker. That's good to know. I'm taking notes here on my list."

"You should. I can be troublesome if you get on my bad side." His laugh is rich and calls to every part of me. "What else was on that intriguing mind of yours?"

153

"You're a damn good runner. I was winded today trying to keep up with you."

"Oh, please. You could probably run circles around me."

"Perhaps . . . but if I did that I'd miss the spectacular view of your ass from behind you."

I swat at his arm while my insides melt a little . . . and my insides don't melt. Ever.

"Nice. You get to run in front next time so I can watch your ass, then." I laugh.

"Mine?"

"In baseball pants. That's a requirement," I murmur, knowing damn well how fine his ass looks in his pants because I was more than checking him out when he was behind the plate today.

"Oh really? Making demands, now, are we?"

"I can be very demanding. I mean, you said you want to get to know me better. So now you know." I purse my lips and lift my eyebrows at him. "And I'm stubborn . . . also a stickler for rules. I can't cook at all. And I have a slight obsession with wintergreen Life Savers, biceps, and romance novels. Oh, and I've been known to snore. Horribly."

"I love that you have no shame." He throws his head back and laughs before narrowing his eyes as he takes in my smirk. "But why do I get the sense that you're trying to make me not like you?"

He shifts on the couch and leans toward me, framing my thighs by putting his hands on each side of them. And holy biceps. Right there is exactly why I like them. Firm, sculpted, and so damn hot.

"Who, me?" I feign. "I'd never do something like that."

"Let's add manipulative, too." He quirks an eyebrow and doesn't relent with his stare, despite his smile disarming me in every way imaginable.

"Only the good kind of manipulative."

"The good kind? There's such a thing? Well, I think it's time we get a few things straight," he murmurs, his lips so damn close I can smell the wine on his breath and see the flecks of green in his eyes. "I like demanding and stubborn. It means you don't stop until you get what you want how you want it. You're a rules girl, huh? I'm good with that. Rules are fun because I like to break them, so keep telling me things I shouldn't be doing, Kitty . . . like wanting to date you . . . and I'll keep doing them. And cooking? I'm a bachelor, so I've got every damn take-out menu in town in the top right-hand drawer in the kitchen, and I can make a mean grilled cheese, if need be, so nice try with that one. Wintergreen Life Savers? I prefer the taste of cherry, but as long as I can put it in my mouth and work my tongue into its center, then I'm pretty sure I can compromise." His lips quirk and his eyes bore into mine as every single drop of blood in my body ignites from his insinuation.

My breath hitches as he reaches up and takes my hand that's still holding the fortune and brings it up to the bicep of his other arm. "And biceps. Is this what you're talking about, Scout? Is this what you like?"

He wraps my fingers around as he flexes so I can feel every muscle beneath twist with the movement. I force a swallow and make myself meet his eyes again. "And what is it about you and romance novels? Is it the happily ever after? Is it the man who's too good to be true? Because I assure you, we all have our flaws, even the fictional ones. But the happily ever after depends on what you put into it. The hard work, the listening instead of talking, the laughing instead of crying, the sticking it out instead of running away, the knowing that sometimes silence is best but having her wrapped in your arms can still solve a lot of problems. So, you can have your romance novels while I have my King and Follett and Patterson because I don't want to read about having that kind of love someday. I'd rather be over here trying to take a chance at it in real life."

I open my mouth to argue, but nothing comes out because I don't know what to say. He effectively just stole a little piece of my heart when it was still under padlock and steel.

155

"Oh, and snoring? When you're with me, we'll both be too damn tired to even worry if you're snoring, so that's a moot point. But, uh, nice try."

"Oh."

"Yeah. *Oh.*" His grin is lightning quick as he leans in and brushes his lips ever so tenderly against mine. It's achingly soft and causes a warmth to spread from my center out, seep into every fiber of my being, and then leave me a little shell-shocked and wanting more. "You smell good," he murmurs.

"Ewww. I haven't showered since my run today. I was sidelined by the same person who's telling me I smell good, so I'm quite sure something is wrong with you."

He chuckles, and then surprises me by placing an open mouth kiss on my neck and then licking a line up to just beneath my earlobe. The sensation, the act, *the everything* about it is like a livewire exposed to water. "You taste salty. And all I smell is your shampoo." He tugs on my earlobe with his teeth, and that slow, sweet ache between my thighs burns bright. "Sweat on you is sexy."

"Men." I laugh and push against his chest, all the while enjoying the feeling of him sinking against me.

"I offered you the shower."

"Yeah, well, good thing I didn't take it, or else I'd have been standing in your kitchen in a robe or one of your T-shirts when your dad showed up, and we both know how that would have looked."

"He won't say anything to anyone."

"Uh-huh."

"And I kind of like the idea of what you'd look like in my T-shirt."

I can't resist. I lean forward and take the initiative by kissing him soundly on the lips. It surprises him. But I love that he lets me take the lead. I love that he allows me to control the depth and the demand and the softness of it. I pour everything that I'm feeling but can't express into our connection.

We shift some, but the pace never quickens, the urgency nonexistent; it's just us, with a setting sun at our backs and the fortunes from our cookies crinkling on the couch when we move. No hands wander, no fingers itch to touch more, because our lips, and everything their connection evokes, is simply enough.

It's intoxicating. It's unexpected. It's everything in a kiss I never knew I needed, and yet somehow knew was missing.

It's not a means to an end, but rather a slow, sweet seduction of the senses, and when it finally ends—when he leans his forehead against mine, with our breaths feathering over each other's lips, and our minds trying to process the moment—he speaks.

"I'm going to hate myself for this the minute the words are out of my mouth," he murmurs.

"Then don't say it and just kiss me again," I tease before I lean in and bring my mouth to his.

His groan sounds tortured when after a few seconds he tears his lips from mine , sits back on his haunches, and squeezes his eyes tight before looking back at me. "I don't think I've ever said these words before in my life."

Now he has my attention. "What words?"

"No."

"*No?*" I laugh; the pained look on his face is more than comical. "No to what?"

"No to what I want to do to you right now. *Desperately.*"

"What do you want to do to me, Easton?" My voice is coy, my eyes inviting.

He clenches his jaw, and the muscle that pulses at its corner is so damn sexy. He laughs, a sound like audible restraint. "I want to fuck you, Scout. I want to take you in my bedroom and make you so tired your body forgets to snore. Okay?"

And now it's my turn to clench my jaw—and my thighs— together as he stares at me with an intensity that only adds to his allure. "So, why don't you?"

His smile is half-cocked when he speaks, "Because I made a promise to myself and to you. I told you we were going to get to know each other better, build up some trust, and see where this thing takes us . . . and so that's what I'm trying to do. Even though, currently, where I really want it to take us is my bed."

"I don't know what to say." I'm flattered. I'm dumbfounded. And, holy hell, how I'm turned on from that kiss and the feeling of his thighs caging mine.

"Tell me you understand the sacrifice I'm making, because right now, all I want is you. Under me. On top of me. Any way with me."

"Then let's—"

"You don't get it, do you? I can see it in your eyes, Scout. I can tell you're spooked, with one foot out the door and one foot in my bed because it's easier to be in either of those places than it is to be in this position. The one where you have to talk to me, where you have to let me get to know you better, instead of shying away from it. So even though it's said under serious protest, the answer is *no*, we're not having sex tonight."

"That's admirable," I murmur as I lean in and tease his lips with mine, "but we've already slept together, so does it really matter?"

He chuckles. "Yes, it does matter because you're trying to distract me with those lips of yours when all my mind keeps thinking of is all of the other things you could be doing with them."

"Like what?" I purr.

He leans back and shoots me a warning glare. "I told you, Scout. We're getting to know each other."

"So even if I go like this . . ." I run the tip of my fingernail over the more than obvious outline of his hardened cock through his jogging pants.

He groans my name, his body tenses, and his head falls back as I complete one long stroke of my fingertip. And just when I think I might have won the battle, his hands flash out and tighten like a vice around my wrists to prevent me from tempting him any further.

"Not going to happen," he grits out.

I try to move my arms, but he doesn't let them budge. And there's something about his reaction and the strength of his hands on mine that urge me to try again.

"And I couldn't persuade you if I did this?" I lean forward and circle my tongue around the flat, bronzed disc of his nipple before sucking on it gently.

"Goddammit, woman." His tone is sharp, but the groan that follows it is so damn sexy I grow wet between my thighs.

"What?" I feign innocence as I look up at him and bat my lashes with my lips still pressed against his chest.

His grin is full of warning, and yet his erection is pressing against my thigh. With our gazes locked, I lean forward to lick the other nipple, knowing I've put him in a quandary.

And just as I make contact, he makes his move. The element of surprise, and probably my own escalating desire, gives him the opportunity to pull me onto his lap, twist me around so my back is to his chest, and wrap his arms around me so that I can't move mine.

"There."

"You bastard." I chuckle because now his cock pressing against my lower back is his reciprocated torture.

"Is something the matter?" he teases, hot breath against my ear.

I wiggle my ass over his dick and feel his thighs grow tense. He repositions and adjusts so his arms are tighter around me, and he brings his legs over my calves to quiet my wriggling.

All I can do is laugh.

He sighs. "See? Perfect position to watch a movie together."

"A movie? That's the first thing that comes to mind right now?"

"Yep." He shifts so that he can hold the remote in one hand and me between both of his arms. "We're going to sit here and watch the first movie I come across on the menu."

He scrolls through the on-screen guide. "Your hair is in the way . . . what's that one say?" he asks, and I smile, knowing exactly what movie it is. *Perfect.*

"Click that one."

And when he does, and the guide cuts to the movie, the screen fills with a very involved sex scene. Moaning and nudity and thrusting and licking. How was I to know it would be at this scene already?

"Jesus fucking Christ," he mutters with a laugh. "Perfect."

"It seems fate is trying to tell you what you should be doing."

"Fate or a manipulative and determined woman."

"Maybe a little of both. But this is actually a movie adaptation of a hugely bestselling romance novel, I believe," I say, tongue in cheek, while my body is reacting to the visual porn in front of me and tangible porn against me.

"Ah . . . and now it becomes clear why you like romance novels." He laughs.

"It has a great story line," I say in jest.

"I can see that."

"Seriously. You can have hot sex and a great story line." I try to gesture to the television, but my arms are still restrained. "Or we could just have the hot sex, instead."

"I'm not budging, Scout. You told me I needed to read a romance novel, so no time like the present to watch one. With you."

"I thought you only liked King and Follett and Patterson?"

"I do, but I've recently been told that romances are where it's at."

"Oh, please." I roll my eyes and laugh but only get a kiss on my shoulder in response.

So, we sit like this and watch the movie.

And another one after that.

But more memorable than the movies that I can't quite pay attention to is the fact that when I fall asleep in the late hours of the night, my last thought is I've never let myself fall asleep in the arms of a man before without there being sex first.

But this time I did.

And when I wake up the next morning with his body behind mine on the couch, and his arm still holding me tight against him, I realize this isn't so bad.

But more importantly, as scared as I am to let him in, I'm more scared of walking away.

CHAPTER NINETEEN

Scout

"**I** just needed to hear your voice." It's all I say but it's the truth.

"I'm here, Scouty-girl. I'm here." His voice rumbles through the connection and soothes my heart that was having a mini-panic attack over needing to talk to him for no other reason than to know he was still there.

I sag against the wall beside me and close my eyes, willing away the tears that threaten.

"You okay?"

No.

"Yeah. I'm good." I clear my throat and look around the empty hallway outside of the locker room. "Sometimes a girl just needs her dad."

"Understood. This time of year is always tough for you," he murmurs. "I'll sit here on the line as long as you need me."

"Thank you." My voice is almost a whisper as I try to contain my emotions. We both sit on opposite sides of the connection, we don't speak, and yet I find comfort in knowing he's there.

"I need to get to work," I say after a few minutes even though I'd stay like this all day if I could. "Thank you for . . ."

"Anytime." He clears his throat. "Remember, clear mind, hard heart."

"I know," I say before the line disconnects and then whisper, "I love you." I know he's no longer there, but I say the words anyway.

I take a moment to pull myself together—frazzled female emotions make gruff men uncomfortable—before I head into the locker room to prepare for Easton's first of two training sessions today.

But it's when I walk into my office to grab the notes on my desk that the fake smile plastered on my lips becomes genuine.

Sitting on top of my notes is a mess of wintergreen Life Savers, crudely arranged to look like a flower. There are three white mints making up each petal, and they all connect into the center Life Saver. Except the center candy isn't wintergreen white.

It's red.

Cherry red to be exact.

And there's a Post-It note beside it that has '*Have a day*' scrawled across it.

It's a simple something that at a glance looks like candies tossed on a desk but speaks volumes to me. It says *I'm thinking about you*. It says *remember what I like to do with cherry Life Savers*. It says *I'm still here, still determined to prove you wrong*. It says *remember that first time we* 'had a day' *together? Well, here's to more of those.*

My heart does a little flip flop in my chest. There's only one person who could have done this. One person who had no clue that I needed something like this right now but who gave it to me anyway.

I pull the wrapper off one of the wintergreen Life Savers and look up through the training room window to see Easton standing at his locker, looking my way. Our eyes connect for the briefest of moments so as to not give away what's happening between us, but it's long enough for me to slip the candy between my lips and offer a ghost of a smile. His nod is ever so slight before turning to say something to J.P. as if our exchange never occurred.

But it did.

And as I look down to the flower (less one Life Saver) I'm left struggling with how to accept all of the good things happening in my life—the rehabilitation contract, my time spent off the field with Easton, the prospect of a long-term job that will allow me to stay in one place for more than a few months—when I should be thinking about my dad instead.

The guilt eats at me when I know I can't let it. I just have to take things one day at a time.

Another quick glance Easton's way drives the point home because while I may not want to admit it to myself, the time I spend with him is the highlight of my day.

CHAPTER TWENTY

Easton

"Where've you been lately?"

I glance over at Drew and wait for him to say what his eyes are insinuating. "You guys have been on a road trip, so I've been here, and you haven't." I snap my towel at him to emphasize my point.

"It wouldn't have anything to do with that hot little trainer you've got rubbing you down, now would it?"

"Fuck off, Drew. You're just jealous I get a female."

"Damn straight, I'm jealous. Please tell me you've tried to round the bases with her, because, dude, I'd be worried if you hadn't."

Heads have turned our way, ears listening, the locker room full of players as they come back in from batting practice, the game's first pitch a little over ninety minutes away.

"Shot down, brother," I lie, and he bumps my fist and laughs. "She's all business, all the time. Last week I thought I had a shot when she showed up at my place after I threw hard for the first time . . . but nope. I had my phone off and hadn't answered her, so she swung by to make sure I'd iced my arm. Not exactly the kind of front-door service I was hoping for."

"There's hope for me yet if Wylder still gets shot down."

"That's cold, man."

Comments ring through the room right beside the disbelieving laughter at the fact that I'd been rejected by Scout.

Little do they know the damn woman has owned my thoughts more than I'd fucking like to admit. It could be that I get to see her every damn day of the week. That I've badgered her into having a few dinners with me. That getting drunk on her kiss is what I look forward to.

But hell, this "getting to know you" shit has to end soon, because a man only has so much restraint and his balls can only get so blue. Besides, there's only so much satisfaction in jerking off when the one you're fantasizing about does something like she did today, showing up in a tank top that makes you want to cave on your promise.

Oh, fuck, how I'd wanted to cave. And not because it was revealing, but rather because every time she rubbed against me during our stretching routine, all I could think about was that I know what her tits look like beneath it. Perky. Pink. Suckable.

The drought definitely needs to end.

And soon.

But isn't that the damn problem? Just when I thought we've gotten to know each other better, that sex is just what the doctor ordered, she showed up today with that fucking spooked look in her eyes. The one that had her so antsy she left right after we cooled down and she was done with me.

I play it off that she's having a bad day. Maybe her uncle is still sick. Who knows, though, because she won't say shit to me about him.

Then again, maybe she's just freaked.

Fucking women.

"Well, one thing for sure," Stanza says from across the locker room, "Santiago is going to get some chin music tonight."

I meet his eyes across the distance and just nod—a quiet thank you for letting me know that when he pitches tonight, he's going to throw a few inside to push Santiago off the plate. A little "fuck you" for hurting me.

Those who say there's no retaliation in baseball have never played. A pitch aimed a little too close to the head. A tag thrown just a tad too hard. A shoulder lowered or cleats angled up when going in to slide at a base. You fuck with my teammate, we'll fuck with you back, is the motto for most teams.

Especially mine. Especially for me because the play was dirty.

"Fuck that fucker," J.P. mutters, getting a rise out of the guys.

"You staying to watch?" Drew bumps my shoulder and asks.

I pull my shirt over my head and chew over the idea I've considered more times than I'd like to admit. "Probably not. Last thing I need to do is run into him in the hallway. A few months isn't long enough for me to not want to rip his goddamn throat out." The guys around me laugh. "Besides, if I did, I'd probably just fuck my arm up further . . . so, nah, I'm gonna watch from home."

"Gonna meet us after?"

I glance over to the empty training room. The one Scout ran out of earlier. She's the one person I'd rather hang with tonight, but fuck it, going out is probably just what I need to feel like my old self again instead of this overthinking, whiny bitch I'm feeling like right now. "Got nothing better to do than hang with my boys."

And then I see him. The rookie who was just called up from the Triple-A team outta Bum-fuck, Nowhere. He's sitting on his stool, staring in awe at the locker with his name placard on it, much the same way I did my first time here, all those years ago.

"Hey, Gonzo!"

The kid startles as he turns around and sees me across the room. "Yeah?"

"Thanks for filling in for me. You'll do great. Knock 'em dead tonight." I smile at him and nod. A little something to ease the pressure of his first time in the big leagues, and a subtle reminder not to get too comfortable in the gear because I'll be back.

I'm not sure who I'm trying to convince more, him or me.

"Thanks," he stutters, eyes as big as saucers.

"We'll see you at Sluggers after the game. The guys'll show you where to go. It's not every night you make your major league debut."

His smile widens, and he nods. And I'm left sitting, staring at my own locker, contemplating what it would be like to have that feeling back—the awe of walking into the stadium for the first time, the nerves that roll your stomach, the jog of your knee as you sit in the dugout for the first time, and the knowledge that when you hop over that chalk baseline there are thousands of people in the stands who would kill to take your place.

All of it is a reaffirmation of how damn lucky I am, when I've been sitting here feeling goddamn sorry for myself.

The chatter begins to die down as the guys head for the dugout. Some slap me on the back as they leave, some give a fist-bump. Good lucks are given. Shit-talking is required.

And when I'm the only one left in the locker room, I head out, hating the feeling that I'm missing all of this with them. That they're moving on—the next game, the next play, the next city in this long season—while I'm still sidelined and going fucking stir crazy over a game I love but can't play and a woman I want but can't seem to get.

Talk about being majorly fucked.

I laugh at myself as I stand in the tunnel and decide if I want to go to the right and past all the VIP fan events happening, where I'll get wrangled into PR, or asked to head up to the announcer's booth for a bit and add some color commentary, as I've done a few times over the past few months, or if I want to veer left and take the long route.

Left. Definitely left.

I'm not in the mood to deal with fans right now. Not when I'm pissed and just want the hell out of this stadium that suddenly feels like a prison I can't escape from fast enough.

My shoes echo against the concrete as I make my way through the maze of tunnels. My thoughts are all over the place. On my shoulder. On Scout. On watching the game today, the first time Santiago has been in the starting line-up against us since he fucked me over.

"Don't you go anywhere near him."

The voice comes from the next hall up, and the threat in it resonates down to where I am. By the time I wrap my head around the notion that it sounds like my dad, I'm standing in the opening of the passageway, staring at him and Santiago.

Standing side by side.

My dad's hand fisted in my enemy's shirt.

There's a tense second where it takes everything I have not to close the distance and smash my fist into his smarmy fucking smirk that has never said anything near an apology.

"What the fuck is going on here?"

He's suited up to play. Just like I should be, but can't.

Because of him.

"Dad?" I address my dad, yet I can't help but stare at Santiago and try to figure out what in the hell his deal is.

Santiago turns to look back to my dad, eyebrows raised. "Thanks for the chat, Cal, but I've got a game to play. See you on the field, Wylder?" he says as he looks toward me. "Oh. Wait. *My bad.* You won't be there."

And with a fucking chuckle that is like acid in my gut, he pats my dad on the back and jogs the other way down the tunnel. We both stare after him without saying a word.

"What the hell was that all about?" I grit the words out, clenching and unclenching my hands to prevent me from punching the wall.

"I saw him walking down the hallway toward your clubhouse. I asked him where he was going. When he wouldn't answer, I figured he was coming to see you. I told him he better not go near you or I'd have him thrown out of the ballpark."

I stare at my dad, but rage clouds my judgment to the point that I'm questioning whether he's telling me the truth. And of course he is, he's my dad, but it's so much easier to listen to the anger and pick a fight with him.

"You should have let him come at me," I mutter as I scrub my hands over my face and pace a few feet past my dad, toward the opposing clubhouse's locker room and then back the way I came.

"For what, Easton? So you can get hurt again and piss the club off because your DL stint just got extended? Nothing good ever comes out of anger. Nothing." He walks up to me, puts his hand on my shoulder, and squeezes. "I know you're frustrated. I know it's taking everything in your body right now to not storm in there and kick his ass. And I know more than anything you just want your norm back. Keep doing what you're doing, and you'll be back in six weeks' time, according to the report that Ms. Dalton gave the front office."

Six weeks? How did I not know that?

I push it away. The thought. The excitement. Because I was given a return date before and never hit it. A man can't recover on a clock.

But something else becomes clear. For the first time in what feels like forever, my dad is being my dad, not Cal Wylder. It's just what I needed right now, even though he might not know it.

"I'm going fucking stir crazy."

"It's hard being cut off from what you love."

I look up to him, meet eyes that mirror mine, and see the concern. "Yeah, well, thanks to *him*." I pace back and forth once more. "You know what I don't get, though, is *why*? Why take me out? Why hurt me? Why any of this?"

My dad clears his throat and chews the inside of his cheek as he thinks it over. "I just don't know, Easton. The guy's bat is on fire. He has a helluva on-base percentage. His arm's flawless, and no one dares steal with him behind that plate. His style reminds me a lot of yours, yet he's probably making a third of what you make."

"You think this is a jealousy thing? There's no way. I mean, there's hundreds of us taking the field every night across all pay grades and starting positions. If that's the case, then why single me out? It just doesn't make sense."

"Nothing seems to these days, son."

"The fucker went three-for-three tonight. What the fuck is up with that?" Drew mutters as he takes a nice long drag on his bottle.

"Bad juju, man," I mutter, tired as fuck but with zero desire to make it the few blocks down the street back to my place.

"Yeah, but we won, so it couldn't have been too damn bad," Tino chimes in with a clink of his bottle to mine. "I think I deserve to get laid for that homer, though."

"Then go home to your wife," I say, the same as I do every time we go drinking. It's innocent enough, I know, because Tino worships the ground his wife walks on, but he never fails to say it.

Almost like a routine.

Pretty much the same as the four of us sitting here after a home game, reliving the highlights, bitching about the ball that wouldn't drop, or the shitty call that cost us the game, and taking time to unwind for an hour or two before we head home to our non-baseball lives. Tino, his wife; Drew, his three dogs; J.P., his girlfriend; and me to my empty bed.

"I plan on it," Tino says with a quick grin, "but I was waiting for Gonzo to get here so we could buy him a beer and fuck with him a bit."

"Yeah. Where is he?" J.P. says, craning his neck around the crowded bar to look for him.

"He's probably still sitting in the dugout, sporting wood and try-ing to believe he actually just made his debut in the show," Drew says, and the image has us all thinking back to that first time and the rush of nerves and adrenaline that lasted for days.

"The kid did good." I nod. "Real good."

"Not as good as you, East," Tino says. "When're you going to get your ass back on the field?"

"Soon. Four, five weeks. It's up to Scout to clear me."

"Ah, the mysterious Scout," J.P. taunts, but I don't take the bait. Because fuck yes, I've thought about her tonight. When I was sitting at my place watching the game, shouting at the television, and flipping off Santiago every time the camera panned to him, it was her I imagined laughing at me. Even when I came down here to grab our table in the back and wait for the guys, sure, the women who approached were attractive, but all I kept doing was comparing them to her.

I've got it fucking bad. Christ. Talk about feeling pussy-whipped when you aren't even getting any pussy.

"You mean *that* mysterious Scout?" Drew asks with a tilt of his beer toward the far side of the room.

I look immediately, hating that my heart fucking slams into my chest as violently as confusion does when I see her on the other side of the dimly lit bar.

"Dude, is she with . . .?"

"Well, we definitely know what team she wanted to win tonight," J.P. murmurs, just above the chatter of the crowd.

I shift in my seat to see better and try to wrap my head around why she's sitting with Penski and Cameron, whose asses we just kicked tonight. I think of her Facebook page. Of picture after picture of her with other players.

It's her fucking job, Easton. Dealing with other men is her job.

So why didn't she say anything to me about them when I asked her if she wanted to do something tonight? If there was nothing to hide, then why fucking hide it?

And if you're trying to hide something, then why come to

Sluggers when you know that's where the whole team goes after a game to blow off steam?

You don't own her, East. She's not yours. You don't have the right to know what she's doing when she's not with you. You don't get to lay claim to her.

Fuck that. I damn well do.

I've put the time in. I've gotten to know her. I've taken more care than I ever have with a woman, and so, fuck yes, she's going to be mine.

Wasn't that the whole point of this?

And it's not lost on me, I can't do shit about any of it. I can't stare long enough to see that she has on a denim skirt, with some sexy ass cowboy boots on her feet. Or that her hair is curled and down, when usually it is thrown up in a ponytail. Or that she has some top on that makes my mouth water thinking about what's beneath it.

She gets dressed up for them, but not for me?

My blood boils knowing that they're over there enjoying the sight of it, getting turned on by her, when I'm over here trying to figure out what the fuck is going on, because I can't do anything about it.

Not with three guys staring me down. Hell, the guys wouldn't give a shit if I was sleeping with her; the only reason they'd care is because that means they can't get with her. But if they knew and accidentally told someone, and it got to the front office, then that could cause problems for Scout and Doc's contract.

Besides, I promised her I wouldn't say anything. And with a woman who has a hard time believing promises, this is one I need to keep.

The problem is, it doesn't seem she's keeping her word, either.

Her *word*? Have another beer. She made no promises. All she agreed to was getting to know each other, to seeing where this might take us . . .

And spending every day together on and off the field doesn't qualify as that?

What is going on here?

"You okay there, Wylder?" Tino bumps my shoulder with his and pulls me from my thoughts, and I realize I'm still staring at her.

"Yeah. Sure." I down my beer and lift my hand to the waitress for another. "Just trying to make sense of it."

"She didn't say anything to you during rehab today about knowing them?" Drew asks, glancing over to her again, and I hate that I want to follow suit, but can't without being way too obvious.

Because every time I look her way, my temper burns brighter. I try to justify that she knows I'm here. Christ, they weren't sitting there an hour ago when I got here to save our table, so she had to have seen me when she walked in. Why hasn't she acknowledged me? I get keeping a public distance to protect our professional relationship and her damn contract, but a simple nod of her head wouldn't scream "We've fucked," either.

"Did she tell me she knew them? Not a word." I thank the waitress for the new beer and take a long swallow of it.

"You'd think she'd have said something about sleeping with the enemy," J.P. jokes. He gets the laugh he was going for, but all it does is piss me off even further.

I lose sight of her through the crowd and tell myself that's a good thing. The conversation moves on like it should, even if all I can think about is what she's doing here. With them. And why she didn't mention it to me.

"I'm gonna hit the head." Drew stands, and when I glance Scout's way, she's staring at me.

There's a shot glass up to her lips, but she doesn't offer me a smile, doesn't acknowledge me at all; her face is expressionless—distant. And my fists clench in reaction to the fleeting thought that she's ferreted. That she somehow got spooked and didn't have the balls to tell me to my face we were over, so instead she came out tonight and sat where she sat on purpose, so I'd see her with them. And then I'd know.

But as she tilts her head back and downs the shot in one impressive swallow before slamming it down on the table among the countless empties I can now see, all I can think is that there's no way she's moving on without me getting to have a final say about it.

"Where're you going?" Tino asks as I tilt my own beer back and down its contents.

"Gonna buy the lady a shot, since it seems to be her poison of choice tonight."

CHAPTER TWENTY-ONE

Scout

The burn of the shot numbs the significance of today's date and yet does nothing to ease the shock to my system when I glance around and meet the ice in Easton's eyes.

I should have expected him to be here. It's the postgame hangout, after all. But I could have handled him if things had stuck to the plan—just Penski and Cameron and me taking a few shots in my brother's honor on his birthday. Yet another piece of my history that I keep tucked away.

But things didn't stick to the plan.

Because now I'm seated across from the one man I want to be nowhere near but can't ask to leave, considering he's Penski and Cameron's teammate.

"That was two," Cameron says with a nod. "Two more and Ford would be pleased."

"Pour me one."

I look across the table, and just the sight of him disgusts me. "No." I snap the word out, causing Penski to nudge my knee under the table.

Santiago just stares at me. The mixture of his dark features, the dim light of the bar, and the fact that he's in the corner of the booth (thank God) so the shadow of the wall falls over his face makes him seem like the asshole I've conjured up in my mind.

And keeps him out of Easton's line of sight.

Because if there is ice in Easton's glare at seeing me here with members from the opposing team—or maybe just men in general—then seeing Santiago here would set him off.

No doubt.

Because it sure as hell set me off when he walked in and sat down with us. I protested, told the boys that this was a ritual we've always done with just us—the only ones who really knew my brother—but they said it was harmless for Santiago to stay.

But he's anything but harmless. Not with his curious eyes always watching me. Measuring me. Making it clear he wants me.

The neck of the bottle of tequila clinks against the shot glass as Penski pours Santiago the shot.

"To Ford," Cameron says, lifting his glass. "It's been three years without you, brother. It feels like a fucking lifetime since I've heard that laugh of yours. Fuck you for leaving us. We miss you."

"Fuck you, Ford," the three of us murmur in unison, and then we toss back the shot. This time, the burn is a little less, but the memories are still painful as ever.

In fact, something about this year's get-together to remember and curse Ford for leaving us behind seems so much harder than the last two.

Maybe it's because what started out as a promise one drunken night when they were trying to make me feel better over my brother's death is tonight reminding me that next year I might have to perform two of these memorials instead of just one.

I raise my shot glass. "To my brother," I whisper as the tears threaten. "You have no idea how much I miss you right now. How much I need your friendship and advice. How, if you were here, I wouldn't think everyone leaves. What I'd give for one more hour to lie in the long grass at Dad's and pretend we were the only ones left on Earth. I miss you."

"Fuck you, Ford," we say in unison, but when I finish my shot, as my head grows fuzzy and a lone tear slides down my cheek, I add in a whisper, "I love you."

"I guess shots are the order of the night." Easton's voice snaps me from my melancholic fog, and for a split second I forget we have eyes on us. I forget that we are supposed to be trainer and player. Relief floods through me from the presence of the one person I've unknowingly started to need.

But just as quick as the relief is the reality that slams into me like a wrecking ball. That Santiago is here. Across from me.

This is trouble.

But Easton's eyes hold mine, search my face, and when he notices the lone tear sliding down my cheek, he shoots an accusatory glare to Penski and then Cameron. But when his gaze shifts, when he comes to the person cloaked in the shadows of the bar, his expression morphs from curiosity to rage.

"What the fuck is he doing here?" His voice is a growl of unrestrained fury as he pushes his way to the table, testosterone raging and temper raw.

"It's not what you think." The words blurt out of my mouth as Penski shoves up from the table, sensing chaos is about to unravel, and steps between Easton and Santiago just as Tino and Drew arrive.

"Not what he thinks?" Santiago chuckles in a low, baiting tone that makes me realize what exactly I'd just implied.

"Leave her the fuck out of this." Easton tries to push Penski out of the way, his fists clenched and body vibrating with a rage so palpable it rolls off him and slams into me.

"Easy now, Easton." Penski pushes against Easton's chest as Drew pulls back on his good shoulder. They can try all they want to prevent the fight, but it's been brewing for so long I'm not sure anything can stop it now.

"You fucking the trainer now, Wylder?" Santiago baits Easton, his name a marred sneer loaded with disdain. "A little locker room lovin'?"

Easton lunges at Santiago, the empty glasses on the table crashing to the ground as Penski uses all his strength to keep them separated. "You fucking bastard!" Easton grits out.

"You got that right, pretty boy," Santiago taunts, his chuckle grating over my nerves.

"Are cheap shots the only thing you're good for?"

"You'd know, wouldn't you? Too bad your lady was planning on going home with me."

"Bullshit!" I shout in the confusion that's now causing a crowd to form.

"Shut him the fuck up!" Penski barks to Cameron as he lifts his chin to Tino and Drew, silently asking them to get Easton the hell out of here, because it seems Santiago is going to keep provoking until he gets just what he wants.

In seconds, Drew and Tino have flanked Easton and are forcibly pushing him toward the door. There's a mass of chaos and confusion swirling around me, but it's the look on Easton's face when he meets my gaze before he's shoved out the door—the look that says, "What the fuck, Scout?"—that sticks with me more than anything.

"We'll get him home," J.P. says before looking at me and shaking his head in disapproval. "Not the brightest of moves, Scout."

With that reprimand, J.P. walks away, leaving me standing in the middle of Sluggers with the man I want more than anyone being escorted out one side of the bar, and the man I despise for his nasty demeanor and the stunt he just pulled being shoved out the other door.

I sink back down into my chair, the remaining shots of tequila looking damn tempting. But they're not the answer.

"I'm sorry." Cameron's voice is behind me, resigned and apologetic as he scoots into the seat next to me. "Not exactly how we'd planned to remember Ford tonight."

I glance his way, at my brother's best friend and college team-mate, and know he misses Ford just as much as I do. That this annual ritual means as much to him as it does me. And that neither of us will go back on the promise we've made my dad to always celebrate Ford's birthday to ensure his memory stays alive.

But how would we ever forget the boy with the goofy grin, ob-noxious laugh, and heart as big as the ocean?

"I know," I sigh. "The timing was perfect though. How the three of us were in the same city, the same time, on his birthday. Besides, Ford always liked a good fight so . . ."

"We should have made Santiago leave. I wasn't thinking. Not with you working with Wylder or us coming to Sluggers . . . it's my fault."

I toy with an empty shot glass, wonder how Easton's doing, and worry that one of the guys may have wrenched his bad shoulder.

But more than anything I just want to see him. Need to see him.

"You want me to walk you back?" Cameron asks, and I'm so grateful that he knows me so well.

I nod.

CHAPTER TWENTY-TWO

Scout

"Scout?"

I look at Cameron. "It's fine. Thanks for walking me back."

"You sure?" His eyes dart over my shoulder and then back to mine.

I nod and welcome the huge bear hug he pulls me into. "It was good to see you again, even if the night went to shit."

I laugh, the tears threatening, as I squeeze him back. "It was. And it did."

"Fuck you, Ford," he murmurs and causes me to hiccup out a laughing sob.

"Thank you for never forgetting."

"Never," he says as he gives me a peck on my cheek, squeezes my hand, and glances one more time over my shoulder before walking away.

I draw in a deep breath before I turn to face the dark silhouette highlighted by the lone light still on in the parking lot. He's leaning against the side of my car, his arms folded, his body tense. We stand there with distance between us and discord roiling around us.

"You want to tell me what the fuck that was all about?"

And the funny thing is, as much as I wanted to see him, as much as I feel like I need him tonight, he just pushed every wrong button possible by coming at me with anger when I did nothing wrong.

"Excuse me?" My voice is a quiet steel as I take another step toward him and his irrational temper.

"You heard me, Scout. What the fuck were you doing with Santiago?"

"First of all, I wasn't with Santiago. And second, did I miss a point in time where you laid claim to me?"

"Not. At. All." He rolls his shoulders. He shifts his feet. But between the dark night and the brim of his ball cap, I can't see his eyes when I desperately wish I could.

"Great. Then you can move out of the way. I can leave. And tomorrow, when we meet up for your training, we can forget all about this whole *getting to know you* shtick and move on."

His laugh fills the night, but falls flat. "It's just that easy for you, huh? Run. Dodge. Avoid. Nice try, Scout, but I'm not letting you use that on me."

"You don't get a say in what I do or don't do, Hot Shot." I take a step closer to him, partly hurt, partly relieved that whatever he's pissed about isn't deterring him from whatever is happening between us.

"Nice skirt," he says, completely throwing me for a loop with his change in conversation. There's an underlying edge to his voice, though.

"Your point?"

"Can't a man tell a woman who got dressed up she looks nice? I mean, I sure as shit know you weren't dressing up for me. I get Nikes and sports bras, but Penski or Cameron or fucking Santiago gets a short skirt, long legs, boots, and fixed hair. 'Dress to impress' must have been the motto for the night, huh?"

My temper snaps.

"I don't have fucking time for this. Or you." I storm over to my car, hands on my hips. "Move."

He doesn't budge, just stands there with a clenched jaw and murder in his eyes that reflects how I feel. "You talk to Santiago with that mouth, too?"

"Fuck you!" I shout. He's pushing for a fight, and you know what? I'm so game for one right now. I have a tornado of emotions whipping around inside of me—grief, loneliness, desire, need, uncertainty, fear—and it's so much easier to be angry than to face any of them.

Or to admit that I'm hurt he could think I'd want Santiago when the only person I want is him.

I want him.

It's a fleeting thought, one my temper overrides, but it's loud enough to add fuel to the fight. Because if I fight, then I don't have to acknowledge that, though I'm used to shutting everyone out, he might be the first I want to let in.

"Come on, Scout. Are you playing me?" I can hear the hurt in his tone, know he's had a few drinks, like I have, and know that nothing intensifies bravado like alcohol. "Are you using the contract as an excuse to keep this your little secret? Do you keep pushing me away, holding me at arms' length because you're really dating one of them and you don't want either of us to find out?"

What? My temper's too far gone for me to think rationally, and so I do what comes next in line—lash out at him.

"Playing you? Glad to know you think so highly of me." I step into him, our bodies inches away from each other.

"Well, you sitting there with Santiago tells me exactly what you think of me." His words are guarded armor when he grits them out, quiet but loaded with vitriol.

"The way you're acting, I shouldn't think of you at all."

We glare at each other. Hurt waging against hurt. Anger swirling in the cool night air. And neither of us attempt to back down.

"You know what? Fuck this," he mutters, looks at me one last time through eyes laden with sadness, shakes his head, and strides out of the parking lot.

It takes me a second to process what's happening. To realize he's walking away from me. And at first, all I can think is that with him gone, I'll be able to breathe for a second. Have a clear mind.

Let him go, Scout. If you do, then you can't get hurt any further. Because people leave. They all do. Ford. Mom. At some point soon, Dad will, too. Chalk up Easton to *having fun while it lasted*. Some good sex, a new friend, but nothing harmed in the end. He's too close. You're too close. Push him away or you're going to end up devastated. And alone.

Walk away now, like he will from you.

Clear mind. Hard heart, Scouty-girl.

But what if I don't want a hard heart anymore?

My feet move. Toward him.

My heart, hard as it may be, jolts into my throat.

And I really wish I had my damn Nikes on instead of my cowboy boots.

"Easton!"

His shadow's up ahead, the streetlights hitting his hair a beacon for me to follow.

"Easton!" I call as I chase after him.

"Forget it, Scout. Just forget it."

"No, wait."

"At some point, it's not worth the trouble anymore."

Tears burn and my vision blurs as I catch up to him, just as he hits the lobby of his building. Conscious of the other people, I don't yell like I want to for him to stop. Instead, I move a bit faster. He steps into the elevator and turns to face me with shoulders square, body tense, and eyes that say everything he doesn't speak.

Step in now or turn around and keep walking. Now or never.

My pulse pounds, knowing the answer but fearing it at the same time.

I step in.

Easton blows out an audible breath as he pushes a button, and I'm not sure if that's a good sign or a bad sign, but it doesn't matter because my heart urged me to step in when every sensible thought screamed for me to stay out.

The elevator jerks and then surprises me when it begins to descend. I glance over at him, but he's just staring straight ahead—jaw clenched, hands fisted, face intense.

So damn handsome.

I want him.

In more ways than *let's have fun 'til it ends.*

Because I want to take a chance on this. On him.

Sure, we've known each other for a couple of months, but when I look at him now, when I think about him when I'm alone, when I anticipate seeing him, it makes me want to push all fear out the window. It makes me want to step into him rather than step away. It makes me realize it's okay to want more, when before, I've never even allowed myself that chance at all.

And I get it now. What he said the other night about making your own happily ever after. His implication that it's not easy. That sometimes it takes time and patience and shutting up instead of shouting louder. That it might be the hardest thing in the world, but it can also be the most rewarding.

We just fought in the parking lot. He walked away, and I chased, for the first time ever. That should tell me something . . . but it's bigger than that. There is the notion that, even though he was livid, even though he told me he wasn't doing this, he still stood in the elevator with his finger on the open-door button and gave me a choice to be with him. The idea that he was mad at me, but still wanted me. That he walked away, but that didn't mean he was leaving me.

This all hits me in the few seconds we have during the elevator ride down—it's suffocating and invigorating.

When the doors open to the private field, I follow as he steps into the lighted entry, the rest of the space still in the muted dark. The elevator dings, the doors close behind us, the silence returns.

"Easton." It's a plea. A question. A "talk to me."

"Don't 'Easton' me," he says as he turns to face me, eyes alive but posture guarded.

So we stand and stare but don't speak. My heart is in my throat. My emotions a train wreck inside of me.

I expect him to tell me to leave.

I expect him to shake his head and say no more.

Wouldn't that be fitting, considering I now want more?

But he does neither. We just stand there as the air around us shifts and changes, reacts and charges. It's hard to draw in a breath, and yet I know damn well it's not the air that's making me feel that way but rather the look in his eye.

Then in the space from one beat to the next, he has me against the wall, his lips on mine, his body pressed against me in the most delicious of ways. Our hands grab and pull and squeeze and *feel*.

He wages an all-out assault on my senses with his lips alone. There is nothing gentle about the kiss. There is nothing passive. It's packed full of greed and need and hunger and a violent desire that ignites every nerve inside my body.

I react in kind. My anger at his accusations earlier, my sadness over Ford's birthday, and the realization of my feelings—they all curl into an explosive ball of harbored energy that gives just as good as it gets.

There are sparks of hunger on his tongue when it brushes against mine. Each connection is like a livewire hitting water—evocative, incendiary, inescapable.

And just when I feel like I can't catch my breath—when I'm drowning in everything that is Easton Wylder—he tears his mouth from mine, hands fisted in my hair, knee between my thighs, and eyes a burning kaleidoscope of colors.

"Fucking Christ, I'm so mad at you right now."

And that's all I get—the growl of his anger—before I taste it on my tongue as he dives back in, catching me off guard and taking what he wants, what I offer him, once again. His stubble scrapes my skin, his fingers tighten in my hair, and his teeth nip my lips, swollen from his.

I fight against him. Not because I don't want more, but because I need to explain.

"I wasn't there for Santiago," I pant as he lets us resurface for air. His eyes narrow, his tongue darts out to lick his bottom lip, and his fingers twist in my hair so he can pull my head back.

He struggles with words. I can see them form, then fade, and so he speaks with his lips again, but by putting them back on mine.

But it's not enough. As much as there's no hesitation in his actions, I can still feel it from him and know he doesn't believe me whole-heartedly.

As hard as it is to stop him again, I can't do this without him understanding the truth. "I was there for my brother," I explain between kisses.

His lips move for a few seconds more, but as soon as the words sink in, his hands still in my hair he leans back to look at me. "You have a brother?"

I swallow loudly and realize there's hurt in his eyes that I never expected to be there. I don't understand it. Moreover, I choose not to because if it's there, then I'm responsible for it being there.

So, I lean in to kiss him again. To try and pretend like I didn't see it, or the confusion in his features. To absolve myself of being the asshole I suddenly feel like I've been.

"No, Scout. No. You don't get to hide behind your sweet fucking kiss. You don't get to hide your life from me when I keep giving you more of mine. Jesus fucking Christ." His growl of frustration echoes around the concrete walls as he paces a few steps away from me, shoves his hands through his hair, the distance between us reinforcing how far away from me he feels right now. "You don't get it, do you? This. You. Me. *This*. It goes both ways."

His words fade and die in the space around us. The look on his face—resigned, uncertain, disappointed—causes the panic to flood full force through me. And the panic this time isn't because he's getting too close, but rather because I fucked up. Because I didn't give him the benefit of the doubt and just assumed he'd run.

"What do you want from me?" I've never spoken a truer statement and been more afraid of the answer.

"More than I think you can give me." His voice is even, but it feels like he just shouted at me at the top of his lungs. The rejection is blindingly real and scary and overwhelming to a point that fear speaks for me this time. Shame carries the tune.

"What do you want to know, Easton? That I had a brother who was two years older than me? That he was my best friend, my everything, and three years ago he died? That I had a mother who went to get milk when I was five—left my dad washing the dishes and my brother in the bath and me in my Strawberry Shortcake pajamas waiting for her to come back and read me my bedtime story—and never came back? That we were too much work for her? That we weren't worth coming back for?" I yell, each word escalating in pitch, my body vibrating from the words I hate to admit but now can't stop from tumbling out. "Or let me see . . . What other juicy secrets can I tell you that no one else knows? What can I confess to prove to you that I really am trying to let you in instead of push you away?"

"Scout. Please. Stop so—"

"Nope. Just giving you exactly what you want." The catharsis is real and frightening and feels like a thousand-pound boulder is being lifted from my chest with each word. "Like how my dad is sick. He's dying, Easton. Is that what you wanted to know? Or how it's taking everything I have to get this goddamn contract with the Aces that I don't give a fucking rat's ass about, but have to get because that was his one request? And once I do, he's going to leave me, too? Is that what you want to know?" I scream the last words at him, tears sliding down my cheeks, anger burrowed in my heart, and all of me laid on the line. "Is that enough for you? You now know that every single person I've ever loved, who I've ever let in to know the real me, has left me. How I'm cursed, and petrified that if I let you in, I'm just dooming myself because you'll leave me, too?"

My voice is hoarse. My heart bared. My fears exposed.

My shoulders shudder with the sobs I won't allow to come. My mind reels with my confession as the dust settles, and I realize everything I just said.

Oh. Shit.

Those two words are the only thing running through my head like the tears running down my cheeks as Easton just stares at me, his face a picture of shock, his eyes a sea of compassion.

"Scout." His voice is broken when he says my name, much like how I feel.

"Don't. Please don't," I beg of him.

I can't do this right now. I don't want to hear the sympathy in his voice. I don't want any pity. But more than anything, I just can't take the hurt anymore. There's a reason I've locked all this emotion up and not touched it for years. This is the explanation for my hard heart.

So, I shut it out to shut him up and step into him. With my hands in his shirt, I yank him down to me and bruise my lips on his, needing to feel him. Needing to feel wanted. Needing to know that, even though he knows my fears, he still wants me.

He kisses me back, but I can feel his hesitation, sense his discomfort, his wondering what in the hell I'm doing. My heart falls, and his hands lift to frame my cheeks. He holds my face still as he leans back. "Scout." Our eyes meet, and I see honesty so raw I can't handle it. I also see the pity. The sadness.

And I can't see any more of that.

I shake my head back and forth, and he leans forward and

brushes his lips tenderly against mine, almost as if he thinks I need nice and sweet right now, to go along with my sadness.

"No." I need the exact opposite from him. "No," I reiterate, gripping the back of his neck, not allowing him to back off, adding some urgency to our kiss. And he lets me take the reins again. Allows me to pour my unsettled emotions into the kiss until I'm breathless and the tears have started to dry on my cheeks. "Make me feel, Easton. I don't need sweet. I need real. I need to know you're here. I need to know you want me. I need to forget. But more than anything, *I need you.*"

He leans back again. I watch his Adam's apple bob, see the clenching and unclenching of his jaw, and watch the realization sink in.

"I need you," I mouth the words to him, and it's like I've just thrown kerosene on a lighted match.

We meet each other in the middle, a mass of hands and tongues and commands and haste. We move to our own music: shirts over heads and bra unclasped and jeans unbuttoned and shoved down while he pulls my skirt up and his fingers find their way beneath the lace of my panties.

"God, yes." His fingers part me, play with me, enter me. There's no niceties. There's no seduction. There's just him doing exactly what I asked him to do—make me feel. Push my mind into the free fall of orgasmic oblivion so I can't think.

He's everywhere at once, hands and teeth and lips and skin, and it's nowhere near enough. We shift backward somehow, our feet moving as our hearts race, until I bump into the net of the batting cage behind me. My feet tangle in it until I fall against it, leaving my body supported by the net itself. My laughter at the predicament shifts into a moan as his teeth nip at my jawline and his thumb slides over my clit.

"Mmmm, hold tight, Kitty," he orders as he pulls his fingers from within me and moves my hands to hold onto the woven rope above my head. "You holding on?"

My eyes flash up to meet the salacious look in his, and I nod and try to comprehend why he's asking; he shakes his head in warning and slides his fingers into my mouth. I taste my own arousal, suck on them, as he slides them back and forth between my lips.

"Don't talk, Scout," he murmurs. "Don't question. Don't move your hands. *Just do.* Just let me. *Just feel.*"

I nod as my breath grows shallow. His teeth are biting into his bottom lip as he watches, his free hand working back and forth over his cock. But it's the look in his eyes, desire personified, that makes my back bow and beg for more.

"You want me to touch you?" He leans in and murmurs against my ear, his body close enough that I feel the crest of his cock bump against my lower belly as he strokes it in his hand. Talk about the sweetest torture, knowing the havoc that cock can wreak on my system, having it just within sight, and being told not to touch it.

I moan when he rubs it against my clit, and push my hips forward to get the feeling again. He half laughs, half groans as I take his dick between the tops of my thighs and show him what I want.

"Mmm, that feels good," he says as he pushes between my thighs and adds to the friction on my clit.

But it's not enough.

Nowhere near enough.

And he must agree because, unexpectedly, he lifts my hips and sets my ass back in a framed alcove of the netting. The moment my butt is settled on the shallow shelf, Easton drops to his knees, spreads my thighs, and looks up at me.

"You want to feel? Well, I want to taste you. Hold tight, Kitty."

Without another word, and with his eyes fastened to mine, he uses one hand to part me and then licks a line from my clit all the way down to my opening and then back up. And with the perfect amount of pressure and frequency, he begins to flick his tongue over the hub of nerves there. Soft and slow at first, and then faster and a bit harder.

I writhe beneath his touch. I sink into the pleasure and soar in its haze. Every sensation works my nerves—the warmth of his tongue, the tickle of his breath, the pressure as he slides his fingers inside me to give me the one-two punch of tongue on my clit and fingers rubbing my G-spot.

I moan and buck and pull on the netted ropes, all to ease the mounting pressure inside of me. To hold off my orgasm so that the pressure can build even stronger. I'm a mess of contradictions, and yet every one of them feels so damn good that the moan from my mouth can't even express how incredible they are.

I'm aroused. Needy. Greedy. Desperate for more. Selfish. Eager. And every single one of those feelings is amplified by the hunger in his eyes as he looks up at me with his tongue buried between my thighs, my arousal glistening on his skin, and his fingers buried deep within me.

A lick of his tongue. A rub of his fingers. The groan from his lips. The carnality in his eyes. The rope biting into my skin.

My breath grows faint. My body pulls tight. My head grows dizzy.

And then lightning strikes—from my center, out to my toes and fingers, and then all the way back in until the reverb slams back for a second, more powerful wave.

My cry fills the room as he laps at the wetness between my thighs, his groan of pleasure sounding as good as the orgasm feels. He milks it out for me, the licks of his tongue grow softer, and his palms slide up my belly to cup my breasts, gently tug on my nipples, and sustain the ecstasy pulsing through my body.

And when he stands, when he brings his mouth to mine and takes my lips with as violent a desire as when his tongue brought me to climax, I'm immediately desperate for the feel of his dick sliding into me.

I can't speak, even if I wanted to, and so, with my taste on his tongue, I suck on it. His groan, broken and begging, is all I need to hear to know I'm going to get my wish.

"Fuck me, Easton."

I broke the rules. I spoke. But I don't give a damn because when he lines his cock up and dips the tip inside of me, my head is already rolling back against the net, and my lips are already falling open into a garbled sound of *yes, please, now,* and *thank you.*

He fists his hands in the net beside my hips and pulls it to him so that he stands still but I slide slowly onto his rock-hard shaft. When he's sheathed root to tip, our mutual groan is the only sound in the room, as he lets me enjoy the feel of him filling me before he pushes the net back so he slides out.

And then, without warning, he yanks the net back toward him, and I slam against him, and him into me. The action sends shock-waves through my already hypersensitive nerves.

This time, when we're as close as can be, his lips find mine and devour them, murmuring, "Hang on, baby."

"Please."

And before the plea is even finished, he already has me pushed back and then pulled back into him again. He sets a bruising pace by manipulating the net around me to control the depth and the angle of his thrust. All I can do is hold on and watch how damn sexy he looks as he works himself up to his own release.

Those biceps of his flex and release with each pull and push. The tendons in his neck grow tight. His teeth bite into his bottom lip, and his nose scrunches up as he concentrates. But his eyes stay steadfast on mine. All the way up until the very end, when his head bucks back as his hips thrust forward, his hand holding me as close as I can be to him as he grinds his hips against mine and loses himself.

Completely.

And I don't think I've ever seen anything sexier than Easton Wylder come undone. I can't take my eyes off him. I can't stop think-ing how I did that to him.

With my words.

With my confession.

With my body.

And when he lowers his chin and meets my eyes, everything I was fighting against the past few months dissipates.

I surrender.

Heart.

Body.

Mind.

Fear.

CHAPTER TWENTY-THREE

Scout

"We can go upstairs, you know." Easton's voice is murmured satisfaction as he speaks a full sentence for the first time since we moved from the nets to lay naked atop our discarded clothes on the turf baseball field.

"I kind of think this is fitting," I muse, grateful to hear his laugh. His silence has been eating at me, because I know I unloaded a ton on him, and now that our tempers have cleared, I must explain more, but need a few more minutes before I do.

I appreciate his patience. I am grateful for his silence. But with both of those also comes the unsettled quiet in my head that riots around on how to begin, since this sharing thing is all new to me.

"It would be more fitting if we were lying on home plate," he chuckles as his finger trails lazily up and down the length of my spine, pausing to smooth over the curve of my ass before starting the whole process all over again.

"So, why did you bring me down here, anyway?" I ask to buy more time. His hand pauses, then continues.

"Because, if you were going to walk away, I didn't want you in my place. Memories are a bitch, and the last thing I needed was to make more of them there on the kitchen counter."

"The kitchen counter?"

"I figured that was as far as I'd get you in the door before I had to have you, and the kitchen counter is the closest horizontal surface so . . ."

"Do you always want to sleep with someone when they make you that angry?"

"Only you, Kitty. Only you." Silence descends again. He plays with a strand of my hair while my fingertips draw aimless circles on his chest.

I feel at peace. It's such an odd feeling for me. New. Foreign. And yet the panic I've lived with for so very long is nonexistent. It's unsettling but also so very welcome.

"My mom is an alcoholic."

His confession into the peaceful silence has me shifting so that I can see his face, but his eyes are staring at the ceiling above us.

"Easton, you don't have to do this."

"Yes, I do. You shared your secrets with me, and so you deserve mine," he says with a nod. I watch his Adam's apple bob. I hear his unsteady exhale. And he continues, "She's not a mean drunk, but she's a drunk nonetheless. There's no gentle way to pretend she isn't. She's stuck back in time, not wanting to let go of the past, so much so that most days she doesn't know what day it is."

"Does she live close?"

"Mm-hmm." He falls silent, but I know there is more, so I give him time. "She lives about an hour outside of town. Seventy-eight minutes to be exact. I know because I often get late night calls when she won't leave the bar in the trailer park that she lives in and refuses to let me move her out of."

"That has to be frustrating for you."

"So many things about it are," he sighs. "It would be different if she were a mean drunk. It would be easier to hate her for it then.

But she's not. She's sweet and lonely and just wants me around more. And I feel guilty that I don't spend more time with her . . . but at least sleeping on her couch a night or two during the week is enough for her. She deserves the world, but her world is her double-wide trailer, cluttered with her things and my games on replay on the TV, and so that's what I give her."

My heart swells at the audible love transparent in his voice. The measure of a man is often unquantifiable, and yet, with Easton, it's everywhere. In his love for his mother. In unpublicized visits to Children's Hospital. In his charitable organization for literacy. In his patience with a spooked woman.

"You love her." It's a stupid statement but so very true.

"Yeah." I can hear the smile in his tone. "You know, my dad wasn't around much when I was a kid. Sure, he was here in the offseason, or I got to spend time in the clubhouse with him, but she was the day-in, day-out parent. It would be easy for me to be mad at her for her drinking. It would be easy when the bar calls to let them get her home . . . but that's my job as her son. She took care of me, now it's my turn to take care of her."

Emotion clogs his voice, and all I can think to do is to press a kiss to his chest to let him know what I think of him.

"Was that the reason she and your dad divorced?"

"I don't know. I don't remember her drinking back then, but it's easy for parents to hide things from their kids when they're that young."

It's easy for them to hide things from their kids when they're old, too. Like my dad has for the past year.

"My parents never discuss their divorce. I don't remember them fighting. I don't remember any ill will. I just remember coming home from practice one day and my dad sat me down and told me that things were going to be changing a little. That was it. Later, I learned from friends how weird it was that neither of my parents tried to pit me against the other . . . but they just didn't."

"Lucky for you . . . I guess," I amend, realizing how wrong that sounds.

"No, you're right. I understood what you meant." His finger begins to trace over my back again.

"You're a good son. A good man."

"I'm all she has, Scout."

I press another kiss to his chest. "She's lucky."

"My biggest fear is a trade. She'd have no one to take care of her."

Easton shifts some and rolls onto his side, head propped onto his elbow, and looks at me for the first time since the conversation started. "Why didn't you tell me about your dad, Scout?" The compassion is back in his eyes, and I can't hide from it this time.

I sigh, shrug, and squirm under the intensity of his stare. "Because he made me promise not to tell anyone. Hell, he only told *me* a few months ago." I shake my head and remember the defeat I felt when he'd told me. "His heart is failing him. Heart disease, which sounds so weird to me because he's always been so healthy, but I guess he's had it for a long time and never took the steps to slow it down. He's on a donor list, but so are a million other people who have stronger bodies that can withstand a transplant, while doctors have determined that at this time his can't. Why waste a precious heart on someone who might not make it through the surgery, when they have ten other matches who can?" The tears threaten and burn, but I keep them at bay. Hold them back like I do the acknowledgement that this is all happening and real and my dad really is sick.

"I'm so sorry." Easton leans forward and presses a kiss to my forehead, the gesture so natural, so sweet, that one of the threatening tears slips out and slides down my cheek.

"When he first told me, I argued with him. Told him he was lying. And to this day, I still hope that's true, but he's living proof you can't recover from a broken heart." Easton's eyes narrow as he links the fingers on his free hand with mine and waits for me to explain. "My mom leaving was hard on all of us, but especially him. He had to figure out how to travel for weeks at a time for his job while giving us as normal of a childhood as possible. And then when my brother Ford died, I don't think his heart ever recovered."

I can see his eyes jolt as everything starts to connect for him. "Wait. Ford? As in *the* Ford Marsden drafted from UCLA? The wonder boy who used to play with Cameron and Penski?" he asks, sounding more shocked with each word.

I nod, my smile bittersweet. "He didn't want any show of favoritism because he was Doc's son, so during college and the MLB draft, he decided to use my grandmother's maiden name."

"I remember when he collapsed on the mound." The dreamlike quality reflects how I feel about it still today. Like I wish the whole thing were a dream instead of the nightmare it is.

"Hypertrophic cardiomyopathy." I murmur the term I'd never heard before I received the hysterical phone call that afternoon. "A massive heart attack from a condition he never even knew he had."

"All of us players had always thought we were invincible. We ran every day, ate healthy, were in top physical form, and then that happened to him. It freaked a lot of us out for a while. Like, if it could happen to him, then . . ."

"It could happen to you. Yeah, I know. I think I've had my heart checked every which way possible to make sure I don't have the same condition." I nod, the nagging worry just something I live with. "And obviously, my dad was checked too . . . but his situation is a different issue all together . . . and now it's going to take him from me, too."

Easton reaches out and pulls me into him. And this time, I let him. I accept the warmth and comfort and reassurance of his arms around me. I listen to the beat of his heart and memorize the feel of his skin beneath my cheek as I nuzzle his neck.

"When Ford died, it broke my dad. He was his pride and joy. He was the light in our house, the one we looked to for our laughter. And then, like that, he was gone. I was left to try and pick up the pieces and fill the holes that seemed to surround us constantly. So, I changed my major in school. I'd always been interested in following in my dad's footsteps, but my dad wouldn't let me. He told me I had to go take the world by storm and do my own thing. But when Ford died, it was like he wanted to keep me close to make sure I was okay, and so he finally agreed to let me learn the trade. Once I was given the chance, I threw myself into everything about it to make him proud. To try and make him happy."

"He's proud of you, Scout. I have no doubt about that," he murmurs into the crown of my head, the heat of his breath hitting my hair.

"Pride doesn't mend a broken heart, though." I speak my thoughts out loud and am grateful that he doesn't refute them, doesn't disagree with my opinion, no matter how irrational it may seem. "So that's why I'm here in Austin. Securing the last job for him, so he can know he fulfilled the one career goal he still had remaining."

"That's honorable and selfless."

"I'm terrified that I'm going to let him down."

"You won't," he murmurs. "Not if I have anything to do with it."

I snuggle further into him, appreciative of the reassurance, but more than aware that the front office has the final say. Not him.

"Is there anything else we need to lay on the line before we get up from our naked ball-field confessional?" I tease. His chest vibrates against mine with his laughter, but when he doesn't say anything, I'm suddenly paranoid. "What is it? What else do you need to tell me?" When I try to lean back and look into his eyes, he just holds me still.

"For a girl who spooks easily, you sure ask a lot of questions. Didn't anyone ever tell you to not ask questions you can't handle the answers to?"

"Easton." His name is a playful warning, but my pulse quickens with his comment. "Please tell me you don't have a wife in every city, or I'm going to be royally pissed."

"Hardly."

"Then what?" Impatience rings in my tone as my body comes to life with the feeling of his naked body and dick slowly hardening against me. I try to tickle him to get an answer. We wiggle and squirm away from each other, but he has the upper hand in the strength department.

"Let's just say, you're not yet ready to hear what I have to say," he laughs out amid my tickle torture, but the simple statement knocks all the fight out of me as my mind races with possibilities. Good possibilities, ones I never dared to think could even be possible but which flicker and fade through my mind nonetheless.

And he uses my momentary lapse in attention to scoot away from me. I scramble on all fours to go after him.

"I know how to make you talk, Wylder." My voice is full of suggestion, and my body is renewed with desire as I crawl slowly toward him.

"Naked batting practice?"

It's sad that there's hope in his voice when he says it, but I burst out in laughter. And it feels good to laugh after everything tonight—my trip to visit my brother at the cemetery, the tension with Santiago, our fight, my confession, him making me feel, the last hour we spent talking—that I welcome the humor.

"Mmmm," I murmur with a raise of my brows. "That's not exactly the bat and balls I was thinking about using right now."

"They weren't?" He fights his grin but lets his eyes roam over my breasts as I crawl over his legs so my face is perfectly poised above his cock.

"Nope. Besides, I'm more fixated on making you talk than proving I can swing a decent stick."

Easton shifts his hips beneath me. "Fixate away."

It's my turn to give him a lightning quick grin as I slowly dip my head and take him into my mouth and all the way to the back of my throat.

His groan fills the room as his taste assaults my senses in the most intoxicating of ways.

"Good God, woman. You're going to be the death of me."

CHAPTER TWENTY-FOUR

Easton

She's gorgeous.

An absolute mess of gorgeous chaos with her hair fanned around her, pillow creases in her cheeks, a soft smile on her lips, and a well of emotion in her eyes.

God. Damn.

Chaos has never looked so damn inviting.

I won the battle last night, but I know there's a war still ahead of me. She's been left, is going to be left again, and there's nothing I can do to protect her from it.

But it all makes sense now. Her not wanting me to get too close. Her closing herself off. Trust being a hard thing and fear being a reality.

Her fears are valid. I get them but don't understand them. And yet I need to figure out how to make her not feel them when she thinks of me.

Last night was the first step in a long journey, but fuck if I don't want to take it with her.

Look at her. She's fiery. Beautiful. Funny. Intelligent. But more than all of that, she gets me—my thoughts and my love/hate relationship with this game. She gets this career I have, which to most others is exciting but disruptive as hell to relationships.

I reach out a hand and wipe a strand of hair from her face as those lips of hers spread into a sleepy smile and she snuggles a little deeper into the covers.

What in the hell am I letting myself fall into?

If she doesn't scare the hell out of you, East, then she's not worth the trouble.

And last night she scared the hell out of me. When I thought she'd moved on. When I thought she'd played me. When I thought I'd lost her.

"Morning." Her eyes light up at the sound of my voice, and I'm a fucking goner.

Toast.

"Morning," she murmurs, in a rasp of a voice that feels like fingernails scraping ever so gently over the underside of my balls. It makes me want. She makes me want, when I should be so damn exhausted after last night that even my dick should be fast asleep.

"Just because my cleats will hit the dirt again, doesn't mean I'll move on from the people in my life." The words are a truth she needs to hear the morning after confessing her secrets, her fears, to help reassure her that I heard her and I'm still not going anywhere. I run my hand down the line of her torso, rest it on her hip, and squeeze it for emphasis. "You're not one who can easily be forgotten, Scout Dalton."

Her eyes cloud with emotion, but it's her shaky inhale that catches my attention. "Uh-uh. I'm not going to let you do it, Scout. I see that look in your eye. After last night . . . you don't get to spook anymore. I know why you're scared. I get it. But you don't get to shut down, you don't get to shut me out. Talk to me. Tell me what's going on in that beautifully, scared mind of yours."

"You can't control our lives, Easton. I may not get the contract with the team. You could get traded. There are no guarantees." Her voice is soft, the emotion I couldn't read is obviously fear.

"You're right, I can't. But it's the possibility that should keep you going, not the guarantees. And I can tell you this—you're going to get the contract. I'll do whatever it takes to get back on that field so Cory sees you got your job done, and I'll put in every single good word I have for you to get the job." She shakes her head, starts to refute, but I just lift my finger to her lips to quiet her down. "And as for being traded, that's always been my biggest fear because of my mom. So, I hear your spooked-ness, Scout, but I'm matching your bet, so what else are you going to throw at me that I can debunk."

Our eyes hold, and I'm shocked to shit when she reaches out, wraps her arms around me, and snuggles into me. The woman who keeps pushing me away has finally pulled me in. And fuck does it feel good.

The only thing that rivals the feeling is her body snuggled up against mine.

My dick stirs to life—how can it not—and every little move she makes, combined with the scent of her shampoo in my nose, makes me want to have her all over again.

"I need to get to work," I groan, hating my own lips for even speaking it.

"I hear you have a mean, wretched trainer who likes to crack the whip." Her lips move against my neck, their heat only making the urge to bury my dick into her tight, addictive pussy that much more enticing.

"You have no idea," I murmur, and press a kiss to the crown of her head as my hands slide down to the curve of her ass, pulling her thigh up and over my hip to open her up for me. "She's demanding."

"And manipulative," she chuckles, and then sighs as my fingers touch ever so softly over that perfect, pink flesh between her thighs.

"Mmmm." Fuck. She's already wet for me. I can feel it and I haven't even slipped my fingers in yet.

"Or we could go bat another round downstairs." She spreads her legs farther, granting me access as my fingers slide inside.

Her hands tense on my shoulders. Her teeth nip into my collarbone.

I chuckle at her comment. "It's not the same. It will never be the same again," I murmur as her breath hitches.

"What won't?" I love how she's trying to act unaffected, but when my fingertips hit that little rough patch inside of her slick, wet pussy and her nails dig in reflexively, I know I've got her.

"Every time I set my helmet in that net shelf, it'll be my face between your thighs I think about." Rub, stroke, slide. Her moan fills my ears. The heat of it sears my skin. "Every time I stand at the plate to take a swing, it'll be you I picture. Naked. Swinging the stick like you own it and hitting that line drive back at me."

"East." A sigh of pleasure. My thumb to her clit. Her coming all over my hand.

"And then your little happy dance as you jogged around the bases." Tits bouncing, hair down her back, laugh filling the gray space.

I angle my body, open her wider, and line the head of my dick up right where I want it.

"No, it will never be the same."

I push into her. Become consumed by her.

Her feel.

Her touch.

Her sounds.

And I'm well aware that when I speak the last words, when her hands tense on my back and her mouth finds the curve of my neck, I'm not just speaking about my field downstairs.

I'm talking about me.

CHAPTER TWENTY-FIVE

Easton

"**L**ooking great, Easton. I don't see anything in the X-ray or otherwise that would impede your recovery any further."

If I could kiss my doctor, right now, I would.

"Whew." I blow out a sigh of relief. "That's good to hear, because it's getting stronger every day."

"Still stiff?"

"Less and less each day."

"I don't feel the click anymore when I move it. I don't feel any resistance either. Your surgeon must have done a wonderful job, if I do say so myself." He winks at me and chuckles.

"No complaints here."

"I'll file my report with Cory. Let him know I see no reason why you shouldn't be able to move to the active roster by the end of the month."

"Music to my ears."

"It's up to your PT though. He has the final say, since he's the one working with you, day-in and day-out. Does the club still have you working with Doc?"

I smile automatically. "I'm working with Scout Dalton." Images flash through my mind of her earlier. At least I know I was right about the kitchen counter theory.

"I hear she really knows her stuff."

"Seems to." I meet his eyes. Hope he doesn't see that I'm talking about a helluva lot more than just her job.

"Haven't heard much from Doc though, lately. Rumor is he's planning on retiring."

"I've heard the same," I murmur as I stand and pull my shirt back over my head. I think of Scout yesterday, and the tears she tried to hide when she hung up the phone with him. She won't talk about it, and I won't push her. That's her dad. It's her frustration over wanting to be with him and him being a stubborn cuss and telling her to finish the job first.

To get me back on the field first.

Fathers and their unexplained actions.

I shake Dr. Kimble's hand and say good-bye.

Let's hope he's right. That my arm should be good to go. While the X-rays may be clean, sometimes it's the things you can't see that are waiting to bring you down when you least expect it.

I'm on fucking cloud nine.

Dr. Kimble gave me his clearance.

The Literacy Project just got approval for a huge grant that's going to help us expand our reach to more inner-city schools.

Scout and I practiced throwing down to second base yesterday and not a single fucking thing hurt.

Then, of course, Scout rewarded me for my progress. Surprised me with a little takeout on a picnic blanket on the private field, gave me a full body massage to work out any muscles that may be tight, and then let me work *her* out.

And Christ did we work out.

So, I add a few extra reps in while I'm down here putting my time in and take advantage of all the things that are falling in line for me.

"You should be activated by the end of the month."

Kimble's words echo in my head as I scrub a towel over my face and head toward the locker room.

Three weeks.

Looks like my stint in hell—the disabled list—might be coming to an end.

"I thought you'd already put your time in?" Miguel says as he passes me in the tunnel, an odd expression on his face that I chalk up to surprise.

"Yeah. I did. But Mathers told me I could come in and catch bullpen if I want to warm the pitchers up and help get my reflexes up to speed."

"*Nice.* That close, huh?"

"I want back on the field so bad I can taste it. I might even give up sex at this point." He looks at me like I'm crazy and we both laugh. "Nah. I'll never give that up." I laugh as we pass each other.

"Hey, Wylder?"

"Yeah?" I turn around to face him. He's standing in the middle of the tunnel, the daylight from the field at his back as he just stares at me.

"Nah. Nothing. We'll be glad to have you back."

"Thanks. Me, too."

Pumped to be getting my gear on and be part of the game in some way, I head into the locker room, ready to shower and check my phone to see if Scout's going to swing by.

"Hey." I lift my chin in greeting as I pass Drew. He startles when he sees me and flicks a glance over to J.P. across the locker room, a concerned look on his face when he meets my gaze again.

What the fuck is going on?

Is this the prank I've been waiting for? Are they finally going to man up and get me back for that stunt in Cleveland? Bring it on, boys.

But when I meet J.P.'s eyes and he glances across the room, I start to doubt it. I follow his line of sight and see a group of guys, some with towels wrapped around their hips, others with just their jock on, some in sliders and their jersey shirt.

Something's up.

Gonzo's locker is empty and the placard with his name is gone. Poor kid. He had a good run but has probably been sent back to Triple-A. Dr. Kimble was quick with filing his report if they already sent him back.

But then who's behind the plate for now?

Just as the thought crosses my mind, I notice the bag on the floor in front of the locker, about the same time the entire room falls silent. Fucking bad juju. I can feel it instantly but have no clue why . . . until a man strolls through the center of the square room. His head is down, he's using one white towel to shake the water out of his hair, and another towel is around his waist.

But I'd know that tattoo on his bicep from anywhere.

And as if he can sense the whole locker room is staring at him, he lowers the towel from his head and looks up and straight into my eyes.

It's not a prank.

Santiago.

Mother. Fucker.

"Tell me it's not fucking true, Finn," I grit the words out.

I keep my head down, the bill of my hat pulled low over my face as I weave my way against the flow of the crowd milling around the ballpark, here to catch batting practice.

I don't know where I'm going, but I know I need to walk. Run. Fucking punch something. Anything to abate the rage controlling me right now.

"I'm trying to get answers."

"That's not fucking good enough."

"It's fucking bullshit is what it is," he sneers, and thank fuck for that because I need him to be just as livid as I am. He was about to be fired if he wasn't.

"Cory wasn't there. The front office was the first place I went for answers." *Neither was my dad.* "And no one had any answers for me other than 'Cory will be back late tonight.'"

"It's probably best you didn't talk to him right now."

"He's a chickenshit fucker to make the trade and not give me a heads-up."

"I'm in agreement with you there."

"They know the history here. He's the bastard who took me out of their starting roster, and then they go and sign the fucker?"

"I know, Easton. It's not making sense." I'm so angry I start to walk one way, and then start back the other way, not sure where I'm going, what to do now, or what to do next. "How bad was it?"

My laugh fills the connection but sounds anything but humorous. "I didn't land a punch, if that's what you're asking. Not from a lack of trying, though." I scrub a hand over my face, my feet eating up the squares of the sidewalk like they're endless. "Tino and Drew were on me before I could throw it. The other guys grabbed him. It was a clusterfuck."

"I've got calls in. I'm hearing it was Gonzo and two other Triple-A players plus Maddox."

"Maddox? They traded fucking Maddox?" My head spins at the news.

"He had a big salary and isn't having that great of a year."

"Fucking Cory."

"This is what he's known for, playing moneyball—he comes in, cleans up, tightens budgets, and he wins pennants."

"We win them. *Not him.*" I pinch the bridge of my nose, trying to process how the hell Santiago is an Ace. "Please tell me I'm ironclad."

"With that book of a contract we negotiated, you're solid."

"Finn . . ." I sigh as I cross the street and cut right, far enough from the stadium to breathe a bit freer, where I can talk a little less guarded, but am conscious that I'm still in the city I play for.

"I don't know," he murmurs, answering my unspoken question: why trade for another catcher when I'm getting my clearance soon? "He's a damn good left fielder, too. Circe's been weak this year. Maybe they're thinking of shifting him there when you come back. This is a business, East. You know that."

"Bad juju, man."

"Fucking juju," he mutters. "Just tell me you can handle being in the same clubhouse as him and that I'm not going to get a call to come bail you out."

"I'm not making shit for promises."

"Good to know and glad to hear it. I'll text you when I hear something."

I look at the blank screen on my phone for a minute, wanting to call my dad but at the same time not wanting to. And when I look up, I realize where my feet took me.

Scout.

I stare at the front of her little townhome for who knows how long, trying to make sense of the trade and the club where I've devoted my career.

And all I feel is defeat. I've busted my ass for months to get back, and just as I get there, my team trades my enemy to my team? To play my position?

I should go have a few drinks.

I should turn around, head back toward the stadium, find a dark hole-in-the-wall bar and drink myself into oblivion while I watch the game. While I watch Santiago in my position. In my team uniform.

Fuck me.

I should leave Scout out of this. I'm not at my best, not what she needs to deal with.

I look around. Spot a bar across the way and down a little bit to the left.

Drink.

Scout.

Drink.

Scout.

I need both.

CHAPTER TWENTY-SIX

Scout

"Easton? *Where have you been*? I've been trying to get ahold of you for the past hour!"

Relief courses through me at the sight of him standing in my doorway, still in his practice uniform, almost as if he heard the news I found out about a little bit ago and walked right off the field. He's a little bleary eyed and a lot unsteady on his feet but it's his face that etches itself into my mind—part lost little boy, part defiant teenager, and a whole lot of pissed-off man.

"I needed a drink. I needed you first, but figured I should have a drink first." He half slurs, half laughs and shakes his head. "I'm not making sense. Welcome to the motto of my day: nothing makes sense."

"Come on. Come in." I grab onto him, pull him inside, and lead him by the hand over to the couch. "I flipped on the TV to catch the game, and he was an Ace. I've been out of my mind trying to get ahold of you."

He plops on the couch but doesn't say a single word as I prattle on, trying to ease the anxiety I've had for the past hour and a half over whether he was okay.

"Talk to me. Please," I beg as I look down at where he's sitting in front of me. I need to know what to do to help him.

The silence stretches except for the low hum of the announcers' voices in the background of the game, and I debate whether or not I should turn it off. His discord is more than obvious, magnified by the drink or ten he's most likely had, and I feel helpless standing here staring at him while he's staring at his hands clasped in between his legs.

"I'm going to get you some water," I say, and just as I take a step, Easton takes me by surprise, grabbing me by the waist and pulling me into him so that his arms wrap around my hips, and he rests his forehead against my belly, his hat falling backward off his head.

My heart breaks for him, for what he must be thinking, because I've been thinking the same. So I do the only thing I can: I thread my fingers through his hair and just let him hold on to me and take whatever it is he needs from me.

Half an inning expires while we stay like this and I try to figure out what it is I can say to make it better. Then I laugh at how stupid that sounds. So I say the next best thing I can think of.

"I talked to Dr. Kimble today. We'll give Santiago three weeks to rent that spot behind your plate and show his skills. Then you'll be back, and when you step on the field, the difference in your skill level will be so obvious, everyone will realize how much they missed you."

He chuckles. The heat of it hits my belly as his fingers tense and flex against my hips before he slowly leans against the back of the couch. His hands pull on my hips and guide me to straddle him. I follow his lead, my eyes steadfast on his, waiting for him to look up so I can get a glimpse of what he's thinking.

He doesn't.

Instead, he rests his head back and closes his eyes; his thumbs, now resting on the sides of my hips, rub circles against the denim of my jeans. "I turned my phone off. Sorry I didn't pick up, but I thought it might be best to not talk to anyone for a bit."

I nod my head, and then realize he can't see it. "Understandably. I'm sure your dad is worried about you. Did you talk to him at all?" He doesn't reply, just gives a half-hearted shrug that doesn't give me any insight.

"You know what gets me?" he asks with an audible skepticism I can understand. "What did I ever do to him? Get a better contract with a better team? There are a hundred guys out there who have better contracts . . . so why pick me to fuck with? Is it just because I'm the privileged legacy son, so he doesn't think I deserve it? Is it because he thinks I was born with a silver spoon in my mouth and a gold bat in my hand when he had to struggle? Doesn't he get that it wasn't all fucking cherries being Cal Wylder's son? That I'd give my eye-teeth to have one moment of my baseball career that wasn't over-shadowed by the fact that I better perform as expected from the Iron Giant's son?"

He lifts his eyes and looks at me for the first time, weary and a little lost.

"You know what's even more fucked up? You know what I thought about as I sat in the bar across the street?"

"What?" I ask gently.

"I love this game, Scout. I told you the other day that I played because of my dad, and fuck yes, I do . . . but I also play because I *love* this game. Baseball is so much more than just a game to me. It's sights and sounds and smells—the roar of the crowd when you crank a home run, the tack of the pine tar on your bat, the smell of the popcorn in the air, the pop a glove makes on a screaming fastball, the sting of a broken bat vibrating through your fingers and up your forearm, the awe on the little boy's face standing above the dugout when you toss him the game ball as you jog off the field . . . Shit, Scout. I could go on forever, but that is the soundtrack, the movie, the everything of my life. *It is my life.* How stupid was I that it took Santiago showing up to reaffirm the love I have for something that's been a part of me before I was even born?"

There are tears in my eyes that I don't even bother to blink away. The reverence in his voice speaks louder than all the things he just said, and they were pretty damn loud.

I lean forward, bringing my hands to frame his cheeks, and press a tender kiss to his lips before resting my forehead against his.

"I promise you that we'll have you back in top form. You're already there—we just need to work your arm up to playing a full game."

He nods, his breath hot against my lips, and the scrape of his stubble rough against my fingertips.

"Santiago being on the team means nothing. Maybe there was an old trade that linked to this one. The 'a player to be named later' kind. Maybe they brought him on to spur your ass into gear."

"Or maybe Cory's an asshole and just wanted to fuck me over."

I know that's the alcohol talking, but he still has a point. "I get why you feel that way, but at the end of the day, you're Easton Wylder. The Aces' franchise player. You're not going anywhere, so why cause trouble just to add strife. There has to be a valid reason."

"And I'm sure if I listen to my thirty messages, there will be, but right now I don't care. Right now, I just want to feel sorry for myself, have another drink, sit here with you, and figure out how exactly I'm going to see that fucker every goddamn day and not break his nose."

I chuckle and press my lips to his before shifting and nuzzling my forehead against the side of his neck. "Ignore him."

"Easier said than done."

"True, but the best way to get back at him is to come back and blow him out of the water. The assumption is that you're injured and won't be one hundred percent. Won't it be the ultimate 'fuck you' to be just the opposite?"

"The mother fucker deserves it."

"He does."

"Do you really think I can get there?"

The cautious hope in his voice digs its claws into my heart and doesn't let go. "I know you can."

"There are no guarantees."

"You're right, there are no guarantees," I repeat his words back to him, "but it's the possibility that should keep you going."

When the guys call him after the game and ask him to meet up for drinks, I encourage him to go. He needs their camaraderie right now. He needs their reassurance that they have his back.

And I need time to myself.

To think.

To process.

To reread the email that Sally forwarded, explaining how they've pulled my dad's name from the transplant list.

It's not like I didn't expect this. A new heart was out of the question. His body is too frail, his immune system too weak to accept a foreign organ.

But while his name was on the donor list, there was a false sense of hope.

And now there's not.

My heart just needs more time to accept what my mind already knows.

But there will never be enough time to accept this.

CHAPTER TWENTY-SEVEN

Scout

My feet stop the second I spot Easton.

The moms pushing strollers have to swerve around me and a little boy bumps against me, but I stand still, trying to comprehend how the mere sight of him eases the stress of my day.

He's lying on a slope covered in grass beyond the left field fence, his legs are crossed at the ankles, his hands are braced behind him, and an Aces baseball hat sits low over his brow. His attention is focused on the Little League game playing in front of him where little boys about five or six years old are trying their hardest to master his game.

The boys are adorable and the man observing from his incognito spot in the outfield even more so, and yet I can tell something is bothering him. He's never missed a training session like he did this afternoon, and the simple text he sent me offered no explanation.

I should leave. The fact that he didn't reply to any of my texts should be a big enough indicator that he wants to be left alone and me being here is anything but leaving him alone.

But I don't move. Can't. And I'm not blind to the fact that my inability to walk away stems from so much more than wanting to know why he bailed on his workout today. The kind of *so much more* that often wakes me up in the early morning hours and challenges me to pull up a thought that doesn't involve Easton in some way, shape, or form, all the while being lulled back to sleep by the even rhythm of his breathing beside me.

The kind of *so much more* that has me standing in the middle of some recreational park a few blocks away from the stadium questioning why I chased after a man when normally I'm the one running the other way.

But there's something about seeing him in this element, watching the game he loves in its purest form that tugs on my heartstrings and has me making my way over to him.

"You just can't stay away from the game, can you?"

"Seems like it," he muses without so much as a look my way as I take a seat on the grass beside him.

We sit in silence as the inning plays out and watch the extremely patient dads trying to coach their sons on how to swing the bat or field a ground ball. I can't help but wonder what Easton's thinking about. Would he trade his experiences for ones like this? Ones where the game was about having fun and absent of the pressure that came with realizing you're expected to live up to the standard of play your father has set? Is that why he's here?

Another inning ends. Another round of high fives is handed out as the teams enter or leave their respective dugouts. And I'm still in the dark about what's going on with the man beside me.

"You blew me off today," I say after a bit.

He nods. "I did."

"Everything okay with your mom?" I ask, fishing for a connection with him when he feels so far away right now.

"Yep."

"Just needed to get some fresh air?" I ask, scrambling for anything to keep him talking.

"Yep."

"Care to elaborate?"

"Nope," he says and then hangs his head for a beat before scrubbing his hand over his jaw. When he lifts his head up, he glances at me momentarily, expression guarded, before he looks back to the game, but I can see he's upset now. It's in the sag of his shoulders. The defeat in his posture. The stress etched in the lines on his handsome face.

"You want me to leave?" *Please say no.*

"Nope."

My sigh of relief is audible. All I want to do right now is rest my head on his shoulder, make a connection with him somehow, but know I can't because of the ever-prying eyes of the public. It only takes one person to recognize the man in the outfield is Easton and take a picture with their phone and . . .

"Manny?" he asks pulling me from my thoughts with his guess on how I knew where he was.

"Yep," I say, taking a page out of his book of one-word responses and earn a soft chuckle from him.

"My first season with the Aces was rough," he begins to explain. "I had a few games that really tested me and messed with my head. Without confidence, skill can only take you so far in this game, and my confidence was shot. I was this huge prospect surrounded by all of this hype and I wasn't delivering. Teammates and coaches were throwing advice my way but all I heard was white noise. After one particularly shitty game, Manny walked into the locker room and told me to follow him. I thought he was crazy. It was almost midnight and here I am traipsing after him through the streets of the city until we ended up here. He made me sit in the middle of the empty field and told me to tell him what I remembered about playing as a kid."

"He brought the fun back," I murmur. I can picture the two of them in the darkness out here and it brings a smile to my lips.

"He did. He made me remember all those first moments when I

finally fell in love with the game. And then he told me to come back the next day at ten o'clock. I did." He smiles and shakes his head at the memory. "There was a T-ball game starting. The kids were running to the wrong bases, swinging the bat backwards, and playing with the weeds in the outfield. It sounds stupid, but watching those little guys drowned out the white noise for a bit."

"It is oddly relaxing," I admit.

"It is," he murmurs, "and ever since that night, this is where I find myself when I need to clear my head."

"It's a good place."

"It is."

Easton falls silent again, while I replay the story in my mind and wonder what he's trying to clear from his head today.

Another inning passes. The red team scores a run, and Easton belts out a loud whistle in congratulations.

If they only knew the random bystander with the Aces hat on sitting in the outfield was Easton Wylder.

"I just couldn't do it today," Easton says unexpectedly.

"Do what?"

"Be in the same space as that fucker. The locker room. The field. The gym. He's everywhere. I'm sick of having the guys babysit me. I'm sick of not being able to walk in my own clubhouse without wanting to throw a punch every time I hear his voice." He pauses but his frustration continues to resonate. "I'm sorry for bailing on you, but I just couldn't do it today."

There's nothing I can say to make him feel better. Honestly, I don't know how he's occupied the same space as Santiago for this long without a serious fight breaking out between them.

So, I don't say anything.

Instead I move my hand to rest in the grass beside his and then hook my pinky around his. He looks over to me, his eyes a well of unexpressed emotion, but when he tightens his pinky around mine, it's all I need to know that my silent show of support and little bit of affection is enough for now.

So with the sun slowly moving toward the horizon, we sit and watch the rest of a Little League game while trying to remember what life was like as kids. Back when my dad wasn't sick and his shoulder wasn't injured. Back when there were no contracts to abide by and we could just be a girl and a boy sitting on a grassy slope enjoying the warm Texas evening together.

We don't feel the need to talk just to fill the silence.

Our pinkies are linked.

And the simple connection is all we need right now to reassure each other that we'll get through this.

CHAPTER TWENTY-EIGHT

Easton

"**S**hit. Maybe I need to get a shoulder injury, if that's how you come back and swing the stick."

The next pitch comes. I swing and connect. The crack of the ball against the bat is the most satisfying sound in the world. And even better, there's still no pain. No pinch. *Just like new*.

"He's the only lucky fucker who could pull it off, though."

"Bunch of fucking cackling women. Leave the poor man alone. He needs to reacquaint himself with his balls right now."

I laugh as I take a swing and miss the fat pitch Coach Walton lobs from the mound. All three guys say, "whiff," in unison.

I hold a batting-gloved middle finger up to J.P., Tino, and Drew standing behind the portable backstop as I take my hacks. The Santiago Brigade. Following me around like the three musketeers anytime I hit the field at the same time as Santiago.

They're trying to keep my nose clean and my temper at bay. It doesn't look too good when the unofficial team captain goes fist-fucking his replacement's face. But shit, how satisfying would that be since the asshole seems determined to annoy me every chance he gets.

Another pitch. I channel my anger at Santiago, my drive to return, my need to prove to Scout that I'm good to go.

And when I hit the next pitch—a line drive that goes right through the five-point-five hole between third base and shortstop—I know I'm back.

"What do you think she's telling Walton out there?" Drew chimes in, trying to get in my head as I watch Scout lean in and say something in Walton's ear. He nods.

"Oh, Walton, you handsome devil. If you hit that pain in the ass Wylder in the nuts, you can take me out to dinner tonight," Tino says in a high-pitched voice. I step out of the box, my hand up to hold the pitch.

"Fuck you, Tino," I laugh as both Walton and Scout look to me from the mound, wondering what the hell is going on.

"It's just the asshole brigade," I shout to them and wave for them to pitch.

Used to our antics, Walton winds up, throws the pitch, and when I let loose on my swing, the crack echoes in my ears as I watch it clear the wall into the stands in left field.

Hell yeah, I'm back.

"Looking good out there, Hot Shot," Scout says as I walk into the training room.

"Felt damn good." I roll my shoulders and smile at her.

"I can tell," she laughs. "You got your swagger back."

"My swagger?"

"Yep. That cocky little smirk you used to get before you stepped into the batter's box was there today. It's the first time I've seen it since I started training you."

"I don't get a cocky little smirk when I step in the box," I say with a chuckle as I slide onto the table. *Do I?* She steps up behind me to work the muscles in my shoulder as I try to think of my batting routine and smiling is not something I do.

"Yes, you do. It says, you better bring your best stuff, Mr. Pitcher, or I'm gonna take you downtown," she murmurs. And there's no way I should find what she says sexy, but the fact that she can talk baseball terms while her fingers slide over my shoulder is definitely a turn-on. It doesn't matter how many times she touches me—here in a rub down or at home in my bed—because every fucking time she does just makes me want her more.

It doesn't hurt that that murmur of hers reminds me of when she climbs on top of me, straddles my thighs, leans forward, and says in my ear to *get ready* before she takes my cock for a ride.

"You're all kinds of swagger and arrogant when you play. It kind of turns me on," she says under her breath, but I catch every damn word.

"You know what I like more than hearing you say that?" I reply with a groan as she digs her knuckles into the knot in my shoulder.

"My magic hands?" she laughs.

"Well, those, too, and that's not the only thing on you that's magical . . . but I like knowing that before you were my trainer, you were watching me. That you knew I had a cocky little smile."

The hitch in her movement tells me she didn't realize she just gave that little fact away. "You also wiggle your ass two times."

"I do not," I deny, but know damn well that I do. It's unintentional but always there.

"Yes. You do. Everyone knows your routine."

"Oh please." I roll my eyes, even though she can't see it.

"I'm serious. Everyone stops and watches you when you walk to the plate, Wylder. They can't wait to see what you're going to do next. The lightning in the bottle you create. You're just that kind of player."

"*The player*," I murmur more to myself than her, remembering that first week we worked together.

"We've come a long way since then," she says, knowing where my thoughts have gone.

And yes, we have. I laugh, though, playing it off, because just like she gets spooked easily, I am, too. This has been too easy, how we've fallen into sync with each other, and I don't want to jinx it.

Don't want any bad juju fucking this up.

I tilt my head back so I can look at her. "I'm still waiting for that lap dance, Kitty."

"If you play your cards right," she murmurs under her breath, "you just might get one tonight."

Hot damn.

"You looked good out there today, East."

I glance back to the doorway of the press box where my dad stands, arms braced on both sides of the doorjamb with a proud smile on his face.

He's looking old. It's my first thought when I see him. The lines in his face are deeper, his eyes serious, his trademark cheer muted.

"Thank you. It felt good." I angle my head and study him closer.

"You looked stronger than I've seen you. The time you've put into your rehab has paid off." I wait for the 'but' from him—in classic Cal Wylder backhanded compliment fashion—but it doesn't come. He just stands there for a beat, shoulders square, with pride on his face. "I'm proud of you and how you've handled everything."

The implication behind *everything* is there, and I smile softly and nod my head, knowing he went to bat for me against Cory, even though I never asked him to and knew nothing about it until after the fact. The Iron Giant, Cal Wylder, tried to throw his weight around and let it be known that you don't run a front office or win a pennant by making a trade that divides a team when they're mid-season.

Luckily Manny had let me know about the conversation he'd overheard between Cory and my dad, or I would've never known. To say it shocked the shit out of me is an understatement. The fact my dad hasn't said a word about it to me even more so.

But knowing he tried without wanting glory for it makes it mean that much more.

"Thanks. Someone once taught me I can only do my job to prove them wrong."

His smile is slow to spread from his lips to his eyes—the sadness not fading completely—as he nods his head when he hears his own words repeated back to him.

"You want to join us for a bit, Mr. Wylder?" Bruce, the Aces' on-air sports announcer asks him, pulling me back to what I'm about to do. An on-air, pregame chat with the team's broadcast network to update the fans on my progress, how I'm feeling, and when they can expect me to return. I wait for my dad's answer, already scooting my seat over as I adjust my headset because he's never been one to turn down talking about baseball.

"No, thank you. Easton, here, has the team covered. The fans want to hear about him, not me. I'm old news." He winks with a soft smile before meeting my eyes and nodding to me.

"Maybe another time, then."

"Maybe," my dad says before turning and walking out of the press box, leaving me to look after him and worry why he seems so subdued.

"Okay, let's get started, Easton. Here is the list of questions in case you want to prep for them ahead of time."

"Nah, I'm good." I don't even glance at the sheet of paper he hands me. "There's nothing you're going to ask me that I can't answer on the fly."

"Even about Santiago?"

I look over to him, and his eyes tell me that he's behind me and my displeasure with the team's bullshit move.

"Let's leave Santiago off the table," I joke. "This is a PG show after all."

He laughs, shakes his head, and pats my back. "You could always knock him out and leave him on the floor if it's easier."

"I like the way you think, Bruce."

"Thought you might. You ready?" I nod. "We're good to go in five, four, three, two, one."

Chapter Twenty-Nine

Scout

"Goddammit, Wylder!" The voice rings out and then a few more curse words, followed by a riot of laughter rumbling through the clubhouse.

I peek out of my training room, and once I see that all of the guys are covered and decent, I head out to see what's going on.

"Where is that asshole?" I think it's Tino's voice, I'm not sure though because the players are all standing together and blocking my view of what's going on.

"That's one way to sparkle and shine on the field, Tino," J.P. says through the laughter that doubles him over.

"Aw man, this shit is *everywhere.*" It's Tino again and the guys around him slowly begin to back away as they laugh and shake their heads. *"It's like I'm fucking Tinker Bell."*

"You always said you were light on your feet, now you just have the fairy dust to prove it," Drew says drawing another round of laughter from the guys.

This time when the crowd parts, I can see what they are all laughing at. Tino is standing at his locker in just his undershirt and sliders on with his baseball cap in his hand, and every inch of him is covered in sparkly blue glitter. From the amount that is concentrated in his hair and down his back, it appears to have been put in his hat so when he put it on his head it fell all over him.

"Tinker Bell Tino," someone chimes in and when Tino looks up to glare at them, he sees me standing there.

I can't help but laugh as he moves toward me, his whole body shimmering and shining under the locker room lights.

"You're a girl," he says.

"Way to state the obvious, Einstein," Drew says earning him a death stare from Tino before he looks back to me.

"Yes, I am," I say fighting the smile on my lips. Now that he's closer, I can see the glitter is that very fine type of powder that's basically impossible to get rid of.

"How do I get this shit off me? The more I wipe it off, the more it sticks." His eyes plead with me, but it's so hard to keep a straight face when I notice even his eyelashes are coated blue.

"Why would you want to wipe it off? I think blue's your color." I bat my eyelashes and feign innocence as the guys hoot and holler in response around me.

"Why you gotta be like that, Scout? Wylder's starting to rub off on you isn't he with his . . ." His voice fades off as he looks down to his hands coated in blue sparkles and does the only thing he can, laugh.

"You can shower, Tino . . . but you're still going to sparkle under the lights for the next few nights, if not weeks," I tease as I turn to head back to my training room.

There's more ribbing as I walk away but there's one comment that rings louder than all others to me. "Wylder's almost back, boys. That much he just proved."

He sure did.

The thought makes me smile more than anything has all day long. Well, since the last time I saw him that is. Because if Easton's pranking the guys again, that means he's getting back in his groove—mentally and physically.

"One scoop of chocolate peanut butter in a cup, please," I say to the girl behind the counter waiting for my selection with her ice cream scooper in hand.

"Make that three scoops." I yelp at the sound of Easton's voice and before I can turn around, his hands slide around my waist and pull me back against him. "Hi." His breath is hot against my ear, and after a long day it takes everything I have not to sink against him and just close my eyes.

"Hi." My smile is automatic when I turn to face him and take a step back, ever conscious of being noticed together in public. I take him in and wonder if there will ever be a time that I look at him and don't feel that flutter in my belly. "Blue glitter, huh?"

His lopsided grin turns full-blown, eyes light up with mischief, and he gives a little boy shrug in his grown man's body. "Peanut butter and chocolate, huh?"

I nod. "Yep."

"Treating yourself for anything in particular?"

My day flashes through my mind. The update from Sally on my dad. My double training session with Easton. The frantic call from my dad's long time client, the Red Sox, asking me to drop everything and fly there to evaluate their ace pitcher who hurt his arm last night. My refusal and then agreement to hop on a video conference call so I could help develop a regimen for them to follow. Then there was the report I had to put the finishing touches on for Cory—my proposal for how I would handle the players' day to day routine if I were to get the Aces' long-term contract.

"Yeah. I survived." My smile is soft when I respond. "It's been a day."

"That bad, huh?" He asks as he steps forward to pay for the ice cream despite my protests.

"Not bad, just crazy."

"I like that you treat yourself to ice cream," he says with a smile as we sit across from each other in the small seating area.

"I like that you chose glitter to showcase Tino's talents under the lights tonight." I raise my eyebrows and take a bite of the heavenly ice cream.

"If you're trying to get me to admit I did something today," he says as his shoe taps mine beneath the table, "then you're barking up the wrong tree. The first rule about pranks in the clubhouse is that there are no pranks in the clubhouse."

"Oh, please." I laugh and roll my eyes. "Well, it was pretty damn funny and the poor guy is going to be scrubbing that off himself for the next few days."

"Good. I'm glad to hear because the Nutella he hid inside my back pockets at the start of the season really sucked ass." My eyes widen as the gasp falls from my lips. "Yeah. It was that bad. I was late getting changed after an interview ran long. I threw on my clothes and hauled ass to the field. First inning, I go to put something in my back pocket and all I feel is this gooey stuff. So now I'm behind the plate with a crowd at my back and something that's the color of crap on my fingers. Where exactly was I supposed to wipe it? On my pants? That would be a great story for the announcers to create as they try to explain why Easton Wylder is crouched behind the plate with these mysterious brown smears all over his pants that appeared out of nowhere from one pitch to the next."

I laugh so hard my eyes tear up because between the disdain in his voice and the image he's painted in my head, I can see it all perfectly. And he's totally right. "So what did you do?" I ask when I can finally speak through the giggles.

"I rubbed my hands in the dirt to try and cover it up some," he says, the devilish look returning to his eyes again. "So . . . glitter."

"Did you just break the first rule of the clubhouse?" I tease, realizing this was the perfect way for me to end the day. His only response is to take a big spoonful of ice cream and shove it in his mouth so he can't talk. "Whoa. Wait. How did you know I was going to be here?"

"I was taking a walk toward your place to see if you wanted to grab a bite to eat and saw you in here."

"You could have just called, you know?"

"I know, but I figured if I came in person, you'd have a harder time saying no." His smile turns shy and it takes everything I have to not lean across the table and brush a kiss against his lips.

Doesn't he realize he's the only one I say yes to?

CHAPTER THIRTY

Scout

"Will he be ready?"

I startle at Cal's voice beside me, but try to keep my cool, forget the *she's a piece of ass* comment, and turn my attention from where Easton's currently crouched behind the plate in full gear.

"Mr. Wylder." I nod and go to turn my attention back to his son but the look in his eyes—the genuine concern—stops me.

"He's looking good, like his old self, but do you think he's really back to where he was? The top of his game?"

"Are you asking me as his father, or as the club's liaison?" I ask, trying not to sound disrespectful, but at the same time needing to protect Easton.

He narrows his eyes and angles his head as he looks at me, lips opening and then closing a moment before he nods as if he gets what I'm saying. "I deserve that."

"I'm not trying to be disrespectful, sir, nor am I trying to overstep my boundaries. I'm just asking so I know which report to give, because with all the crap that's happened over the past two weeks, I think he needs you to be his dad more than be on the side of his employer."

He nods and then looks back out to where Easton makes a perfect throw down to second base that clearly beats the runner trying to steal. Yes, it's just a practice. Yes, it's his teammates helping him get back in the groove. But his talent is unmistakable. His natural ability is phenomenal.

"I know you must think I'm a pushy asshole. A guy who only thinks about the game, about his own image, and not his son who plays it." He pauses, watches Easton throw to third base with laser perfection. "Easton's the best thing I've ever done. I only want the best for him."

The emotion in his voice stuns me and is such a contradiction to the hard-ass I've seen bits and pieces of.

"What's best for him or what's best for your legacy?"

He whips his head my way, and I know I've overstepped here, but it's Easton, and he deserves to have a relationship with his dad. The kind I have, which I'm going to lose soon.

"For him." He says the words, but I can see he's questioning himself by the furrow in his brow and swallow in his throat. "This is a hard business, Scout. It's not your right to judge me." His tone is stern. The features on his face tell me he's offended.

"You're right. I don't. I overstepped." And I hate that a part of me feels the need to back down to make sure I don't screw up my chance at getting the club's contract, since he's such an integral part of the front office. "But I've grown to care about your son, sir. You don't spend all this time rehabbing someone, training them, celebrating their small victories to get them back where they can play the game they love without caring about their continued success. And I do care about it with Easton. He has more talent in his pinky than most guys would dream of having."

"He's definitely more talented than I ever was," he murmurs, both of our attention pulled back to the field. To the man we both care about, whose swagger is back and unmistakable. We watch him for a few minutes, the silence settling between us.

"Maybe you should tell him that."

In my periphery, I can tell Cal has turned his attention back to me. "He knows it."

"Does he, though?" I meet his eyes. "He's clawing his way back from an injury that was so severe it would be career-ending for most players. His team, which he's been a part of for most of his life, traded for the man who caused the injury, currently in his position while he's on the DL. Physically, he's getting ready to take the field and kick ass . . . but it's his mental game I'm worried about now. It takes a lot to come back from an injury and not be timid of reinjuring it and suffering through the pain again. Add to that the bullshit with Santiago, and a father who is the Iron Giant of baseball, perfect in every way. That's a lot to swallow all at one time."

"I was and still am far from perfect," he murmurs, in a faraway voice that tells me he's speaking of way more things than I am.

"Not in your son's eyes."

There's a crack in Cal's armor as he blinks away tears that well in his eyes.

There's a commotion on the field that pulls our attention. The guys are practicing bunt plays, so that Easton has to run out from behind the plate, barehand the bunted ball, dying in momentum right in front of the plate, and then throw it in an off-kilter stance down to first base.

It's a hard play for sure. One that makes you throw with your arm at odd and often inconsistent angles. It'll be a test to his arm's range of motion. If there is any scar tissue that's going to cause a problem, he'll notice it now because the guys are watching him, the adrenaline is pumping, and he's nowhere near thinking about how to properly throw the ball. He's acting on instinct, falling back on the motion he's done hundreds of times over his career.

I cringe as he scrambles out from behind the plate, calls the other players off so they know he has it, picks up the ball with his bare hand, and then throws down to first base on one foot and off balance. And the throw is perfect, beating the runner by a few feet.

But more important than the ball's placement is Easton. I watch him as he walks back behind the plate, raising his hand to acknowledge something that was said to him by J.P. before pulling his mask back down on his face.

"He's an iron giant in his own right, too, you know." Cal speaks so quietly, but the emotion packed into every word is unmistakable. "I never pulled his kind of stats. I never had his strength or understood the game like he does. I just used my natural ability, but Easton . . . he has the ability and then some. He'll surpass every record, every career high I ever had, way before he retires from this game."

"And how does that make you feel?" If I'm going to overstep, I might as well clear the line with a flying leap. I turn to watch him as he watches his son play the game he no longer can, and wonder what that does to a man's ego when their ego has been on one of the biggest stages of the sports world for so many years.

He doesn't turn to look at me, and I'm more than surprised when he answers. "Every parent wants their child to have more than they did. More opportunities. More success. More happiness. More life. More love."

"It's hard constantly living in the shadows; maybe it's time you helped him step out from under them. Telling him what you just said to me might just do that."

CHAPTER THIRTY-ONE

Scout

"**A**re you going to tell me where we're going?"

I glance over at Easton in the driver's seat and take him in. And I'm just as knocked back by how attractive he is now as I was when he unexpectedly knocked on my door forty minutes ago with a bouquet of handpicked daisies and a request that I get dressed because he was taking me on a proper date.

"I'm not going to tell you, but I will say I like the skirt," he murmurs as he reaches out and rests his hand on my bare knee and slides it slowly up my thigh, the fabric bunching with it. "And the boots."

Without thinking about it, I slide my hand on top of his and link our fingers. It's a natural gesture, so indicative of how he makes me feel. Comfortable. At ease. Okay with whatever this is.

We drive for a bit longer, leaving the city behind us with each mile. The houses grow farther apart. The wispy grass grows longer. The trees grow bigger. It's so different than the brick buildings and high rises of the revamped downtown district around the ballpark. And while I love the new, trendy feel of the buildings the developers tried to make look aged, this is real. The country around us. It's peaceful and idyllic beneath the blue sky, sitting beside Easton with Sam Hunt playing softly on the stereo.

"*Scout and Ford.* Did your parents have a thing with cars?" he asks out of the blue, and I laugh at the random but very valid question.

"Says the man named Easton," I tease.

"No mystery what I was named after." He laughs.

My smile widens as the country whips by outside my window and the memories come back. "Ford was conceived in . . . well, in the back of a Ford truck, from what my dad has told us. I guess he and my mom were having a hard time with names, and on the way to the hospital, he racked his knee on the bumper in excitement. As he was leaning over in pain, hand braced on the tailgate, there was the Ford decal, and so Ford was named Ford."

"Logical," he muses. "And you?"

"My brother loved the neighbor's car. It was a bright yellow Scout International, but being two, all he could say was Scout. So, when my parents told him he was going to have a little brother or sister, he said, 'No, I want Scout,' and would point to the car next door." Easton laughs. "And I guess he continued to say that all the way through my mom's pregnancy, so at some point it became a joke and they would refer to me as Scout. Needless to say, they thought I was going to be a boy and thought Scout would be cute with the name Ford."

"But you are definitely not a boy," Easton says playfully, that hand of his sliding a little farther up my leg.

"No, I'm not, but the name stuck."

"I like it. It suits you."

"Yeah, well . . . people think my parents had a thing with *To Kill a Mockingbird* and named me after Scout Finch. I always disappoint them when I explain that my name has much less significance than that."

"It's unique. Just like you."

I glance over to him and smile. "Thank you. I used to hate it but now I love its originality. I'm glad my mom went along with my dad's suggestions."

"Do you miss her? Shit. Fuck. I'm sorry. Don't answer that."

It's cute watching him stumble all over himself. "No, it's okay. People always want to know, but then don't know how to ask."

"Yeah, but it's kind of a shitty thing to ask. I'm sorry."

I nod to accept the apology and wonder exactly how it is I feel when it's not something I think about much these days. "Do I miss her? Hm. I guess in a sense I do, because she's my mom, and I hear other women talk about how they do this and that with their moms and how lucky they are . . . and I don't have that. In fact, I have the exact opposite. I'm close to my dad. I work in a business dominated by men . . . so maybe subconsciously I've surrounded myself with people who won't remind me constantly and unknowingly that I don't have a mom."

"It has to be hard, though. I mean, I have a mom. She makes things hard for me, makes me have strings most grown kids no longer have . . . but she's my mom," he says, the love evident in his tone, just as sincere as the look in his eyes two nights ago when he received a phone call at one in the morning, crawled from my bed, and went to take care of her.

"I think. . ." I begin, and then pause before I start again. "I've spent a lot of time over the years wondering if I'm glad she left when she did or if I wish she'd waited and I'd gotten more time with her. And I think I'm glad. If she'd stayed, then I'd have gotten used to her. I'd have missed her more. The way she did my hair, or the way she made me lunch for school. I remember the songs she'd sing me good night, but I don't remember much about the predetermined ways she did things, and that means I couldn't miss them. I couldn't compare them to my dad trying to fumble his way through them and learn . . . it was harder for Ford since he was older. And it may sound strange, but if she was going to leave, I'm glad she did it when she did. As much as I missed having a mom around, I think it would have been harder if I'd known what I was missing, if that makes any sense."

He rubs his thumb back and forth on my thigh in reassurance. "Yeah, it makes sense. Thank you for talking about it. I know it hasn't been easy . . . there's no way it could have been, but it also tells me that your dad is as good of a man as I always pegged him for. Raising two kids on his own, giving them as stable of a life as possible, all the while being the best of the best in his job. I respected him before, but now . . ." He shakes his head, and his kind words about the best man I've ever known make me smile.

"Yeah, he's pretty fantastic. I'm a lucky girl."

We fall into our own thoughts again, our fingers linked as we hum mindlessly along to the music and just enjoy the comfortable silence between us.

"Speaking of dads, mine paid me an unexpected visit yesterday."

His words ring out, and while I'm immediately curious, I'm also unsure whether I should tell him about my conversation with his dad, too. "Hmm. Is that not normal?"

"Not this kind, no." He squeezes my thigh, and when I look over at him, his eyes are hidden behind his sunglasses, but his smile is soft. "He said you two chatted the other day."

"You were on the field, and he asked me if I thought you'd be ready to play by the club's date. That's all." I hate that I lie, but think it's important for him to think whatever Cal may or may not have said was because of his own recognition, not because his son's lover said something to spur it on.

"I'm sure that's not the half of it," he murmurs.

"What do you mean?"

"He told me that if I were smart, I'd figure out how to keep you around . . . after your rehab assignment is over."

"Oh."

"Pretty much." He laughs. "And then he told me how proud he was of me. How it must have been hard growing up in his shadow, and that I need to handle the transition back into the game, with Santiago being on the team, with the exact same amount of grace as I did growing up as his son."

He clears his throat, and there is nothing I can say to express how thankful I am that Cal heard me and actually said something. I can tell that it touched Easton, even though he's trying to play it off in his gruff way. The fact that he's not speaking right now is saying it all.

"Here we are," he murmurs as he turns down a tree-lined drive set back from the road. Dust plumes up behind us as we drive, and my neck feels like it's on a swivel as I try to take in my surroundings.

When the trees part, we pull up to a two-story brick house that spreads in all directions over the plot of land. Dogs are barking, I can hear a lawnmower somewhere in the distance, and cottonwood seeds dance all around us in the breeze.

I narrow my eyes at Easton as he hops out of the truck and rounds the front to open my door. He takes my hand in his, and the minute he shuts the door of the truck, he pulls me against him, into a kiss to rival all kisses. It's soft and sweet and tender and has the heat, desire, and need that's never too far from reach.

"We're not in the city," he murmurs against my lips. "There's no one to see me kiss you, so I'm taking advantage of it."

I laugh, loving that he's so protective of our little bubble, and put my free hand to the back of his head to pull him back down. "Me, too." I brush one more kiss against his skillful lips before letting him tug me along by my hand toward the house.

He has the cutest grin as he pushes the doorbell and just stares at me, shoulders against the wall behind him, one foot angled and resting against it. His eyes dare me to figure out what we are doing, and I honestly have no clue.

The door opens, and a slight woman with long, gray hair stands inside. Her smile widens to epic proportions when she sees Easton. "Mr. Wylder. Thank you so much for making your way out here to come and visit us."

"The pleasure is mine, Melinda. Thank you for letting us come out on such short notice."

"It's such a long way from the city."

"It's a beautiful drive," he says as he steps in, kissing her on the cheek in greeting.

"And you must be Scout." Her voice is full of warmth as she wraps her arms around me in a brief hug. "So nice to meet you."

I'm a little startled by her overly friendly welcome but follow Easton's lead and hug her back, still so in the dark about what we are doing at this woman's house. "You, too."

"Let me show you to it," she says as she leads us through the large but cozy family room of the house. "I had to kick Timmy out with the boys, or else they would have just gawked at you—the real live Easton Wylder in our backyard. Noses smashed to the windows. Eyes wide as saucers. They'd grab at any reason to head out back and interrupt you, and I couldn't have that."

"You shouldn't have. They would have been fine," he says with absolute sincerity. I get that this is Easton's public persona, have seen it time and again at the field, but this is also the real him. "Maybe they'll be back before we head out. Meeting them is the least I could do after you so graciously let us come here."

"Are you kidding me?" She laughs, her fingers nervously fidgeting with her hair. I want to put her at ease and tell her we all get that way around Easton. "Your generosity is enough to keep the sanctuary fed for the next year. It's us who should be bending over backward for you."

"It's well deserved," Easton says as Melinda pushes open the door to the backyard. The sound of dogs barking hits us immediately, before I even clear the threshold, and when I do, my eyes widen and the smile is instant on my lips.

"You brought me to see dogs?" I ask, my voice escalating in pitch with each word. I look around the yard, where, organized in a hexagonal type fence, there are about fifteen dog kennels angled off one large play space. And the play space is currently occupied by about ten dogs of different colors, breeds, and sizes. Tongues loll, tails wag, and bodies wiggle in excitement.

"Not just any dogs," he says with a laugh, "but mutts."

My feet move on their own, down toward the fence where the fur babies are all vying for attention, hopping on top of one another, trying to lick my hands through the fence. "Can I go in?" I ask as I turn to look at Easton and Melinda, who are both smiling at me.

"That's the whole point," Melinda says as she walks the short distance toward me and directs me to go in the first set of gates that closes me off from the rest of the free yard, before opening the second set that leads me into the play pen. "These babies need some extra attention, and Easton said the two of you would love to come out and give it to them."

"Seriously?" I look over to her and then glance at Easton as the gate is opened, but my attention is diverted as I'm assaulted in the best of ways by licking tongues on my hands and tails whacking against my legs. There are grunts and whines and a few growls.

Time passes in wiggles and pets. The pack slowly calms down; their interest and eagerness is still there, but not as desperate. And I'm so lost in giving and receiving attention that it's a while before I notice Easton standing inside the play area, staring at me with a beagle snuggled in his arms.

There is a soft smile on his lips, a quiet awe in his eyes, and there's something about his expression that makes those butterflies in my stomach take flight, tickling my insides as they flitter about. His face is typically all hard lines with his dark features, but right now, with the sunlight on his face, all I see are his soft edges—soft edges that call to me to push myself to my feet and let him know how much this means to me.

And he must sense that I want to be near him but am currently serving as a chair to Lola, the slobbery pit bull with a scarred face and the sweetest disposition of the lot. As I nuzzle Lola with my forehead against her back, Easton makes his way over to me.

I laugh when he's overrun by the wags and licks like I was when I first sat down, but when our laughter subsides and I look his way, those butterflies hit me again.

"What is this magical place?" I ask as I reach over and squeeze his forearm as he pets the belly of a scruffy three-legged mutt.

"It's a dog sanctuary for abused and abandoned dogs. Melinda used to work for the ASPCA . . . and she wanted to do more after she ended up adopting some of the dogs she'd nursed back to health herself. She couldn't turn them away, so she started with one, and then another, and then . . ." He shrugs. "You get the picture."

"That's incredible. This *place* is incredible." I laugh as I get nudged by a fluffy brown dog demanding attention. "Such a good girl," I coo, but my next words trail off when I look up to see Easton's head cocked to the side, eyes on me. "*What?*"

"Nothing." He shakes his head as if he's trying to rid it of a thought, and links his fingers with mine. We smile like goofy teenagers for a moment, like there isn't a care in the world and this is the only thing that matters.

"I just thought, with how hard you've been working to get me back on the field, and everything with your dad, that you could use some extra loving."

"It's perfect." I feel like I've used that word a million times while we've been here, and I'm not sure if I have, or if I've just thought it, but it's true. The trees. The sun. The clear sky. The furry flurry. And Easton. How much better could it get?

"I guess Melinda typically has some high school kids come out and volunteer to help her here at Pet Haven. They give the dogs some extra attention or give them baths when people are coming out to possibly adopt them, but there's some big school function this week, so they're not available . . . and so I volunteered us."

"How long have you been involved with the organization?"

"Since about two days ago." He laughs and goes to lean back

on his elbows, quickly realizing what a huge mistake that is as he's smothered in canine tongues and pawing paws. His laughter carries over the landscape and sounds so carefree, so relaxed, it makes me smile. When he can finally sit back up, after giving equal loving to the dogs around him, it hits me what he just said.

"Wait. Just two days ago?"

He nods. "The night I had to head out to take care of my mom? Melinda was there to help rescue a dog who broke free one street down. I ended up helping her get him back, and we started talking. I told her about you and how you were missing puppy love."

"But wait . . . didn't she just say something about a donation that would help feed the animals for . . ." I narrow my eyes as I put two and two together, and he nods slowly, trying to figure out where I'm going with this. "Easton Wylder, how much money did you donate so I could pet dogs?"

"I love when you get all *Easton Wylder* on me." He laughs at the same time I realize how ungrateful I sound. I begin to backpedal and explain that I don't need to be impressed, because I already am—with everything about him—but he just shakes his head, takes my hand in his, and brings it to his mouth, pressing a kiss to the backside of it, which cuts me off before I can get the words out. "First of all, Kitty, I never donate to charity to impress a girl. I donate because I want to. Because I've been blessed beyond measure in my life. It didn't hurt that I know you love dogs. And it definitely doesn't hurt that bringing you here might get me extra brownie points I can cash in for my benefit." He lifts his eyebrows and one corner of his mouth curls up. "But I did it because I wanted to *and* because they need more love than most to prove that not everyone is going to hurt them or leave them behind."

I look at him for a split second, hear the subtle parallel he's drawing to my life, and wonder what man does this. What man would pay enough attention to what I need and then go out and find a way to reassure me the one way he knows I'll hear?

I scoot next to him, the grass cool beneath my skirt and the sun heating my skin, but it's the man whose shoulder I just put my head on that keeps on warming my heart. And so we sit there for a bit and just enjoy our canine company and the fact that we don't have to speak to fill the silence. We can just sit here in a field of grass with the breeze on our cheeks and let the idea of there being an *us* settle between us.

"You brought me to see doggies," I finally say, and there's no other way to describe my voice other than completely enamored with him and what he did for me.

"I figured it would tide you over until you can get one for yourself."

If it were possible for my heart to break free of my rib cage and flop onto the ground, then that's what it would be doing right now. That hard heart of mine doesn't seem so hard any more. Not when it comes to Easton Wylder, at least.

And as much as I want more of this with him—as much as I think I'm ready—it still scares the shit out of me. The idea that I'm cursed is still alive in my mind, despite the most incredible past month.

"I love this."

I love you.

The thought is there. And once it's there, it takes hold and won't let go, no matter how hard I push it away, try to run from it, try not to be freaked by it.

Because I am.

"Thank you so much, Melinda, for letting us come out here today."

"Thank you, sweetie," Melinda says to me, but I don't think she's heard a word I've said, because her attention is on the field to the left of the house. Her two boys, ages ten and twelve, are standing there with bats in their hands while Easton gives them pointers about their stances. The looks on their faces are priceless, complete idolization, and yet Easton continues his lesson, making them laugh and kidding around with them.

He's good with kids.

And with dogs.

And with his sick mom.

And with spooked women.

Is there anything this man can do to make me not like him?

Because I'm beginning to think he might need to do that, so I don't start believing he hung the moon.

Or stole my heart.

CHAPTER THIRTY-TWO

Easton

"**Y**ou smell like dog." She laughs, leaning over to kiss me on the cheek before settling in the passenger seat.

"You're one to talk. Lola got more kisses than me. It seems she claimed you as hers," I tease as I push a hand playfully against her face when she comes close and makes a show of sniffing at me. She grabs my arm, her laugh ringing out above the warm night air rushing in the windows, and she tries to wrestle it away.

I let her win. Let her grab my hand and link her fingers through it, tangle us as if we're not already entwined. Am I a sap if I admit I like this? A relaxing day, a casual dinner at a roadside diner, and a beautiful woman in the cab of my truck. There's only one thing that could make this day better, and I sure as fuck plan on making that happen once we get back home.

A skirt and cowboy boots? What sane man says no to that?

"What are you thinking about?" she asks.

"Today."

"What about it?"

"How it was just what the doctor ordered."

"How so?"

"It was good to get away from the city."

"It was." She nods.

"And it was nice to get to do something for you for a change." She squeezes my hand in response as I roll up the windows. "You have spent so much time and effort on me."

"That's sweet. Thank you for being so thoughtful."

"You deserved a proper date."

"You just wanted to see me dressed up in my skirt and cowboy boots again," she laughs.

"Now that . . . I won't deny." Images of her laid out in the batting cage with her legs spread, skirt pushed up around her hips, and her hands wrapped around the netting fill my mind. "Seeing your legs in anything is a turn-on."

The truck falls silent as I check my mirrors and take a right on the lone highway back to town.

"You mean these legs?"

I glance her way to find her shifted in her seat, back against the door, with one leg bent so her thighs are spread. But with the dimming sky and the shadow of her skirt, I can't see shit.

And fuck how I want to see what's beneath it, even though I already have the taste, the scent, the feel of her pussy imprinted on my damn mind.

"Yes. Those. Legs," I murmur, as desire fires my blood and my dick hardens at just the thought of her. I glance up to find her eyes trained on mine. The damn woman is testing me, taunting me, and it's hot as hell.

"About those brownie points . . ."

Music to my ears.

"Yeah? What about them?" I may feign nonchalance, but fuck if she can't hear that restraint in my voice snapping string by string.

She doesn't answer, not with words, anyway. It's the hitched sigh of hers that catches my ear and almost makes me jerk the truck off the road when I find her with legs spread wider and fingertips moving in the darkness I can't see between her thighs.

God. Fucking. Damn.

The road, Easton. Look at the road.

I glance to the straightaway then look back to her. To her fingers hidden beneath the white pair of panties. To her teeth sinking into her bottom lip. To her nipples pressing against the thin fabric of her shirt. To her panting breath that turns into a moan as she fingers herself.

"Eyes on the road, Hot Shot," she murmurs.

"Now, that's just not fair," I groan, but obey only for a second before my eyes are back on her.

On her eyes. On that slow, seductive smile with her teeth still biting into that lip.

"Straight ahead," she orders, and damn it's hot being ordered around by her.

"Fuck me," I mutter under my breath, but I obey under protest. Because those fingers are still in her panties. The scent of her is filling the cab of the truck.

"That depends if you're a good boy and do what I say." She chuckles, cranking up the seductress role and turning me on even more.

I groan.

She laughs. Fucking foreplay if I've ever heard it. Deep and suggestive and throaty.

Her seat belt clicks.

I move to look her way, and her hand is right there, guiding my face forward so I remain looking at the road. I start to protest, but I'm met with two of her fingers slipping between my lips.

They taste like her.

Sweet.

Damn.

Perfection.

I suck on them and fight the urge to yank the truck to the side of the road and fuck her hard and fast right here for all to see. Because it's Scout. That's what she does to me.

She pulls her fingers from my mouth and slides them down to my lap. She scrapes her nails up and down my thigh and over my cock pressed against the seam, pushing my thighs wider so she can tease my balls. I groan out loud and struggle not to close my eyes and drop my head against the headrest because it feels so damn good.

"Here's what's going to happen," she murmurs against my ear, the heat of her breath tickling my skin and hardening my dick. "I want your cock, Easton Wylder. I want it right now. I want to wrap my lips around it. I want it hitting the back of my throat. I want all of it. To suck you off. To fuck you with my mouth. I want every last drop you have to give me."

That's about the hottest thing I've ever heard.

"You're going to help me get your cock out of your pants, then you're going to put both hands on the wheel and concentrate on not crashing. Understood?"

My hips are already lifted, my zipper undone, and my pants shoved to my knees before she even finishes her sentence.

"Good God, woman." It's all I can say as she wraps her lips and one hand around my shaft and then takes me all the way to the back of her throat on the first suck. My hips lift to give her as much of me as she can take. My hands squeeze the steering wheel like a vise grip. My teeth grind together as I force myself to keep my eyes open and watch the road.

It's a mixture of sensations. The heat of her breath warming and staying on my skin. The wetness of her mouth as she slides up and down. The suction of her lips as she pulls to my tip, and the little pop I hear and feel as she releases me from her mouth. She twists her hand as she works over my cock in a varying pattern; just as I start to get used to the feel of it, think I'm at the point of no return, she changes the angle, the grip, the movement, and builds me up all over again.

Nice and slow, East.

"You taste so good," she murmurs around my dick, the vibration tickling down to my balls and then back up.

Keep the gas pedal steady.

She goes to town, holds nothing back as she sucks and fucks and licks and tongues every inch of me until I can't hold back any more. I'm either going to crash or come, and fuck if I want to do the former.

Remember the road.

The sensation rushes from my balls and then through my cock. Her moan as she tastes my precum is the final straw that pushes me over the edge.

I break the rules. I put my hand on her head to keep it still as I buck my hips and fuck her lips. And she doesn't fight me. She doesn't do anything more than pump my cock faster and suck harder as I shoot down the back of her throat.

Her name fills the cab. *Scout.* It's a broken moan as she does what she promised—sucks every last drop from me.

And I can't take it anymore. I can't not have my hands on her. My tongue in her.

I jerk the truck to the side of the road. She shrieks in surprise and sits up just as I slam on the brakes. And then I lean over the console in a flash.

My one hand is back in her hair, the other is sliding to the wet heat of her pussy, and my tongue is between her lips.

I taste me.

I taste her.

The two of them together are a drug I can't get enough of.

I need more.

I want more.

I'm going to take more.

Right here. Right now. On this rural country road with fireflies outside the window and the scent of her everywhere.

And just before I lose my fucking mind to lust again, just as I shift in the confines of the cab to slide down and taste the heaven between her thighs, a single thought owns my mind.

I'm so fucked.

I'm so far gone.

Damn, does it feel good.

And I'm not sure if I ever want to come back.

Chapter Thirty-Three

Scout

"D ad?"

"Scouty-girl!"

I sigh in relief. He sounds good. Stronger than he did the last time I spoke with him. And I'll take that any day.

"How are you doing? Are you comfortable? Is—"

"Sally's taking care of me just fine. Stop hovering, child. I'm the parent. I'm supposed to be the one hovering, so knock it off or I'll hang up on you."

"Yes, sir." I laugh and feel so good hearing him do the same. I know it means nothing more than he's having a good day, like Sally already told me, but a good day is a good day and that's what I'm holding on to.

"You're five days out. How's the player looking?" he asks as Easton walks into the room with timing so perfect, he could never have known. I enjoy the visual—the towel slung low on his hips, the water still beaded on his skin, and the flex of his biceps as he runs another towel through his wet hair.

"*The player . . .*" I say, meeting Easton's gaze. He stops on his way to his dresser and narrows his eyebrows at me, a silent inquiry as to how my dad's doing. When I nod my head and give a thumbs-up, his smile chases the concern away. "Appears to be at or above one hundred percent."

In my periphery, I can see the little fist-pump that Easton gives in response to my comment, his grin a mile wide. And I share the same sense of satisfaction knowing that, in a big way, I helped him get there.

"So you're ready to give your recommendation?"

"Yes."

"You need to make sure you have a written report. Type it all up. His range of motion. What percentage you think his arm strength is. If you think he can last a whole game or if he needs to take a few innings at a time."

My cheeks hurt from smiling. You'd think he forgot I was around to watch him do this so many times in his career. But I'm just so thankful to be getting a lecture from him.

So I let him ramble on.

I let him advise me.

I let him feel like he's still in the game when his feet will most likely never touch the field again.

It's the least I can do after everything he's given me.

CHAPTER THIRTY-FOUR

Easton

"Hey, Easton?"

"Ignore him, Easton," Tino warns.

"I see him," I mutter as we line up on the left field line, jog a few feet, and then sprint the remaining ninety feet of baseline. We turn to jog back, and there he is, Santiago, with his arms crossed over his chest, his hips leaning against the left field railing, and that goddamn smirk I want to punch off his face. "The asshole doesn't know how to leave good enough alone."

"He's just trying to fuck with your head. He knows in three days you'll be back behind the plate and he'll be relegated to riding pine or being bat boy."

I laugh. It feels good to know these guys have my back. But when we hit the line again, he's still there. Still smirking. Still goading me.

"Was that your trainer I saw you with the other night? Heading into your building with you?"

My feet stop.

"Easy, E," Tino warns.

My blood boils.

"If that's the type of personal PT the Aces provide, then this is one helluva club. Count me in. I'm gonna request her now for any future injuries."

My body vibrates with anger.

"What's her name again? I need to write it down on my request form."

My temper snaps.

I turn to charge him, but Tino holds me back, and just as I break free, Drew is there. Then J.P.

The goddamn Santiago brigade.

Santiago's laugh fills the air. "Was it Scout? Or Slut?"

I see red.

Fucking blood-red.

And just as I'm about to punch my own friend to get a piece of the mother fucker, I hear one of them mutter, "He's all yours."

Their hands are off me.

And I'm charging.

I lower my shoulder and tackle him to the ground.

All I think about is Scout.

We roll back and forth on the ground.

All I see is fury.

I fist a hand in his shirt. Yank him up.

All I feel is satisfaction.

When my fist connects—

All I feel is pain.

Then there are hands.

And shouts.

Ripping us apart.

Pinning us down.

Damage control.

But I don't fucking care. I've had enough.

And when Tino and Drew push me off the field, it's my dad's face I see in the stands before they usher me down the dugout steps, and I can't quite read what it's saying.

CHAPTER THIRTY-FIVE

Scout

"**H**ow stupid could you be?"

All this work—months of healing, hours of strengthening—and Easton risks all of it by fighting Santiago.

"You should have seen the other guy," he jokes, then hisses when I push his hand with the ice pack back up to his cheek.

"It's not funny."

I slam stuff around the training room. The door is shut so no one can hear us, or the drawers I shove open then close, or the cart of the ultrasound machine as I bang it against the table where Easton's sitting. I hate that I'm pulling out the shit I used when I first started his rehab, because who knows what he just did to his shoulder other than just telling me it hurts.

"It's a little funny."

"Don't. Just don't!" I smack my hands down on the counter and brace them there as I let my emotions roil through me.

The confusion when I first heard the shout of "I'm gonna kill him."

The shock of seeing Tino and Drew physically restraining Easton from running back onto the field.

The bewilderment when they shoved Easton toward where I stood in the training room, when I saw his knuckles on one hand were bloody, his T-shirt was torn, and his cheek had an angry red mark on it.

And then the fury, the goddamn fury, when I saw him wince as he moved his shoulder.

"Scout." He sighs my name, and the resigned defiance mixed with apology only infuriates me further.

"What? What could possibly be your excuse?" I shout as I throw my hands up and turn to face him. "You couldn't control yourself? You couldn't be the bigger man and walk away? At least for a few more days?"

"Ah. Now it all makes sense. You don't give a fuck about my arm right now. All you care about is the meeting. The goddamn contract and what's in it for you."

His words punch out into the small space and slam into me harder than his fists probably did into Santiago's face. Because if he is aiming to lash out at me, he just got a direct hit.

Why am I fighting him? Why? Santiago deserved to get punched weeks ago. Better yet, he deserved it months ago, when he hurt Easton and was only fined and given a four-day suspension.

So why are you so pissed at Easton for actually doing it?

Why are you fighting him so hard?

Because I'm scared.

Over what this means for him and his position here. What this means for me and working with the team in the future. What this means for the two of us as a couple. And most definitely what it means to my dad's final wish.

It's so much more than the contract. Doesn't he see that? And yet, that's how highly he thinks of me right now—that I value the contract over him?

Add some more hurt to the anger, Scout.

"Excuse me?" My body trembles with restless fury. The kind you can feel deep down in your bones and have no clue how to get rid of.

"You heard me." Easton stands and squares his shoulders. His rage toward Santiago is still there, still raw, but right now it is directed at me.

Well, bring it, Hot Shot, because I'm primed for a fight, especially when you say bullshit like that.

"Glad to know that your precious fucking contract is your number one concern right now. Doesn't anything else matter?"

"Yes. Of course other things matter."

"Betcha can't name one." He stares at me, eyes searching and a muscle pulsing in his jaw. For the life of me, put on the spot like this and with his anger misplaced on me, I can't think of one when I know there are tons.

"Are you kidding me?" I screech, hating that I can't answer him, and lashing out in return. "You're going to turn this on me? Was it that hard to keep your testosterone in check? To walk the fuck away from him? Did you even think once that maybe when they reinstated you, it would cement his fate? You'd step back into your position, they'd see you side by side and know your talent blows his out of the damn water, and—"

"And you'd be awarded the contract." His voice is quiet and even now, and I hate the tinge to its edges—disappointment, sadness, hurt . . . I'm not sure what, but it digs deep down in me and makes my stomach churn.

"It's not about the goddamn contract! Don't you get it?" I walk from one side of the room to the other. I'm so angry, so confused, I can't seem to say the words I need to get out. It's like I have so many I'm suffocating on them, and yet at the same time, I don't have any. "It's about the time you put in. It's about getting you back on the damn field. Back to the game you love." My voice hitches. The tears well. "What's more important to you than that?"

He glares at me, the tendons in his neck taut, his mouth pulled tight, his body like a rubber band about to snap. "You just don't get it, do you?" He shakes his head, his voice vibrating with resigned frustration.

"Get what? That you couldn't control your temper. That you just risked everything we've worked for?"

"There you go again." He blows out a sigh.

"Whatever, Easton." I'm done. He wants to act like the asshole, then I don't want any part of it. I turn my back to try and hide the hurt, the confusion, the unsettled feeling that things just changed majorly between us, even though it had nothing to do with us.

"Whatever?" he shouts, grabbing my arm and spins me around so we're face to face, body to body, temper against temper. "*Whatever*? There are more important things than getting the goddamn contract," he growls, his finger poking against my chest.

"Like what?" I challenge.

"Like doing what's right."

"What's right is keeping your nose clean and getting reinstated. There's nothing more important than that right now."

"Jesus fucking Christ, you're frustrating." He steps back from me, shoves a hand through his hair, blows out an audible breath, and then steps back up to me. "What's right, Scout, is defending what you care about."

"And what's that?" Our eyes are locked, tempers bouncing off each other's in the space between us.

"Not what, but who." He pauses, squeezes his eyes shut for a beat, and when he opens them back up, the anger is still there, but there's something else, too.

"Who? What in the fuck are you talking about?" Did something happen with one of the guys? With his dad? What?

"*You.* I care about *you.* And I'd fucking punch him and fuck up my shoulder a thousand times over than ever let him talk shit about you again. You got it?"

"Oh." I stand there, stunned. Never in a million years did I think that Easton and Santiago would get in a brawl, on the field, with the fans there to watch batting practice, *over me*.

How could I have been so stupid when he was saying it all along?

We stand a foot apart, and all I want to do is put my hands on his cheeks and kiss him senseless. Reassure him. Reassure me. Anything to make a connection with him and thank him and tell him in the only way I know how that I care.

But I can't. There's a room full of teammates at our backs, who I'm sure were watching our fight unfold from the room's window. I'm certain assumptions have been made over why we're fighting. I know Easton's had his hands on me one too many times to come off like trainer and player.

And, right now, I don't really care, because he's upset and I want to soothe him. I can't touch and I can't kiss. I can't wrap my arms around him or press my lips to his hurt cheek—the punch he took for me—and kiss it better.

I step forward out of instinct, and he steps back.

"No, Scout." There is so much emotion in my name, I know he's feeling the same way I do, but the look in his eyes tells me his control has been snapped once, and it's best not to test it again.

He's so amped up on adrenaline and need that one touch and he won't be able to stop.

So, I use the only thing I can to reach him: my words.

"There will always be men talking shit about me, Easton. It's part of my job. I know it comes along with the career I chose. There will always be a guy who thinks I'm a Kitty or a Trixie." He sighs, and my heart does, too, right along with him. "Thank you for standing up for me, but you can't slay every dragon I face. It's a full-time job these days, but I'm strong and can handle it."

He cracks a smile. One full of regret, apology, but more than anything, filled with love. It's the first time I recognize it, and I stand there, so overwhelmed with emotions, I don't know what to do about it.

"You may be able to handle it, but that doesn't mean I'm going to stand by and put up with it."

I nod my head, acknowledge it, and know it's a battle I'll have to fight another day, but right now, I need to look at his shoulder.

"Come on, let me see if you did any damage." I direct him to the table and start checking out his shoulder. I can't see his face any longer, but the look that was in his eyes is all I think about.

About how it's ingrained in me to want to run.

But one thought keeps repeating over and over in my mind.

He tried to slay dragons for me.

CHAPTER THIRTY-SIX

Scout

The condo is quiet.

There's traffic in the distance, and the windshields glint from the early morning sun.

The stadium is empty. The grass is groomed in its crazy criss-cross pattern that mesmerizes the eyes from this distance, and the dirt of the infield is dragged to perfection.

The coffee is warm in my hands, and the chair I'm sitting on is sink-into-it-and-never-want-to-get-out-of-it comfortable.

Easton, too amped up about getting to hit that groomed dirt later today, for what feels like the first time in forever, is somewhere in this city, jogging mile after mile to ease some of his restlessness.

Everything seems storybook perfect.

But inside I'm a nervous wreck.

Three hours.

That's all the time I have left before I willingly turn our world upside down. Our quiet nights at home. Our seeing each other every night. The day-to-day routine we've somehow established in this relationship that we haven't admitted is a relationship.

Or maybe we have, and I'm just choosing not to see it for fear of cursing it.

But in three hours, all of that will change.

CHAPTER THIRTY-SEVEN

Easton

"**S**hould I be worried about what I'm interrupting?"

Fucking Finn.

"I'm running, you jackass," I pant.

"Oh," he laughs. "I was going to say, she must not be that important if you're stopping to pick up the phone mid-stroke."

"I love you, man, but there's no way I'm stopping mid-stroke if my phone rings." I lean over and brace one hand on the streetlight to try and catch my breath.

"Smart man. It's D-day . . . how you doing? You good?"

"Dude." I chuckle as I look around and judge; I'm about five miles from the house. "I'm so amped up, even crossing paths with Santiago couldn't fuck it up."

"Well, that says it all." He laughs, then gets a little more serious. "I know you're ready, but how's your arm feeling? Is it still sore from your stunt the other day?"

I roll it out of habit, wait for pain to come, but know it's not going to. Scout was right when she said I'd be at one hundred percent.

Even after throwing a few punches. "I'm ready, Finn. It feels like it's been for-fucking-ever since I had the crowd at my back. Just get me on the field."

"That's Scout's job to decide for them. Not mine. Are you confident she's going to tell them you're good to go? That your arm is able to withstand the pressure?"

Images flash through my mind. The shower. Scout's soapy hands sliding over my skin, down to my dick. Being tested and taunted. Picking her up and holding her against the wall as I fucked her.

Can it withstand the pressure?

I believe it did about six hours ago.

"Easton," he groans, mistaking my silence for uncertainty, and causing my smile to widen. "Please tell me you thought to ask her."

I laugh—can't help it. Torturing him is part of my job as his client.

"I'm not feeling as confident about this as I was when I picked up the phone to call you. I thought you two were close. Why the hell would you not flat-out ask her?"

His torture has gone on long enough. I can hear his anxiety ratcheting up. "Relax. There's no need to worry. It's just fun listening to you carry on like a little old woman."

"So your arm's good, then?"

"I love how you just completely ignore me." I laugh, needing the comic relief this phone call has brought with it.

"Easton," he warns as I laugh again.

"We had one . . . uh . . . final workout last night. It felt great."

If he only knew what I was talking about.

"No side effects or anything?"

Not the kind you can quantify. "Nope. I slept like a baby."

"Good. Good." I can hear his agent's mind start to turn now that he knows I'm ready. "Just promise me from here on out you won't do anything stupid like sign a document that says you'll agree to be back on the field by a set date."

"Are we back to this again? I was in pain. They pushed papers in front of me, and I signed. Does it matter? It all worked out, and I'm back with one week to spare on their deadline."

"We dodged a bullet is what we did."

"Quit being a worrywart. I'm fine. You're fine. We're all fine."

"You're going to kill me one of these days, Wylder."

"No, I'm not. I'm your most favorite client."

His silence makes me smile.

"Just make sure you're in the locker room getting ready to help catch bullpen like you've been doing. That way, when I get the call you've been taken off the DL and reinstated, you're at the field."

"Already planned on it."

CHAPTER THIRTY-EIGHT

Scout

"Wow."

Easton's voice startles me. I've been so lost in my own mind, so busy rehearsing what I'm going to say, what my dad advised me to say, that I didn't hear Easton come back.

"What?" I turn to face him, watch him pull his sweat-soaked Under Armour shirt over his head and toss it in the hamper.

"Work-out-clothes Scout is hot. Cowboy-boots-and-skirt Scout is sexy. But dress-up-for-a-business-meeting Scout is gorgeous."

"Thanks. I'll be in a room full of men. Work-out-clothes Scout makes them think I'm a college intern getting my hours in. Cowboy-boots-and-skirt Scout makes them think I'm there to giggle and flirt and maybe date a baseball player," I say as he lifts his eyebrows. "And dress-up-for-a-business-meeting Scout tells them I take my job seriously, and I'm a professional who wants what's best for the team and the player."

"What if what's best for the team, for you, and for *the player* are all different things?"

"In this case they are the same, so it doesn't matter," I say, knowing he needs the reassurance that I technically can't verbalize due to my contract but have told him in a hundred different ways anyway.

"But what if they were, though?"

I don't like the feelings the question evokes, because they very well could have been when he punched Santiago the other day. But that was a different day, a stupid fight, and we've moved on, so I try to shift from this topic.

"Well, since you said *wow* when you saw me, I'd use my wily feminine ways to woo them into what I thought was best."

"Ahh, there comes that manipulative side of you."

"Not manipulative." I laugh as he takes a few steps toward me. "Just determined."

"You're sexy when you're all business," he says as he slides his arms around me and goes straight for my ass.

"Eww, you're all sweaty." I try to bat his hands away, but half-heartedly.

"You didn't say that last night when I was all sweaty." He leans in, and all my doubts disappear with the brush of his lips and the taste of his kiss.

"Well, that kind of sweaty is welcome," I murmur and then physically remove his hands from my ass before they move to undo the zipper.

He laughs and swats me on the ass as I turn to put my makeup, curling iron, and dirty clothes into my overnight bag. When I turn around, Easton's smile is still there, but he's just staring at me with that look in his eyes like he had at Pet Haven.

My pulse speeds up.

"*What?*"

"You don't have to do that, you know."

"Do what?" I glance around like I don't understand, but the sudden echo of panic within me tells me I do.

"Pack up your things." He waits for a reaction, and when I don't give one, other than not saying a word, he continues, "You can have a drawer here, Scout. You can have a whole side of the closet if you want. Better yet, why don't you just stay with me. You're in that temporary place with furniture that's not even yours . . . when I have all this space."

I just stare at him, eyelids blinking and panic slowly clawing its way in to squeeze my heart. "I . . . we . . . it's not . . . how can . . ."

"Scout." Easton says my name as he takes my hand in his and looks at me with those hazel eyes that are loaded with storm-cloud-gray today. "Don't you get it?"

"Get what?"

"This is the next step for us. Some sort of permanence. We're doing it anyway, so why not just admit to it?"

My chest constricts. It hurts to draw in air. The fear I thought I'd chased away is the weight making it hurt. "Easton."

"No, uh-uh," he says as he steps into me and frames my cheeks with his hands so that I'm forced to look up and into his eyes. "You don't get to spook right now. You don't get to hide from me."

"But things are going to change." I finally find my voice. "You're going to start travelling. You're going to leave."

He shakes his head and smiles. "Just for a few nights at a time. And most nights you'll be there, too, since you'll have the team contract. It's not that big of a deal, Scout. Me getting back on the roster doesn't mean this has to stop between us."

He leans forward and reinforces his words with his kiss. To try and combat the fear. To ease my anxiety.

When he ends the kiss, his eyes are back on mine. "We can make this work."

And I see it before he says it.

Maybe I've been seeing it all along and have just been denying it.

But then he says it.

Out loud.

Concrete.

Can't take it back.

"I'm falling in love with you, Scout."

The elevator doors open, and I step to the side and stand there for a beat. I try to pretend I'm okay. I wave to the doorman. I smile at the college girl with the sorority sweatshirt on, doing her homework in the lobby chairs like she often is. And I concentrate on breathing.

On collecting myself.

On telling myself that Easton confessing he was falling in love with me was not a curse for us. I repeat his words in my head. "Just because I said the words doesn't mean I'm going to leave you, Scout. You're not saying it, but I can see it in your eyes. And I'm going to prove to you that you're wrong. That you're not cursed. That's one dragon I'm going to slay for you, and there's nothing you can do to stop me."

Clear mind.

Believe him, Scout.

Hard heart.

He's slayed them for you before.

Clear mind.

He believes in happily-ever-afters.

Hard heart.

Isn't it time you deserve one, too?

Yes. It is.

CHAPTER THIRTY-NINE

Easton

"**Y**ou ready?" My dad's voice booms through my cell.

Did I just royally fuck up?

"Yeah." My response sounds flat even to my own ears, but I'm too preoccupied second-guessing myself as I stare at the elevator doors Scout disappeared behind minutes ago. *Should I go after her and make sure I didn't just spook her?*

"*Yeah?*" he asks sounding just as confused as I feel.

Because sure as shit, I just spooked the hell out of myself.

"Yeah," I snipe, irritated that he's questioning me.

I told her I was falling in love with her. How fucking stupid could I be?

"Easton?"

It's not stupid when it's the truth.

"Are you okay, son?"

The genuine concern in his voice breaks through my thoughts. It brings me back to the present. "Yes. No. Sorry." I chuckle as I take a deep breath, rattled when I'm never rattled. "I'm good. Just preoccupied with something and anxious to get the call later saying that I've been reinstated."

"Well, I'm glad you have something to keep your mind off things," he says. "Since you're coming off the DL, it's probably best if you have a strong presence tonight. You need to go three for three and—"

"Thanks, dad, but I've gotta go." I don't wait for his goodbye to end the call because I've got more important things to do than listen to what my dad expects from me in my first game back.

Like processing how Scout was standing in my room like she does more mornings than not lately, and my only thought was how perfectly she fit there. How seamlessly she's become a part of my day to day. Then of course, how the words rolled off my tongue.

The offer for her to move in with me.

Telling her I was falling for her.

Damn straight I saw the fear in her eyes, but I was too busy trying to manage my own panic to do anything to help quiet hers. Because thinking you're falling for someone is one thing, but saying it out loud is another. *You can't take that shit back.*

But now that she's gone, I know I don't want to take the words back. Who needs grass that's greener on the other side when you're a huge fan of how green the grass is beneath your feet?

Let's just hope I've proven that to her.

CHAPTER FORTY

Scout

"**G**entlemen."

Nerves rattle and shake through me, and I realize this is fear. This is panic. This is not wanting to screw up.

So very different than how I feel with Easton. So very different than how Easton makes me feel.

And I know I'm ready to slay dragons for him, too.

Starting now.

I meet the eyes of the six men surrounding me at the table, and begin, "I was brought on board to facilitate the rehabilitation of *the player*, Easton Wylder, and assess his ability to return without limitation to the starting line-up. I'm here to report my findings. Shall we wait for Mr. Wylder's agent?"

"He won't be joining us," Cory Tillman says with a resolute nod of his head.

"Oh, I assumed—"

"Let's begin."

CHAPTER FORTY-ONE

Easton

I see it the minute I walk into the locker room.

My pinstriped jersey.

Wylder 44

Pressed and hanging in my locker where it hasn't been in what feels like forever.

A hand slaps me on the shoulder. "Welcome almost back, Easy E."

I turn to see Manny and the twinkle in his eyes. "You better not be jinxing me, Manny-Man." I laugh and shake his hand. "I don't need any bad juju today."

"No jinxing. No bad juju. Maybe I wanted to give ol' Santiago a subtle reminder when he walks in here today who was first. And who will be last."

I shake my head and laugh. Good ol' Manny. He had my back way back when, and he still has it now.

"God, I love you, old man."

"I've missed watching you play. I can't wait to sit in the stands tonight."

I stare at him, eyes wide, mouth open. Did I hear that right? "The stands?"

"Yep." He nods. "That's the only place I like to watch the greats play."

I clear my throat. Such a simple comment means so much to me.

Because it's Manny.

And it's what today means to me.

All the hard work.

All the pain.

All the doubt.

I'm so close I can taste it.

CHAPTER FORTY-TWO

Scout

"**A**nd so it is my professional opinion that Mr. Wylder—"

"Shit!"

Cory says the word but it takes me a minute to process the dark brown pool of liquid sloshing across the conference table in all directions. The room erupts into momentary chaos as we shove our chairs back and try to save the pile of documents littering the table from being ruined by the spilled coffee.

Cory curses again as he furiously blots the liquid off the keyboard of his laptop with a wad of Kleenex while his assistant rushes from the room for paper towels. The gentleman who was seated to Cory's right adds to the litany of curses as his hip hits a stack of file folders right on the edge of the desk and knocks them to the floor.

"Get the stuff on the table," I direct as I drop to the floor to help out. "I'll get these." There's so much bedlam, no one argues or notices that in a room full of men, I'm the one in the skirt and heels kneeling on the floor.

Papers are everywhere. Manila folders are lying open and their contents scattered on the carpet beneath the table. I note the labels on the folders as I collect them—Easton Wylder, Dalton Rehab, Long-Term PT Contract, Options—but am too preoccupied grabbing everything to process exactly what they mean. Or rather, what their contents might be.

And it's only when I have all the documents haphazardly stacked in a pile and am about to crawl out from beneath the table that I notice what the topmost paper has on it. The words. The figures. The implications.

There's no way.

Can't be.

Trying to make sense of it all, I flip to the next page but with the papers being out of order, I find nothing.

I look at the next one. Nothing.

Cory's loafers come into my view a few feet from where I'm kneeling and pull me back to reality—to what I'm doing snooping through his files and to the ramifications if I were to be caught.

It's when I look back down one more time to bury the first page in the stack so no one knows I saw it, that I'm blindsided for a second time.

My mind scrambles to process what I'm reading and why Easton's signature is scrawled across the bottom of it in acceptance.

My hands tremble.

I scan the words again.

My pulse thunders in my ears.

Holy. Shit.

"Do you need any help under there Ms. Dalton?"

CHAPTER FORTY-THREE

Easton

"**Y**ou're just wasting your time suiting up, Wylder." Santiago's voice rings above the chatter of guys shooting the shit and silences them instantly.

Every bone in my body vibrates with the need to smash my fist into his face to shut him up, but I ignore it. I grit my teeth and just stare at my jersey hanging in my locker in front of me. He's just not worth it anymore.

"Why's that?" I ask, more than aware that the entire team is on edge waiting to see how this plays out.

"Because it seems the team has one too many Wylders on the roster these days."

"Hmpf. Thanks for the heads up." I don't take the bait. I don't let him know I haven't got the call yet informing me I've been reinstated so technically, there's no Wylder currently on the roster at all.

"Sure thing. Did you hear that joke that's been going around? What's ten-times worse than a shitty catcher?" he asks and then answers without skipping a beat. "A Wylder one."

Every muscle in my body is tense when I turn around to face him.

"Cool it, Santiago," J.P. warns, sick of hearing his mouth like we all are.

"What?" he shrugs and smiles. "I'm just having a little fun with my new teammate."

I take my time crossing the distance, stopping when I'm about a foot from the bastard. I stare at him for a few seconds before I speak. "You know what, Santiago? I don't know what your deal is and I sure as hell don't know what I've done to make you hate me, but honestly, I'm beyond giving any fucks. I'm a part of this team, have been for years—we're one big, happy family—so every time you fuck with me, remember you're fucking with them too." I jerk my thumb over my shoulder toward the guys and take another step closer to him. "And I guarantee you that life will get awfully hard for you as an Ace if you keep this shit up. *Capisce*?" I stare at him for a beat longer, wait for him to nod his head, and then turn on my heel and walk away.

CHAPTER FORTY-FOUR

Scout

What if I'm wrong?

What if the information on that paper didn't mean what I thought it did?

But what if it did?

I glance around to the pairs of eyes staring at me, waiting for my response, and wonder where the hell Easton's agent is. None of this makes sense to me and I *need* him to help me make sense of it.

The image of Easton's signature flashes in my mind.

I learned a long time ago that front offices rarely do things that seem reasonable to the public, but in the long run make perfect sense. My dad's voice rings loud in my ears and I'd give anything to call him right now and ask him what to do but the gentlemen waiting impatiently across the table from me wouldn't think too highly of that. In fact it would only serve to undermine my credibility.

My stomach churns. There's too much at stake.

For Easton.

And for me.

The whole situation feels off somehow, and I can't help but think it's because I'm still rattled by Easton's confession this morning.

You're too close, Scout. My dad was right, I am too close.

"Ms. Dalton?" Cory prompts.

What if what's best for the team, for you, and for the player *are all different things?*

It's Easton's voice I hear now. His question from this morning comes back to haunt me.

What. Would. You. Do. Scout?

"In your informed opinion, is Easton Wylder completely re-habbed and ready to return as a contributing player to the Aces' line-up?"

CHAPTER FORTY-FIVE

Easton

"First Santiago and now the carpet. Take it easy there, turbo, and save some energy for the game tonight."

I glance over to Drew as he tightens a spike on his cleat while I wear a hole in the carpet of the locker room. "What the fuck is taking them so long?"

"Maybe that lady friend of yours is spilling your deep dark secrets."

I halt midstride and glare at him and his half-cocked smirk.

"You think those of us who know you well don't know you've got the hots for each other? Dude, the way you look at her is enough to make me get a boner."

I roll my eyes. "Fuck you."

"I got you to laugh *and* stopped you from making me dizzy watching you walk back and forth like a caged animal."

"Whatever." As soon as I say it, I realize I'm already pacing again. Shit. All I can do is hang my head and laugh at proving him right.

"My job here is done."

"Such an asshole," I mutter.

"You wouldn't want me any other way." He pats me on the back. "She better hurry the fuck up because if I have to see Santiago behind the plate one more night, instead of your ugly mug, you're going to owe me more than just a round of beer."

"Agreed," I laugh as he heads into the tunnel and out to the dugout where I want to be.

My phone rings.

I can't get to it fast enough.

"Finn. I've already got my jersey on. Tell me I'm good to go."

"Easton."

"Sweet."

"Easton." His voice is harsher. It begs me to stop moving. "I just got word."

"Finn?"

"You've just been traded."

THE END

THE CATCH

Ready for more Easton and Scout?

Find out what happens in the conclusion of The Player duet.

The Catch releases June 29th

ABOUT THE AUTHOR

New York Times Bestselling author K. Bromberg writes contemporary novels that contain a mixture of sweet, emotional, a whole lot of sexy, and a little bit of real. She likes to write strong heroines, and damaged heroes who we love to hate and hate to love.

A mom of three, she plots her novels in between school runs and soccer practices, more often than not with her laptop in tow.

Since publishing her first book in 2013, K. has sold over one million copies of her books and has landed on the *New York Times, USA Today*, and *Wall Street Journal* Bestsellers lists over twenty-five times.

In April, she'll release *The Player*, the first in a two-book sports romance series (*The Catch*, book 2, will be released June 29th), with many more already outlined and ready to be written.

She loves to hear from her readers so make sure you check her out on social media or sign up for her newsletter to stay up to date on all her latest releases and sales: http://bit.ly/254MWtI

Connect with K. Bromberg
Website: www.kbromberg.com
Facebook: www.facebook.com/AuthorKBromberg
Instagram: www.instagram.com/kbromberg13
Twitter: www.twitter.com/KBrombergDriven
Goodreads: bit.ly/1koZIkL

71230893R10168

Made in the USA
San Bernardino, CA
13 March 2018